MW01287533

A TOUCH OF LIGHT AND DARK

#3 TILDAS ISLAND SERIES

TAMSEN SCHULTZ

Copyright © 2020 by Tamsen Schultz

Published by Devil's Gate Press, LLC

Cover Design by Melody Barber
Edited by Rebecca and Woody Fridae

Print ISBN: 978-1-955384-12-4

All rights reserved.

No part of this book may be reproduced in any form or by any electronic or mechanical means, including information storage and retrieval systems, without written permission from the author, except for the use of brief quotations in a book review.

ALSO BY TAMSEN SCHULTZ

THE WINDSOR SERIES

THE TILDAS ISLAND SERIES

For more information visit www.tamsenschultz.com

To the people of the Caribbean who survived Irma and Maria, your spirit is indomitable

ACKNOWLEDGMENTS

This book is being finalized and released as my state burns with unprecedented wildfires. I've always been grateful for the community I've surrounded myself with, but when events like these wildfires happen, or Irma and Maria in the Caribbean for those who lived through the devastating sister hurricanes, community becomes everything.

First and foremost, to the sisters of my heart who are checking on me daily, Sarah Carlan and Angeli Weller—we say it to each other often, but now I'm putting it in print, this journey through life would not be the same without you.

To the community of Winters, CA – we are small, but we are mighty, and if we have to go through something like this, I'm glad it's with you all.

To the Rotary community – your willingness to jump in and help with just about anything that needs doing is inspiring, and why I'm so grateful I joined. Being this year's president is going to be a challenge, but also an opportunity to serve, and I couldn't be doing it with better people.

And last but not least, to my family. You are what sustains me, full stop.

I know most acknowledgments acknowledge those who have helped with a book, and there are many that I am very grateful for, including my editors Woody and Rebecca Fridae and my PA, Stephanie Thurwachter. But in this book, and at this time, I especially wanted to acknowledge those who, mostly without even knowing it, and mostly just by being the people they are, have helped me be the writer I am.

CHAPTER ONE

Dr. Nia Lewis pulled into a parking spot at the Caribbean Marine Research Center and turned off her car. As it always did, the sign that proclaimed the spot "Reserved for Dr. Lewis," gave her a little thrill. Against all odds, not only had she obtained her Ph.D. in marine biology ten years ago, but she now headed the biggest marine research center in the Caribbean. It wasn't the best in the world, but it was the best in the Caribbean. And she loved every minute of it.

Well, except for maybe this specific minute.

She glanced down at her skirt and heels and considered leaving. She was due to meet her friends, Jake McMullen and Dominic Burel, in downtown Havensted, the main town on Tildas Island, in fifteen minutes. There was no *real* reason she needed to be at the lab. The samples she'd started running earlier that day on a couple of fish she'd collected the day before could wait until tomorrow.

She wrapped her fingers around the key and clicked the ignition over once. The radio blared from the speakers, and the air conditioning blasted, blowing her curly hair away from her face. But with her fingers on the key, one click away from starting her engine, Nia hesitated.

"Fuck," she muttered, turning the key back toward her and yanking it from the ignition. It wasn't as if Jake and Dominic couldn't entertain themselves without her. In fact, those two could entertain themselves inside of a bucket; waiting for her at the beachside bar of one of the island's trendier hotels would be no hardship. It would be better to just take ten minutes now and check on her damn samples than it would be to wonder about them all night.

Throwing her door open and sliding from her seat, the October heat and humidity hit her like a wall, and she sucked in a deep breath. She'd been raised in the Caribbean—on Tildas Island itself—and so with two more deep breaths of the ocean scented air, her body more or less adjusted. But, no joke, living in the tropics wasn't for sissies.

Adjusting her skirt, Nia made her way from her parking spot to the main entrance of the research center. Using her pass card and a code, she let herself in, pausing just inside the door to let the cool, air-conditioned air caress her skin. The motion-sensing lights flickered on, and though normally a receptionist would be there to greet employees and direct visitors to the visitor center, at nine o'clock on a Saturday night, the building was empty.

Crossing the reception area, she pushed through a door marked "employees only" and proceeded down a long hall. Bypassing several of the main labs, Nia walked to the back of the building and toward a side lab—*her* side lab. It was a small room that was hers and hers alone. A place where she tinkered, tested, and theorized. A place where she discovered, failed, succeeded, and created. She'd recently published her fourth paper based on findings she'd reached in that room. It was no secret that it was her favorite place in the large complex.

As she walked the hallways, her thoughts settled and

centered on the samples that had brought her back to the lab. The tests she planned to run the next day would probably show nothing—at least she hoped so—but even so, how she'd even come to have the samples was a bit of a strange story and one that baffled her.

Making the last turn, she pushed through a fire door and let her mind drift back to Friday afternoon to when she and a few colleagues had been running checks on a small, coral nursery north of Tildas Island. A school of fish had been leisurely circling her and her colleagues when one of the fish had literally swum into her. It hadn't been the first time she'd been booped by a fish, but usually when that kind of contact happened it was in the middle of a frenzy.

Surprised by the gentle, but strong, bump, she'd turned to see what had hit her hip only to find a parrotfish hovering at her side. It had paused, seeming to contemplate what to do about the obstacle in front of it, then after a beat, it had tried to swim through her again. The behavior had been so odd that Nia had stopped what she'd been doing to watch.

And that's when the second fish had entered the picture. It hadn't swum into her like the first one, but it had hovered right in front of her belly, as if confused about how to get around her.

After she'd spotted four more fish acting in the same unusual manner, she'd called them to the attention of the two research assistants diving with her. Perplexed by the conduct, they'd ended up collecting four of the six for testing. There were lots of bacteria and viruses that fish could get that would alter their behavior, but she'd never heard of anything that resulted in what she'd witnessed. Her curiosity as a biologist had been piqued, but so had her responsibility to the people—and marine life—of the Caribbean. If something was negatively affecting the ocean and the animals that lived in it, she had a duty to investigate.

And so here she was. At her lab. On a Saturday night.

Rounding the corner just before her destination, Nia slowed her steps. The motion-sensing lights in her lab, visible through the small window in the door, were already on. She paused, confused as to why that might be. Her lab was locked, and while a couple of the research assistants had keys, none of them had mentioned coming in tonight.

Then again, neither had she. Her decision had been a spur of the moment thing, driven by her curiosity and lack of patience. It was possible one of the RAs had done the same.

But if they had, they would have let her know. Everyone who worked at The Center knew that no one was allowed in her lab without her approval, and there was no way anyone would go against that edict and risk getting fired.

No, something felt, well, *off*.

Looking at the door, and the little window into her space, Nia quickly ran through the options in her head. She could either enter the lab, and hope that whoever was in there was friendly, or she could pull back and call security.

She nearly snorted at that last thought. The Center had security—of course it did—but it was *island* security. The men and women who made up that department were good people, but on an island with very little crime—other than petty crime targeting tourists—their response times were sometimes a little on the slow side. Or a lot on the slow side. Like if she called them now, she might never make it to meet Jake and Dominic because she'd be waiting so long.

But while calling security didn't seem like the most efficient option, charging into her lab didn't seem like such a hot idea either. At least not without a little more information.

Eyeing the small window in the door, Nia made a decision. Reminding herself of the low crime rates, and reasoning that it was probably an RA who'd forgotten to tell her they'd be in, she inched her way closer to the door, keeping her back to the wall.

Her logic was sound, but that didn't keep her heart from

racing or her palms from sweating as she paused in the corner where the door met the wall. Leaning forward, she strained to listen. Surely if an RA were in there, she'd hear the usual lab noises?

Her ear was practically plastered to the door when a jarring crash of breaking glass erupted from the other side. On instinct, she jumped back, pressing her body against the wall. That was most definitely *not* the sound of one of the RAs.

Reaching into her pocket, she palmed her phone. If someone had broken into her lab, the island police were a better bet than The Center security. It took her two tries to unlock the device, and in that time, whoever was on the other side of the door started moving a table and its legs rumbled and screeched against the industrial flooring.

"This is 9-1-1, what's your emergency?" the dispatcher answered.

"This is Dr. Nia Lewis of the Marine Research Center. I think someone has broken into my lab," she whispered loudly, hoping the responder would be able to hear her.

"Are you safe, Dr. Lewis?"

Was she? Probably not. But when the sound of her spectrometer being moved across the counter—a sound she was all too familiar with—filtered through the door, she knew she wasn't going to go anywhere. That was an expensive piece of machinery and damned if she was going to stand by and let someone send it crashing to the floor like they'd done earlier with what she assumed had been one of the holding tanks.

"Dr. Lewis? Are you safe?" the responder repeated.

"For now, yes. I'm also pissed," she said. "They are still here, and it sounds like they are destroying my lab."

"You need to leave the building, Dr. Lewis. As quickly and as safely as possible," the responder directed. "Can you do that?"

Oh yes, she could do that. But she wasn't going to. Not yet, anyway. Her life wasn't worth the spectrometer, but it went against everything inside her to stand by and let something happen to that machine. Perhaps she could create a diversion and scare the person away?

Stepping toward the window, she peeked her head above the frame, all the while cursing biology for not designing people's eyes to be in a location that would allow them to see without having to expose a large part of the head—honestly, evolution could have learned a thing or two from some fish.

The man, and it was a man, had his back to her, and appeared to be contemplating one of the three mini-fridges she kept on the counter. Dressed in jeans and a black t-shirt, he didn't look very tall, but he was built like a tank and definitely not someone she'd want to encounter in a dark ally. He jammed a hand on his hip and ran the other through his shaggy blond hair. There was nothing special about the small appliance he stared at, and Nia wondered what it was that drew his attention.

"Dr. Lewis?"

So fixated on the man in her lab, Nia startled at the sound of the responder's voice.

"Sorry, I'm here," she whispered, shifting so that her back was against the door and her face was no longer in the window.

"The police are on their way. Are you safe?"

That question was getting a little old. "For now, yes," she said. The man had no idea she was there, so until he learned otherwise, she was safe.

"Good. You should hear the sirens shortly. Can you stay on the line with me until they arrive?"

"Yes," Nia answered.

She itched to look back inside her lab again, and as the hours —okay, seconds—stretched, the itch became a twitch. She fought the urge to do something, even if that "something" was just to tap her foot, and forced herself to stillness.

She could hear the responder typing away on her computer, maybe starting the paperwork for the call already. But that was all she heard. Nia frowned. Considering there was a man in her lab who had, until he'd stopped to contemplate the mini-fridge, been moving around, shouldn't she be hearing something else? Or was he still staring at it?

The distant sound of a siren permeated the walls of The Center, and for the first time in what felt like ages, some of the tension left Nia's body. She hadn't heard any more destruction, and the police would soon be there—she didn't know what state her lab would be in once she got a look, but at least it sounded like her spectrometer was going to be safe.

Right?

Taking courage from the imminent arrival of Tildas Island's finest, Nia rolled to her side to peer into the lab one more time. As she did, two things struck her simultaneously. First, she should have remembered that if she could hear the sirens so could the man in her lab. Second, there was no way out of her lab other than through the door she now stood in front of.

The man's face popped up on the other side of the window, and Nia screamed. Which led to a third thing striking her—the actual door. It flew open, catching her first in the head then the rest of her body. She went flying across the hall and hit the opposite wall, her head snapping back against the hard concrete. The man didn't bother to pause as he fled, and Nia slumped to the ground as his figure—looking fuzzy in her current state—retreated. The last thing she remembered thinking before closing her eyes and drifting off, was to wonder whether or not her spectrometer okay.

CHAPTER TWO

"I NEED to get into my lab," Nia insisted as a paramedic flashed a light in her right eye.

"Can't. Cops are in there," the paramedic said, moving the light to the other eye.

"But how will they know if anything is missing if I'm not in there?"

The paramedic sat back on her heels. Nia had refused to lie down on a gurney so she was still sitting on the floor with her back pressed to the wall, not far from where she'd first fallen. It reminded her of high school when she and her friends would take shelter from the random rainstorms and congregate in the halls. Only back then, she never had a headache like the one she sported now.

"Not my job," the paramedic said as she reached into her bag. "I'm not Agatha Christie." No, according to her uniform, her name was P. Jobard.

Nia narrowed her eyes at the woman. "Aren't you supposed to be sympathetic or, at the very least, soothing?"

P. Jobard looked unimpressed as she rolled Nia's head to the side to get a better look at the ginormous goose egg forming where she'd hit her head against the wall.

"What can I say," Jobard said. "You got the B-team tonight."

At a loss for how to respond to that, Nia tried to get a better look inside her lab. The police had left the door open, and she could see two of them talking while a third looked to be dusting for prints. Not long after she'd come to, Nia had given one of the officers, Detective Anika Anderson, a brief statement. But she had no idea what Detective Anderson could be discussing so intently with her colleague when they had such little information to go on. Maybe they were talking about their fantasy football teams?

Nia's grumbling complaint was cut off when a phone vibrated to her right. Looking over, she saw her device just out of arm's reach. P. Jobard didn't look like she was interested in helping a woman out.

"Hand me that phone and you won't hear another word from me," Nia said, not above a little bribery. Or was it blackmail?

The paramedic let out a huff, but she also reached for the phone and handed it to Nia. Shit, there were five texts and two calls from Jake. She was supposed to have met him and Dominic an hour ago, and she was never late. As an FBI agent, Jake wasn't too prone to freaking out, but this was definitely his version of that.

"*Sorry,*" she typed. "*Problem at the lab. Won't make it tonight.*"

She'd barely hit send when the "read" notification popped up along with the little bubbles indicating Jake was typing.

"*What kind of problem?*"

Nia considered not answering the question, but not only would Jake not let her drop it, if she were honest with herself, the fact that he cared—and the fact that she truly *believed* he cared about her—was something special that she wasn't willing to cast aside. She could count on two hands the number of people who ever expressed any genuine interest in her well-being, and Jake was always first on that list. The other six were Jake's teammates and their significant others.

Her life was definitely weird when the people she considered her closest friends were the five members of the elite—and temporary—FBI task force assigned to the island in preparation for The Summit of World Leaders scheduled for the following May. Then again, maybe the fact that they were temporary was the reason she'd clicked with them eight months ago when she'd fished Agent Damian Rodriguez, and his now-fiancée Charlotte, out of the water after their boat had exploded.

And wasn't that a sobering thought.

"*Hello???*" Her phone vibrated in her hand.

"*There was a break-in. My lab is trashed,*" she typed.

"*You okay?*"

"*A little banged up, but fine. Just waiting to get into the lab and talk with the police.*"

"*We'll be right there.*"

"*You don't need to come. I'm fine,*" she said.

"*We don't need to, but we're coming anyway. Let the local law enforcement know.*"

Jake's last text didn't require an answer and so she slipped the phone into her pocket. She considered calling her parents to assure them she was okay, but the thought didn't go any further than that. She'd only be setting herself up for disappointment if she did. Her family didn't fall into that small group of people who cared about her well-being. At all.

"We done here, yet?" Nia asked P. Jobard.

"Yeah, we're done," Jobard answered, rising from her squat. "Ice the goose egg on the back of your head. The cut on your forehead doesn't need stitches, but I put a butterfly bandage on it to hold it together. Be sure to change it every day. It's possible you have a mild concussion, but since your eyes are responding and you're clearly alert, I'm not going to require you to visit the hospital. If possible, you should stay with someone tonight to keep an eye on you." As she'd delivered her diagnosis, she'd packed her bag, and by the time she was done, P. Jobard stood over Nia looking down at her.

"You got someone to stay with tonight?" Jobard asked.

Nia raised an eyebrow at the woman. *Now* she was solicitous?? "I got it covered," Nia lied.

The paramedic eyed her, then nodded. "I'm out, boys and girls," she called to the men, and woman, in blue. "She's all yours," she added when the officers turned her way.

Nia let out a sigh, followed by a much less genteel grunt as she dragged her ass off the floor and stood. "Looks like I'm all yours," she said. "Now, can we figure out what, if anything, is missing from my lab?"

"Tell me again what you know," Dominic demanded as they navigated the streets of Havensted toward the Marine Center.

Jake scowled out the passenger window, startling the person stopped at the red light next to them. He eased the tense expression and winked at the white-haired woman who smiled back as she accelerated away. But he didn't feel like smiling. No, his mind was going all sorts of places it shouldn't, and his whole body was coiled tighter than a cobra since Nia had sent her text.

How hurt was she? Why hadn't she called him? She was one of his best friends and they saw each other three or four times a week, wouldn't that alone warrant a call? Not to mention the fact that he was an FBI agent. But had she been so hurt that she couldn't have reached out to him before she had?

His stomach churned at the thought.

"Jakey, you okay over there?" Burel asked.

No. "Yeah, why?"

"You made a weird sound."

"I'm worried about Nia," he said, amazed his voice sounded somewhat normal.

"I'm sure she's fine," Burel said with an annoying level of confidence.

Jake reined in his anxiety. The truth was, he wasn't quite sure *why* he was so anxious. Nia was obviously well enough to be texting, and her texts hadn't sounded like she was scared. But still...

"Tell me what you know," Dominic repeated, bringing Jake's thoughts back to facts. What few they had, anyway.

"This isn't an interrogation, Burel. I'm not going to have any more, or different, information than the first time you asked me. Or the second," Jake said. He'd told Dominic what little he knew as they'd left the beachside bar. It had been a condition of getting Dominic to leave at all as he'd been a bit wrapped up with a woman visiting the island from Estonia.

"If you want to go back, I can drive myself and you can get a cab home. Or whatever," Jake added. Jake had a bit of a reputation when it came to driving and he rarely ever drove—and almost never drove anyone else's car—and so they'd taken Dominic's car to the bar.

"It's Nia," was all that Dominic said.

Jake's thoughts and emotions might be all over the place, but Dominic's simple statement brought some calm to the storm. When the chips were down, Jake could always count on his colleagues to be all in. And when those chips involved someone that one or all of them cared about, there was never a doubt or question about what would be done. Because they would all do whatever it took.

And there was no doubt that they all cared about Nia. She'd helped them out on more than one occasion, but even more than that, she'd become their friend—and one of Jake's closest friends. Maybe that explained why he was teetering on the edge of a panic attack at the thought of her being hurt? If something happened to Nia, the whole team would feel it. Yes, maybe that explained this weird turmoil he was experiencing—he was carrying the weight of what it would do to his friends if she were hurt. Logical or not, Jake grounded himself in that belief as they parked the car at The Center—he was taking one for the team, and he'd pull on his big boy boxers and deal with it. Surely Dominic was feeling the same as he was, but he was just doing a better job of hiding it.

When they finally walked into the lab, Jake's attention zeroed in on Nia, who was deep in conversation with two police officers. At the sight of her standing on her own, clearly alert, he took what was probably his first deep breath since receiving her text. Letting some of the tension ease from his body, his gaze swept over her. Her sun-streaked hair fell just above her shoulders and she wore a black tank top with thin straps. With her back to them, he took in the familiar expanse of tanned skin—skin that took on a rich golden hue thanks to her Danish ancestors—and the smattering of freckles across her shoulders. Her skirt landed just below the middle of her thighs, and although it was loose enough to dance in, it was still tight enough to show off her curves. And yes, Nia was his friend, but he'd have to be dead not to notice her mile-long legs or curves.

"Doc," he called out. The three turned, Nia wincing at the movement. "You need to take care of that concussion," he added with a smile.

"It's a potentially mild concussion," she shot back. "And how did you hear that?"

"We ran into the paramedic on our way in. Dominic flashed his badge and that smile, you know the one." Jake gestured to Dominic, who complied and graced them with his trademark smile. Both officers blinked, but Nia was unfazed.

"Right. Of course he did," Nia said as they stopped beside her. She'd known them long enough to know exactly what kind of things that smile could get Dominic.

"So, what happened here?" Jake asked. Nia hadn't been exaggerating when she'd said the lab had been trashed. Papers were strewn around the room, two of the mini-fridges had been emptied, and fish guts—or whatever Nia was looking into—and shattered glass were scattered all over the floor. Three empty tanks remained on the counter that ran along the back wall of the room, but one had clearly been tipped and the contents had tumbled to the ground. Filter equipment, sand, and glass lay in a heap, and a large puddle of water reflected the fluorescent lights of the ceiling.

"This is a local investigation, Agent," the male officer said.

Jake lifted his eyes from the scene to Nia. She shrugged. "Jake, Dominic, this is Detective Anderson," she said, gesturing to the female. "And this is Officer Schuyler. Officers, these are Agents Jake McMullen and Dominic Burel."

Since neither of the police held a hand out, Jake went back to perusing the scene. "You okay?" he asked Nia, taking in the violence of the room. She'd said she'd been a little banged up, but with Nia, that could mean anything from a scraped knee to missing an arm. Clearly, it wasn't the latter, but he could see a butterfly bandage on her forehead that he was pretty sure wasn't a fashion accessory.

"I got hit in the forehead by the door when the guy was fleeing," she said. "I got thrown against the wall and hit my head."

"You saw him?" Jake asked. There was a lot in her statement that made him uneasy—not only had she *been there* when the break-in occurred, but she'd seen the man, too. On the one hand, she might be able to identify him. On the other, that meant he could probably identify her, too.

Nia started to nod, then abruptly stopped and took a deep breath. Her eyes were tight and she was a little pale—which, considering her perpetually suntanned complexion, spoke more about how she felt than she would ever vocalize.

"Again," Officer Schuyler said. "This is a local investigation."

14

"He had blond, shaggy hair, brown eyes, and one of those noses that looks a little pig-like—kind of round on the tip with big nostrils. You know the kind I'm talking about?" she said, ignoring the cop. When Jake nodded she continued. "Other than that, I'd guess he was maybe five foot seven? Not tall, but built like a brick shit house."

"Anything taken?" Dominic asked, making his way to the side of the room to get a better look at the remains of the aquarium.

"I'm going to have to ask you both to leave," Officer Schuyler said, straightening his shoulders and adjusting his belt.

"Oh give it up, Ronnie," Detective Anderson said. "She's not saying anything to them now that she wouldn't tell them later. She's had a bash on the head and her workspace violated. Cut her some slack and let her tell us everything at one time."

Ronnie opened his mouth to object, but the women silenced him with the most cutting glare Jake had ever seen. Impressed, Jake turned to see if Dominic had caught it. Dom had his eyes back on the wreckage, but he was grinning.

"Thank you, Detective Anderson," Nia said.

"Yes, thank you," Jake said. "And we're not here to interfere, but Doc is a friend."

Anderson flashed Nia a supportive smile, but the look she shot him told him he better watch his step.

"So, anything missing?" Dominic repeated the question.

Nia's gaze swept the room. Her brow furrowed and she frowned. "I haven't been able to go through the papers, but he did a hard reset on my spectrometer and took off with two fish."

"Hard reset?" Anderson asked.

Nia nodded, her attention going to the large machine in the back corner of the lab. "I think he wanted to trash it, but it's really heavy and I don't think he could tip it over. But the hard reset erases the stored memory."

"So, you lost data?" Anderson asked.

Nia shook her head. "No, it backs up to a cloud drive. If it didn't do that, I would have lost some data, but as it is, it's really nothing more than an inconvenience as we'll have to recalibrate it. But that's the extent of the damage. At least that I can tell right now."

"And the fish?" Jake asked.

Nia shrugged. "Two parrotfish we brought in yesterday."

"He took two parrotfish?" Officer Schuyler asked, deciding to do his job and join the conversation.

"I'm guessing those aren't fancy expensive fish?" Dominic asked.

Detective Anderson shook her head. "You dive off the dock out there," she said, gesturing with her head in the general direction of The Center's small, private marina. "You'll probably see a dozen of them. Why did you have parrotfish?"

Jake walked over to join Dominic as Nia answered. "We were out checking on some coral beds yesterday, and they were swimming around us acting a little unusual. I brought two to my lab because I wanted to check their health, make sure there's not something going on that could threaten the marine life. It was actually some samples from their skin that I was coming to check on tonight. I wanted to make sure my RA finished the prep work so I could run the tests tomorrow."

"These the samples?" Jake asked, pointing to the remains of several glass test tubes and their stoppers scattered around the floor.

"Yep, that's them," Nia said, staring at the mess.

"But nothing else was taken?" Officer Schuyler asked.

Nia shook her head. "Like I said, I haven't had a chance to go through the paperwork, but from what I can see, that's it."

"Can you think of any reason someone would want those fish?" Anderson asked. Jake had grown up in Hawaii and knew exactly how prevalent parrotfish were in tropical waters, and he was as confused as the cop as to why someone would break into a lab and walk away with nothing but the pair.

Again, Nia shook her head. "I honestly can't."

Jake eyed her. She glanced at him, then quickly looked away. He slid his gaze to Dominic, who raised a brow in question, but when Jake gave a small shake of his head, Dom went back to his examination of the lab. Whatever it was that Nia wasn't saying, they'd get it from her later.

"Looks like he broke in through the side door down this hallway," came a voice from behind Jake. He turned to see a third officer, this one clearly more junior than the other two since he looked no more than twenty.

"Don't you have an alarm?" Schuyler asked.

Nia stared at Schuyler for a beat as if trying to determine if the question was a serious one. She turned her back on the officer and made a face at Jake as she answered. "Of course we do. But it didn't go off, or I would have received an alert. We also have surveillance cameras in the reception and visitor areas and at the main door between the public and private areas of The Center. There's also one by Perry," she added.

"Perry?" Jake asked.

"The fridge that holds the few controlled substances we keep at The Center," Nia answered. "It's not a regular fridge. It's heavy and specially insulated and has a couple of different locking mechanisms. It wasn't broken into, though. We checked before you got here."

"But Perry?"

"The Fridge," Dominic said. Jake turned to his colleague for more of an explanation. "William 'the Fridge' Perry, the football player."

"Ah," Jake said. He'd heard the name before, but as he'd never been much of a football fan—living most of his life on a surfboard before joining the FBI—he hadn't made the connection.

"If the power goes out, there's a few seconds before the

generator kicks in," Nia said. "In that time, the doors remain locked, but the alarm is disabled. It's a gap we're aware of but can't really fix. I don't know if there was a power outage earlier this evening, but that's the only reason I can think of as to why the alarm wouldn't have gone off."

"We'll have an electrician out tomorrow to see if we can figure that out," Detective Anderson said. "There wasn't a general outage in this area, but it's possible there was something more targeted."

Nia looked around her lab. "And by 'targeted,' you mean just The Center." It was a statement, not a question. The potential seriousness of the situation was slowly sinking in, but rather than letting fear take hold, Jake could see Nia's mind trying to make sense of it, trying to solve the problem. This lab— The Center—was her life, and he didn't doubt that eventually, the implications of it being violated would hit her. But for now, she appeared to be focusing on the question of "why" like the excellent scientist she was.

"Dr. Lewis, I think we're done here for the night," Detective Anderson said. "We collected lots of prints and will start to run them tomorrow. Since you're a federally funded entity, we have the prints of the folks who work here and we'll eliminate those, but we'd appreciate it if you could come in and maybe look through some photos to see if you recognize the man who was here tonight."

Nia nodded but her attention was still on the mess that used to be her tidy lab.

"We'll also get an electrician out tomorrow to check the alarm," Officer Schuyler said. "Do you have a ride home?"

"Yes, she does," Jake answered.

At the same time, Nia said, "I can drive myself. I'm fine."

"Of course you're fine," Jake countered. "But your head got a little shaken up tonight and you shouldn't be driving."

"So I should ride with *you*? It seems like I'm taking a bigger chance with that than driving on my own," she said.

He grinned. "Fair point, but I promise, I can drive like a normal person when I want to."

Nia looked at him skeptically, then her gaze switched to Dominic, who lifted a shoulder. "He picked Charlotte up from the airport this week."

"Damian asked *him* to do that?" Nia asked, pointing to Jake and clearly surprised.

"Upon pain of death if either Charlotte or the car was damaged, but yeah, he did," Dominic answered. Nia's attention lingered on Dominic, and he shook his head, answering the question in her eyes. "I could take you home in my car, but then he'd be driving yours back to your house unsupervised, and I'd advise against that. You're hurt, I don't generally trust him behind the wheel, but I do trust him with you."

Nia seemed to consider that answer, then finally, she let out a long sigh. "Fine," she said. Jake thought he should probably be offended at her reticence, but he was just glad she was going to let him make sure she got home safely. Besides, his reputation with cars was a carefully cultivated one, and he could hardly blame her or Dominic for thinking of him exactly what he wanted them to think when it came to his driving skills. The truth was, he was a damn good driver. He just hated it—give him a surfboard in a storm and he was a happy camper but ask him to drive ten miles and he wanted to pull his hair out.

With some reluctance, Nia handed her keys over and twenty minutes later, Jake pulled her car into her driveway. She lived in a small bungalow in a newer development that was a mix of locals and a few snowbirds that couldn't afford something on the beach.

"Thanks for the ride," she said, opening her door.

Jake ignored her and exited the car. "I have the keys, it's not worth arguing with me," he said as he jangled them in his hand.

He could see the calculation in her eye—could she grab them if she lunged fast enough? She couldn't, not even on a good day. And wearing heels and sporting a mild concussion, she had no chance. He grinned when annoyed acceptance settled on her face.

"You're such an asshole," she said, walking by him toward her front door.

The epithet rolled right off him. His teammates called him that every day. Usually more than once. As far as he was concerned, it was a term of endearment.

"You want any water or anything?" Nia offered after he closed and locked the door behind them. "Not quite the night I had planned, but hey, I'm alive, so no real complaints." She walked into the kitchen as she spoke and reached for a glass on the drying rack beside the sink.

"Nah, I'm good," he said, leaning against the tile counter. "The good news is that if you still plan to get up at six, I only need to wake you up once in the middle of the night since the paramedic said not to let you sleep more than four hours at a time."

Nia's eyes slid to the clock on her microwave as she filled her glass. It was eleven o'clock.

"How do you know I wake up at six?" she asked after taking a sip of her water.

Jake shrugged. "Remember that night of Carnival when you were out with Dominic and me? You said you had to leave because you wanted at least two hours of sleep before having to get up and go to work the next day. It was three-thirty in the morning, so accommodating the time it would have taken you to get home and adding two hours to that, gives me a six o'clock rising time."

She stared at him. For a weirdly long time. Then she turned and started to walk toward her bedroom.

"That's too much math for me right now. I have a concussion," she said as she walked away.

"It's only a potential mild concussion," Jake called back, parroting her earlier words.

She didn't bother turning around, but he did like the one-finger salute she threw him over her shoulder before disappearing into her room and shutting the door on him.

Nia winced as her bedroom door shut behind her a little more forcefully than necessary. Kicking off her shoes, she wandered into her bathroom, thinking a shower and some ibuprofen might be in order for the night.

She didn't worry about Jake settling himself in. He'd spent enough time at her place to make himself comfortable in the guestroom. In fact, it was practically his room. Not that he stayed over that often, but he was the only person who'd ever used that room.

She popped two pills, then she stripped out of her clothes, letting them fall to the floor. As she did, the events of the night started to catch up with her. She hadn't given it much thought at the time, but the realization of how close she'd come to someone who was clearly comfortable with violence—even if just against property—shook her. She shivered as memories of the night filtered through her mind like a series of snapshots. She wasn't sure if she'd ever forget the wild look in the man's eyes when his face appeared in the window.

Turning on the water, she stepped under the spray, hoping the warmth would soothe her. She forced herself to stop thinking about the man and his crazy eyes and instead started to mull over the question of why. Why would someone break into her lab? The Center itself had a few controlled substances and some very expensive equipment, but he hadn't been after any of that.

The water streamed over her body, and she let those thoughts percolate as she gently washed her hair and body. She had more questions than answers, but at least the process occupied her mind and kept her from dwelling on the man who could have done much more harm to both her and her equipment.

After shutting off the water, she dried off in the shower, then stepped out. As she hung her towel, her gaze caught on her phone sitting on the counter. Should she call her mom? Jackie Lewis wasn't likely to care one way or the other if Nia had been hurt, and she certainly wouldn't care about the damage to the lab.

Nia stared at the phone for a beat, then raised her eyes and looked at herself in the mirror. Her gaze lingered on the butterfly bandage that had survived the shower, and as her attention focused on the edge of the cut visible along the top edge of the bandage, she could feel the rumblings of a pity party starting to happen. Her lab had been broken into, she'd missed a night out with Dominic and Jake, and the only reason she was contemplating calling her mom was because if Jackie found out about the incident from anyone else, it would be yet one more thing Nia had failed to do for the woman who'd gone to the trouble of birthing her.

With a sigh, Nia picked up the phone and dashed off a quick text as she walked into her bedroom. Jackie wouldn't care enough to reply, but even so, Nia deliberately turned the sound off and set the device face down on her bedside table. She didn't need to be confronted with her mother's neglect tonight. Not when she was feeling so raw and the idea of a pity party was feeling more and more attractive by the second.

Pulling a tank top and a pair of boxers from her drawers, Nia slipped into her go-to pajamas then slid between her sheets.

In the next room, Jake's bed creaked, and a pang of longing lanced through her. What she wouldn't give to crawl in next to Jake and have him hold her. There was no doubt in her mind that he'd keep the looming pity party at bay. But even more than that, having someone like Jake—someone kind and capable and endearing—care for her might be enough to remind her that, despite her family's opinions otherwise, she was *worthy*. Worthy of friendship, worthy of care, worthy of love.

But even though the draw to go to him was strong and she knew he'd welcome her—and welcome her platonically—it was a line she wasn't sure she wanted to cross.

Rolling over and hugging an extra pillow to her chest, she thought back to those first few times the two of them had gone out. Jake was a good looking man—tall, well built, with sun-streaked brown hair, slate blue eyes, and a face that looked like every girls' fantasy of the perfect surfer. The spark of attraction she'd felt toward him would have surprised exactly no one, least of all her.

There had been a few moments when she'd thought she'd caught a hint that her interest was reciprocated. But then it became clear that friendship was all he had in mind, and she'd decided that having Jake's friendship was more important than maybe giving something more a go—especially when the *something more* would only have to end once Jake left the island. They'd been more or less inseparable—or as inseparable as their jobs would let them—since she'd committed to the friendship-path, and she didn't regret a moment of time they spent together.

She let out a sigh and closed her eyes, willing herself to forget about the comfort Jake might offer and fall asleep. The pills still hadn't taken effect yet and her head throbbed, but she did her best to ignore the pain. Unfortunately, she didn't have the strength to ignore both the pain and the memories of the past few hours, and within a few minutes, her body started to tremble. Not big shakes, but little ones, little ones that were big enough to remind her that maybe she wasn't as strong as she thought she was.

Jake's bed creaked again, and her mind flitted back to what Dominic had said to her that night. He trusted Jake with her.

And so did she. He had come as soon as she'd told him what had happened, he'd driven her home, he'd insisted on staying to make sure her concussion wasn't a problem. The crazy thing was, none of his actions surprised her. It was what Jake did and who he was. He cared for those in his life as easily as he breathed.

Letting out a long breath, she swung her legs over the side of the bed and rose. She wasn't sure if what she was doing was the right thing, but if ever there was a night she needed, or wanted, someone to tell her everything would be okay, tonight was it.

She left her room and walked down the short hallway. Pausing before his door, she hesitated, then knocked gently.

"Come in, Doc," he said.

Quietly, she opened the door just enough to see him lying on his side, facing her. She stared at him for a moment, a moment of indecision.

"Need a hug?" he asked.

She did, she desperately did. She managed a nod.

"Come here, sugar," he said, flipping back the covers. "I'll keep the demons at bay."

CHAPTER THREE

THOUGH JAKE WAS NOWHERE in sight, a fresh pot of coffee sat in the machine when Nia woke the next morning.

She'd curled into his side all night, and he'd rubbed her head and kept the shakes away until she'd drifted into a deep sleep. As promised, he'd also managed to wake her up once, around three in the morning. He'd given her someone to lean on when she needed it, and she was grateful, more than grateful, for the gift.

But at the moment, if she were honest with herself, she was also feeling a little selfish—she would have liked to see him before he'd left. She had an interesting—and probably not very fun—day ahead of her and she could have used the laughter he brought into her life. He also had that disheveled sexy look going for him in the mornings, and it always perked her up. They may be just friends, but she wasn't blind. And seeing him in her kitchen, in his boxers with a cup of coffee, wouldn't have been a bad way to start her day.

That said, waking up to a fresh pot of coffee wasn't a bad alternative. She poured a cup then went to the fridge to pull out some yogurt for breakfast only to find a note taped to the door.

"Meet at The Shack at four this afternoon," Jake had written, referring to a bar on the southeast side of the island. Owned by Isiah Clarke, the significant other of another agent, Alexis Wright, The Shack had become the de facto gathering spot for the five members of the FBI special task force.

She stared at the note, not because the substance was anything special or surprising, but because she really had no clue where he'd found the tape. She couldn't remember the last time she'd ever used any, so had no earthly idea where it might have been or how long it would have taken Jake to find it. But he'd probably gleefully gone through all her kitchen drawers as he searched. She smiled at the thought. Leave it to Jake to not take the easy way and text.

After eating a light breakfast and finishing her coffee, Nia headed into the lab. Early on a Sunday morning, no one was in to greet or distract her when she arrived, and she got straight to work, sweeping up the glass, plastic, sand, and gravel. By the time the floors and counters were clean, a couple of the research assistants and her associate director had stopped by. Each of them had come in to check on their own projects, but once they'd heard what had happened, they had all offered their help. The intermittent interruptions had been a welcome break —especially once she'd started sorting through the hundreds of papers that had been tossed from her files and scattered around the room, like some kind of bizarre ticker-tape parade.

By three in the afternoon, exhaustion had kicked in, and as she slid the last sheet of paper into a hanging file, she contemplated texting Jake to tell him she'd meet them another time. As she considered her options, her fingers drummed on the metal cabinet—the cabinet that once again held everything it should since, oddly, nothing had been missing. It was too early to go home—if she did, she'd end up grabbing a quick meal and a glass of wine, and would no doubt fall asleep much too early to have a good night's sleep. She didn't relish the idea of being questioned by her FBI friends—because she knew that was the primary reason Jake wanted her to stop by—but it beat sitting around the house. Especially if she could get Isiah to make her some chicken wings. No one made wings like Isiah Clarke.

Decision made, she locked up her lab then made her way to her car, planning a quick stop at the liquor store before heading out to The Shack. It seemed weird to bring alcohol to a bar, but both Isiah and Alexis enjoyed a good whiskey, and if Isiah was going to host her after hours, then he deserved a host-gift.

Forty minutes later, she walked into the bar, bottle in hand. The Shack sat up on a hill, and the outdoor veranda had, in her opinion, some of the best views on the island. It was also far enough from the hustle and bustle of Havensted that very few tourists made their way to the watering hole. Not that that was a problem on a Sunday afternoon when the bar was closed, but during the week, it made for a nice change of pace when she wanted a beautiful place to relax and enjoy a drink and good food without the crowds.

"Just in time, Nia," Isiah said as she joined him at the bar.

"In time for what, is the question," she replied, handing the bottle over.

Isiah glanced at the label. "You didn't have to bring that, but I'm certainly not going to turn down a bottle of Oban," he said, as he placed the bottle on a low shelf. "As to your question, just in time for the food. They're all outside with a big plate of wings, and I was about to bring out some mini-rotis—pork and potato, today. Go ahead and join everyone, and I'll bring you a drink when I bring the rest of the food. You should make them wait until you've had at least one before they start the inquisition."

Nia smiled. Isiah was a retired Navy SEAL who'd taken to bar-ownership like a fish to water and was one of the most chill people she'd ever met. "Make it a double and I should be good," she said, pointing to a local rum.

"On the rocks?"

"Of course," she said.

"You got it."

When Isiah disappeared into the kitchen, Nia joined the group on the wide verandah. With tall ceilings, fans, and screens to keep the bugs out, it wasn't hard to figure out why the large, circular table that sat on one end of the space was a favorite.

She'd just finished greeting everyone and assuring them she was fine when Isiah returned with the food and her drink. Grabbing an open seat between Jake and Dominic, she gave Isiah a heartfelt "thank you" as she relieved him of the glass then raised it to her lips. There was nothing quite like the way a cold rum turned to liquid heat as it traveled down her throat.

The food provided a distraction—at least for a few minutes —as everyone passed around small plates and started to pile wings and rotis on them. She'd been looking forward to eating, but as she watched her friends descend on the food, the reason for her being there crept back into her mind and she found she didn't have much of an appetite. During the day, she'd been able to push aside *really* thinking about how violated she felt—it was easy to focus on cleaning and re-ordering her lab and answering questions from her colleagues. But here, with Jake and all the others, she had no illusions about what was coming, and she almost wondered if reliving it would be worse than living it.

"Eat," Jake said, setting a plate in front of her that held a couple of wings and a small roti. "If for no other reason than to absorb that rum you're drinking since I doubt you've eaten much else today."

She started to protest, but then realized he was right. She'd had a bag of chips and some trail mix from the vending machine in the kitchen at The Center, but nothing more than that since her breakfast.

"Eating isn't normally a problem for me," she muttered,

picking up the roti. "But you're right, I do need some sustenance."

"There's nothing normal about what happened last night," Jake said. The matter-of-fact tone of his voice reassured her that he wasn't coddling her, just stating a fact. Which was good because she didn't want to be coddled. At least she didn't think she did. She'd never really *been* coddled, so maybe she did want it?

"Whatever you're thinking right now, turn it off," Alexis said. Nia blinked and looked at the agent. "Whatever it was," Alexis continued, "we can talk about it if you want to, but first, you need to eat."

Nia glanced down and she still held the roti in her hand. She hadn't taken a single bite. "Right," she said, then bit into it. The flavor of spiced potatoes and pork exploded in her mouth, and suddenly, she was ravenous.

Fifteen minutes later, the table looked like a swarm of locusts had descended, done their best, then moved on. Nearly empty plates were scattered across the surface holding various pieces of evidence of the feast they'd devoured—a remnant of wings here, a few fallen potatoes there. Yes, the food had just been finger food, but it had been plentiful and, of course, delicious.

Nia sat back and took a sip of her drink. Lowering her hand, she let the bottom of the glass rest on the arm of the chair. "Okay," she said. "Lay it on me. I don't know how much more I can tell you than what I told the police last night—which I'm sure Dominic and Jake have relayed to you all—but ask away."

Damian, who sat on the far side of the table with his fiancée, Charlotte, glanced at Beni. Of course, the first question would come from one of those two. In truth, the five members of the task force were all peers and they had a director to whom they all reported. But between them—Damian, Beni, Dominic, Jake, and Alexis—Beni and Damian seemed to take up the role of team leader more often than not.

"Why don't you tell us what you saw?" Beni said, leaning back in her own chair and taking a sip of her beer.

As succinctly and as quickly as possible, Nia recounted everything she'd heard and seen during the short time she'd been in the building with the perpetrator. When she was done, Damian asked if anything had been taken at the same time that Alexis asked if she'd been to the police yet to look through the mug shot books. She answered Alexis's question in the negative, saying that they'd asked her to come by when the main office opened on Monday, then turned to Damian.

"Just the two parrotfish," she said.

"Parrotfish?" Isiah asked.

"Yes, parrotfish," Jake said. "But there was something hinky about them wasn't there, Doc? Something you didn't tell the police?"

She glanced at Jake, not all that surprised that he'd noticed her omission the night before. She wasn't sure why she hadn't mentioned anything to the police. She didn't have anything to hide, but absconding with two parrotfish had seemed so absurd that she didn't think it could be anything more than a joke.

Jake gave her a small nod of encouragement, and she turned back to the table. She didn't think the theft was meaningful, but she took a few minutes to tell them the origin of the fish and why she'd had them in her office in the first place.

"You said you brought in four, but you only had two in your lab. Where are the other two?" Jake asked.

"In one of the shared research labs," Nia answered. "I took two for testing and we wanted the other two for observation. And yes, before you ask, they are both still there and acting completely normal. We were going to release them today, but I decided to hold them and we'll run some blood tests on them tomorrow. I can compare it to the samples I took from the fish in my lab. As long as neither sample shows something that might have a broader detrimental effect on the eco-system, then I'm not that concerned. As I said last night, I have no idea why that man would have taken the two from my lab."

"If it's not something like a bacteria or virus—something that would have a broader impact—what might make the fish behave the way they did?" Alexis asked.

Nia thought for a moment before answering. "It would be uncommon, but the most likely culprit would be something they ate. Honestly, though, it was almost like they were on drugs or something. Their bodies were functioning, but their brains seemed to be shut off. A bacteria, and maybe even a virus, could do that. But if it's not either of those, I'd have to do more research."

Sitting beside Alexis, Isiah stirred. His gaze traveled around the group then landed on Alexis.

"What are you thinking?" Alexis asked softly.

Isiah hesitated, then answered. "She's using almost the exact same words you used to describe Angela Rosen," he said. "The body is functioning, but the mind is somewhere else entirely."

Nia's attention shot to Alexis. Nia knew about Angela Rosen —a CIA agent who'd been shot while she and Alexis had tried to escape a kidnapper—but only because Nia had been on the Navy research boat where Rosen had been brought for emergency care immediately after the shooting. As the case was mostly classified, that was the extent of her knowledge, and until now, she'd had no idea that something other than a bullet wound had been wrong with Rosen.

"Would drugs cause the same reaction in fish as in humans?" Beni asked.

Nia nodded. "Some drugs, yes. The dosage would need to be different to account for size, of course, but it's possible."

"Who else could have known that you had these oddly behaving fish in your lab?" Damian asked.

Nia started to answer that no one other than she, and the researchers with her that day, knew, but then she paused. Because that wasn't entirely true. "A couple of us went to The Taphouse after we finished for the day. We were talking about the fish and how crazy they were behaving. We were laughing about it because we'd never seen anything like it before. Of course, we all knew it could potentially be bad news—like I said, we were, *we are*, most concerned about a bacteria or a virus— but we were all still laughing about it. You know what that place is like," she said, turning to Jake. The Taphouse wasn't a place any of the others would likely go—Damian and Alexis tended to stick closer to home with their partners, while Beni preferred the nightlife in Havensted and Dominic preferred places less, well, gritty. And The Taphouse was nothing if not gritty.

"It's possible any number of people could have overheard you," Jake said, finishing her thought. Nia nodded.

"But who, and what are the odds that it would be someone who would know something about why the fish were acting the way they were?" Beni asked.

Nia shrugged, but it was Jake who answered. "If those fish got into something they shouldn't have—"

"Like maybe finding a stash of drugs somewhere," Dominic interjected.

Jake nodded. "It wouldn't surprise me in the least to find out that someone in The Taphouse would know something about it."

"I've heard of drugs being left at ocean drop spots—tied to buoys or weighted down and dropped near a reef—for dealers to pick up a later, but I haven't heard of it happening *here*," Alexis said.

"It's only a matter of time before a good idea spreads," Dominic interjected with a wry grin.

"When were you at The Taphouse?" Jake asked, pinning her with his dark blue eyes.

Nia lifted a shoulder. "After the dive and closing up The Center. Maybe eight o'clock."

"So chances are that if it was a drug drop gone wrong, whatever is left of the drugs has probably been picked up already since it's been, what, nearly forty-eight hours since you collected the fish?" Beni asked, clearly pondering whether a search of the area was warranted.

"That's certainly enough time to go collect something if there was anything there to collect," Nia said.

"I hear doubt in your voice," Jake said, sliding his unfinished drink over. She glanced at her glass to find it empty. She hadn't remembered finishing it, but she set the tumbler down on the table and shook her head at Jake's offer. A double rum wasn't enough to get her tipsy, but she had to drive home and any more alcohol might do the trick.

"It just sounds far-fetched," she said. "Not the drugs being dropped in the ocean for later pick-up. That actually sounds reasonable, maybe even brilliant. But the fact that maybe some of those drugs leaked and somehow some fish ingested them, and then we happened to come along and see them acting high as kites. And then, not just all that, but that someone who might be involved in the initial drug drop—or perhaps pick-up—overheard us talking about it in a bar? It's possible, I suppose. The scientist in me has to admit that it's a possibility. But the statistician in me also has to acknowledge that the odds aren't good for that chain of events."

Jake shot her a look that made her feel like she'd taken away his favorite toy. He liked adventure, and nothing piqued his interest quite like a good dose of intrigue. But what he was thinking might have happened had a less than 5% chance of being possible, and she wasn't going to pretend otherwise.

"Did you find anything in the blood samples that you took from the fish that went missing?" Jake asked.

Nia's gaze bounced around the table before landing on Jake.

She felt a little chagrinned at the answer she had to offer, but she didn't shy away. "I didn't even look."

Jake wasn't the only FBI agent at the table to frown at her, and yes, now that she'd mentioned it, it did seem odd that the results of the blood samples—the only evidence she still had in her possession of the two missing fish—hadn't been the first thing she'd looked at that morning. But she was a scientist, not law enforcement, and although she wanted to understand why her lab had been targeted, her primary goal for the day had been to get it back up and running before The Center opened to the public on Monday and she got pulled into other tasks.

"I'll look first thing in the morning," she said, avoiding everyone's gaze. She didn't have anything to feel guilty about, and yet somehow, she felt…inadequate. As if she'd failed them.

"Look, it's late and I didn't get much sleep last night," she said, rising from her seat. Everyone but Charlotte and Beni rose as well, startling her with the sudden movement and the cacophony of chair legs scraping against the floor.

As sure as she knew her own name, she knew they were planning something. Something—whatever it was—that she wasn't ready to participate in because it would likely involve her being asked a gazillion more questions, or would require that she consider things—like the man she'd only caught a glimpse of—more than she wanted to.

"I'll give you a call if I find anything tomorrow in the tests," Nia said, stepping away from the table. "Isiah, as always, the food was amazing. Thank you."

He nodded to her and, beside him, Alexis started to speak, but Isiah slid his hand into hers and squeezed. Alexis hesitated, then slipped from Isiah's hold and gave Nia a hug. "Take care of yourself tonight and get a good night's sleep. Call if you need anything," she said.

Nia assured Alexis she would, and as she spoke, Charlotte stood as well and rounded the table. "I have the day off tomorrow. Call me if you want to grab lunch," she said, as she wrapped her arms around Nia and gave her a hug, too. That seemed to shift the focus of the moment and it was another ten minutes and five more hugs before she made it to her car.

As she navigated her way back to the west side of the island, she pondered the strange truth that she was more at home with those five FBI agents and their significant others than with her own family.

CHAPTER FOUR

"I SHOULD HAVE ASKED her where they picked up those fish," Jake said to Beni as he leaned back in his chair. The two of them, and Dominic, were occupying their desks at the FBI office on the north side of Havensted on Monday morning while Damian and Alexis were conducting a security training at Hemmeleigh Resort where The Summit of World Leaders would be held in seven months.

"You're bored and it's been a while since you've been out on the water, so you're looking for an excuse to go diving," Dominic said. "You know you don't do well when you don't get out on the water, so why don't you go? It's slow here today. Take your gear and head out. If you want to feel productive, go diving around Hemmeleigh and see what kind of underwater threats we need to consider for The Summit."

Everything Dominic said was true, but Jake's recent lack of dive time was not the root of his agitation. No, an early morning call from his father—a man Jake would like nothing more than to be estranged from—took those honors. Well, that and still worrying about Nia. Something had happened in that beautiful, complex brain of hers just before she'd left The Shack and despite going over that part of the conversation at least a dozen times in his head, he couldn't, for the life of him, figure out what had put that pensive look on her face.

He switched his attention to Beni. He wasn't sure what he was looking for from her, but maybe something other than "go for a dive," because as much as he wouldn't mind being in the water, he was definitely not in the right headspace for it at the moment.

"I'll give you ten seconds to remember that you shouldn't even bother looking to me for sympathy," Beni said without looking up from the file she was going through.

Her response was curt, but it did the job and made him laugh, pulling him away from his own thoughts. It was so *Beni*. "Beni" and "sympathy" didn't go in the same sentence.

"I'm being whiny, aren't I?" he said.

"No more than usual," Beni answered.

He glanced at Dominic, who shrugged. "I'd say 'annoying' more than 'whiny,' but 'whiny' works, too."

Jake let out a long exhale and craned his head to get a glimpse of the peek-a-boo view of the ocean they had from their office. Fuck, maybe he did need to get out on the water—maybe not for a dive, but maybe a swim? He'd practically grown up in the ocean and it was definitely in his blood. There was nothing, absolutely nothing, like straddling a surfboard and catching the first glimpse of a beautiful wave—the possibilities were endless and the world was wide open.

Of course, he couldn't surf. Not anymore. Even if the Caribbean had the right waves, the knee injury that had taken him off the pro-tour more than ten years ago had also, more or less, forced him off a board altogether.

A familiar darkness started to cut into his psyche as memories of Hawaii, and the career that had ended so abruptly, began pushing their way into his mind. If he let them take hold, what would happen next wasn't a place he wanted to go—not mentally, not physically.

"I gotta go," he said, rising from his seat, his chair scraping against the wood floor. Both Beni and Dominic looked up, but he ignored them. "I have my cell. Call if anything comes up." And with that, he left. He'd catch hell from Dominic later, although Beni would probably let it slide—she was as badass as badasses came, but was also selective about which battles she picked and those she walked away from, and anything having to do with *feelings*, which he was clearly having at this moment, tended to fall into the camp of things she let slide.

He made his way down to his jeep parked in the building's garage and he was pulling out of his spot when a call came in. He considered ignoring it and heading toward the warehouse he rented on the northwest side of Havensted, but he'd told Dom and Beni to call if anything came up. It would be pretty shitty of him not to answer if it was one of them. Besides, he'd only left because he'd needed a distraction—whether it was the warehouse or work, either would do.

But when his cell phone connected to his Bluetooth, his heart stuttered. Pulling to a stop in the middle of an aisle, he hit the answer button.

"What's going on, sugar," he said, keeping his voice casual.

"I don't know, Jake," Nia said, the fact that she hadn't responded to his use of the nickname she—only sometimes—hated, told him how serious her call was.

"Talk to me," he said, putting the car back into gear and exiting the garage in the direction of The Center.

"I ran the tests on the two fish we still have and compared those results to the results I had on the two that were stolen..."

"And?" he prompted.

"They all ingested some drug—the same drug. It was mostly out of the systems of the two fish we still have, but the markers are all the same. But the thing is," she hesitated, and he could all but see her, standing in her lab, staring at the two sets of results.

"The thing is?" he pressed.

"It's like nothing I've ever seen before, Jake," she said, her voice clear and strong. "It's a synthetic drug, for sure. But it's not presenting as any drug we know."

Jake stood behind Nia, looking over her shoulder at the two test results. He could see what she'd been referring to in terms of the similar markers on each of the four fish—and two were definitely higher in concentration than the other two.

"Walk me through what these are," he said, pointing to the little spikes in the graph.

"That's a barbiturate," she said, pointing to one. "But that's a benzodiazepine," she said, pointing to another. "Benzodiazepines largely replaced barbiturates, except in a few cases, so it's unusual to see them in the same sample. But where it gets weirder is here," she said, pointing to two other spikes. "The first is a version of amphetamine, though it's not pure. The second is scopolamine, also knowns as Devil's Breath and the only naturally occurring drug in the sample."

"What would this kind of drug cocktail do?" he asked, mostly to himself, as he stared at the sheets. He wasn't a chemist or even a scientist of any sort, and so the pages wouldn't reveal any more to him than Nia had shared, but still, he studied the peaks and valleys and numbers and chemical markers.

"In a person, I don't know," Nia said. "But I told you how the fish were acting...like their bodies were fully functional but their minds were blank."

Jake considered the implications of that and it didn't give him the warm fuzzies. He thought back to what Isiah had reminded them all of the night before—that Alexis had described the deceased CIA agent Angela Rosen in much the same way—and it didn't take a genius to figure out that someone, somewhere in the Caribbean, appeared to be experimenting with designing drugs.

If it didn't impact Tildas Island and the upcoming Summit, it technically wasn't in the jurisdiction of the task force to look into. But even if the drugs weren't circulating on the island, the drug trade wasn't comprised of upstanding, law-abiding citizens and it *was* the team's job to make sure *those* people didn't pose a threat to the security of the upcoming event.

"Can you show me where you found the fish? Or tell me, if you can't get away right now?" he asked.

Nia set the pages down and turned around to face him. "You want to go look *now*?"

He nodded. Her hazel eyes studied him. True, he might be looking for an excuse to get out on the water, but he also truly did want to see if there was any evidence of a drop point. He didn't expect to find any drugs or a smoking gun or anything like that. But if he could find some evidence as to *how* the drugs were dropped and how the spots were marked, that would be more information than they had before.

"Jake, what's going on?" Nia asked.

He shifted and let his gaze drift to the papers until Nia placed her hands on his cheeks and forced his attention back to her. "Something is bugging you and it's not just that," she said, jerking her head toward the results. "Talk to me. I'll take you to where we found the fish, but I need to know what's going on in that mind of yours before we go, if for no other reason than for our safety when we get in the water."

He tried to pull away at the suggestion that he would *ever* put them in danger, but she didn't let him. In fact, she slid her hands higher and pinched his earlobes between her fingers. "Don't even think of blowing this off," she said.

"That hurts, Doc. I didn't know you were into pain," he tried to joke.

Nia's eyes narrowed. "You have no idea what I'm into, sugar," she shot back. "But I can tell you what I'm *not* into and that's two things. The first is a friend who dodges a simple question, and the second is a dive buddy with something else on his mind. Talk to me, or we don't go."

He considered pulling the FBI card and making it a formal request. He really considered it. But then his eyes locked on hers. Nia was a tall woman and in the heels she wore, the top of her head came up to his eye level. She was inches away from him, her face slightly turned up, refusing to let him back away.

Over the months he'd known her, he'd seen the scientist-Nia, the friend-Nia, and the fun-loving-partying-Nia, but he'd never seen *this* Nia. This Nia that wasn't letting him back away from taking a step toward something more—not *more* in a romantic sense, but *more* in the friendship sense.

Jake was a man who lived his life on the surface, letting the wind—or whim—take him wherever he felt like going at the moment. But as her eyes stayed locked on his, refusing to give him any quarter, a physical change started to pulse and course through him. There were reasons he'd chosen to live his life the way he had, but with her steady hands on his face and her unrelenting presence, he started to feel grounded. And like parts of a complicated lock clicking into place, Nia suddenly made him feel safe.

Slowly, the anxiety that had been building in his system since earlier that morning ebbed away, leaving behind something calmer and clearer.

"We can talk about it in the car," he said, all teasing gone from his voice.

Again, her eyes searched his. "Promise?"

He nodded and slowly, she released her hold on his ears and

slid her hands from his face. She didn't pull them away altogether, though, and her palms landed on his chest.

When her gaze drifted to somewhere behind him and her
finger started tapping a disjointed beat against his shirt, he
knew she was making plans—determining which boat to take,
what equipment was needed, the tides, the dive times, and all
those things an experienced diver, and responsible head of the
Marine Center, would take into consideration. Nia might be the
life of the party when they hit the bars, but she didn't become
the head of the largest research center in the Caribbean because
she could dance the night away. She was damn good at her job
and it was a thing of beauty to watch her do it.

Finally, she stepped away. "We'll take the smaller boat. The
water is smooth today so it should handle fine and it's easier
with just the two of us."

He felt the loss of the connection as she turned toward her
computer. "Before you shut your computer down, can you send
those results to Beni?" he asked, managing to remember at least
some of his professional duties in the midst of what felt a little
like a crisis of identity.

She said nothing, but the clack of the keys told him she was
doing as asked. A few minutes later, she powered down,
unplugged the device, and slid it into a bag. "The boat is gassed
and ready to go. My equipment is in our equipment room,
along with fresh tanks. Do you want to grab your own or see if
we have something that works for you? We keep extras for
when other researchers and scientists visit."

He reached for her bag and slung it over his shoulder. "If you
have something that you think will work for me, let's go with
that since mine is at home and it will add an hour to the day if
we have to head over and get it before we leave."

Nia crossed her arms and let her gaze drift over him. It
wasn't a sexual perusal, not in the least. Yet, something about it
made him wonder what it would be like if it were.

Startled at the thought, he stepped back, putting another few feet between them. His head was definitely messing with him today. He might be able to handle the foray into a deeper friendship, but anything more than that? Uh huh, no way. A deeper friendship was one thing; sex was another. In a perfect world—in the world of Alexis and Isiah, and Charlotte and Damian—the two co-existed. But they didn't in his. Not because he didn't believe that friendship and sex could go together, but because together, that would be *way* more emotion than he could handle. Was he a coward about that? Yes, without question. But he needed his carefully curated life in order to keep from falling down the emotional and mental rabbit hole that he often teetered on the edge of.

"Yes, we'll have something that works for you," Nia said, oblivious to the emotional danger he'd just sidestepped.

"Great, let's go," he said, turning toward the exit.

Nia came up beside him and slipped an arm through his. It didn't mean anything—she'd done it a million times since they'd first started hanging out. But the part of his brain that had just put the words "Nia" and "sex" in the same sentence wondered if it *could* mean anything. And if it *could*, did he want it to? Did Nia?

She bumped her hip against his as they walked—a particular talent of hers—and he turned his head toward her. She was smiling up at him. It was a nice smile, a friendly one. Not one that made him think she'd been thinking the same things he had.

Especially not when the smile shifted into a grin.

"And just because it's only a short drive to the equipment warehouse and dock, don't think you're going to get away with not telling me what's bothering you," she said.

Nope, she was most definitely *not* thinking the same things he was.

43

What had possessed her to grab Jake's face and force him to talk to her, Nia hadn't a clue. Well, scratch that, she did. The errant thought she'd had the night before about him and the team being more like family to her than her actual family hadn't turned out to be so errant. No, it had festered—no, not festered, that made it sound like a disease—but it had fermented overnight and turned into something completely different than the original toss-away thought.

And then Jake had walked into her lab, strung tighter than a bowline in a storm, and suddenly, *he* mattered. Not just as a going-out buddy or someone she had a ton of fun with—which she did—but as someone who *meant something* to her. Of course he always had, but something had shifted inside her when his eyes had met hers. When his eyes had met hers, and she'd seen a flash of pain there. It hadn't lingered and she hadn't a clue what had put it there, but it was clear that Jake was in pain—not physically, but mentally—and she was no more willing to walk away from it than she would be if he'd broken his arm. He meant too much to her.

"So talk to me," she said, leading Jake to the path that ran from The Center to the marina rather than to her car. It took the same amount of time to walk as to drive and so she'd made the executive decision not to coop Jake up in her car for the ten minutes it would take them to get to the dock.

"I was worried about you," Jake said. "You can't think that breaking into The Center was just about the two fish. Nobody is that weird. I've just been waiting for the other shoe to drop and it was making me antsy. Now the other shoe has dropped."

"That's sweet, and I appreciate the concern, but maybe you can do me the favor of not treating me like an idiot and tell me what's really bothering you," she said.

Jake stopped in the middle of the path. She didn't bother to stop and wait for him. She was the master of evasive answers when it came to things that were, well, uncomfortable, and she'd known a half-truth would come out of his mouth the moment he'd inhaled before speaking his first word.

"That was what was going on," he insisted when he caught up with her.

"I'm sure it was," she said as they paused at an intersection and let a safari taxi pass by. "But it wasn't the only thing. Talk to me about that other thing."

They crossed the street and started down the winding walkway toward the water. The smell of the ocean whispered around them, mingling with the scents of the lush foliage that lined the path. Jake was quiet for a long time, but he'd eventually answer—if for no other reason than to ensure he'd be able to join her on the boat for the dive. Of all the members of the task force, Jake would most appreciate how uncompromising she'd be about their safety.

Finally, when the top of the warehouse came into sight, Jake slowed his steps and stopped. This time she stopped with him.

"I got a call from my father this morning," he said. "That's not a way I like to start my day."

Nia searched her memory for anything Jake might have mentioned about his family but quickly realized that, like her, he hadn't ever mentioned a thing. She stared at him, waiting for him to elaborate.

"My family," he hesitated. "We're not close. Not like normal families. Or maybe not like families *should* be." He looked down at her as if expecting her to acknowledge that she understood what he was talking about.

"My family lives here on the island," she said. "Has for generations. There are a lot of us. But I don't see them very often. Or talk to them much. And when I do, I usually end up regretting it. They aren't bad people, but they are bad family. At least to me."

Jake's eyes searched hers. Her heart rate kicked up and a flush that had nothing to do with the temperatures warmed her cheeks. Suddenly, she understood what a difficult task she'd laid at Jake's feet. If his family was anywhere near as messed up as hers, maybe she would have been better off letting that sleeping dog lie.

But then again, she hadn't really had a choice. Not if she wanted to be sure his head was in the game when they both went into the water.

Jake gave a rueful chuckle and started walking again. "Well, my family is bad family *and* bad people. They are sketchy as shit, and it's a fairly regular occurrence for them to call me and ask me to do some favors for them. In fact, that's the only reason they ever call me."

Wow, she wasn't entirely sure what that meant, but she had a pretty good idea what kind of favors someone sketchy could ask of a well-respected and well-positioned FBI agent. "How big is your family?"

"My mom died when I was young," he said as they rounded the bend and the bay came into view. "My dad owns a few luxury resorts on a couple of different Hawaiian islands, and my older brother helps run them. My younger brother has decided to not even bother with using the family businesses as a smoke-screen for their criminal activity and has gone straight for a leadership position in a particularly nasty group that he refers to as businessmen but that I, and my fellow FBI colleagues, and any reasonable person, would refer to as the mafia."

She couldn't help it, it was grossly inappropriate, but she laughed. Jake pulled her to a halt at the side of the parking lot and glared down at her. Which, of course, made her laugh even more.

He crossed his arms and watched. Finally, she pulled herself together and reached for his arms, wrapping her hands around his bare skin.

"I'm sorry," she said. "I'm really sorry about your mom, Jake. That must have been so difficult. But, I just…well, I know this isn't the point, but honestly, how the hell did you get into the FBI?" she asked lightly, fighting another smile. "I mean, what kind of screening did you have to go through? Did you have to turn in a contact to prove your loyalty? Or maybe set someone up? Not that I'm not glad you are an agent and not that I doubt your loyalty in the least, but seriously, how did that happen?"

She kept hold of his arms, his skin warm under her fingers. His muscles twitched then finally, after what seemed like minutes, but was probably only ten seconds, a hint of a grin teased Jake's lips. Seconds later, it was a full-blown smile.

"It was an interesting process," he conceded with a chuckle. "And no, I didn't have to turn anyone in my family in or set them up. Other than that, I can't tell you what more was involved."

"Or you'll have to kill me?" she teased as she let her hands slide away and they resumed their walk across the parking lot.

"Something like that," Jake answered.

They walked in silence until they reached the equipment warehouse door. She spoke as she plugged in the code, "I probably shouldn't have laughed, Jake. It can't be easy for you. But you're one of the best people I know and it's fucked up that that's the kind of family you come from. Although now that I know, I'm even more impressed with you and the way you've chosen to live your life. What did your dad want from you this morning?"

He looked away from her and toward the bay as he answered. "I like that you laughed, sugar. It reminded me of the good things in my life—like friends who can make fun of me and my fucked up family and not hold them against me. I can get…distracted by my family, and sometimes, if I think about them too much, things start to feel, well, dark, and I start to wonder if I'll ever be free of them. Your laughter made that darkness go away."

She reached out and took his hand in both of hers though she remained silent, knowing he had more to say.

His fingers curled around hers as he spoke. "This morning, he asked if I knew anything about Samuel Haines, a young, recently elected state legislator."

Her family was messed up, but she was suddenly glad they had next to no contact. How her family spoke to her was nothing compared to how Jake's seemed to treat him.

"I'm sorry," she said.

His gaze flickered down to her and one side of lips tipped up in a wry grin. "Yeah, me too." He paused, then reached up with his free hand and brushed a curl that had blown into her face behind her ear. "I'm good now," he said. "Really, I am."

She studied his face and knew he was speaking the truth. She wasn't much into new age stuff, but the coiled energy he'd carried into her lab less than an hour ago was gone, and in its place was the steady, focused Jake she knew well. He wasn't quite as lighthearted as she was used to, but she believed him when he'd said he was good. He'd be better, eventually. But for now, he was good.

She smiled up at him. "Then let's go see if we can find any more stoned fish."

CHAPTER FIVE

"So, where are we going exactly?" Jake asked as they motored out of the bay and headed west. It hadn't taken long to gather gear and tanks—they'd even found a spare pair of clean board shorts for him to change into—and now that he was relaxing in the passenger chair beside Nia, he realized she still hadn't told him where they were headed.

"A small bay on the north side of Lovango Island," she said, raising her voice over the sound of the wind and the engines.

It would take a little over an hour to get to Lovango—a small island to the northeast of St. Thomas. It was privately owned now, but back in the colonial times, it housed nothing but brothels—brothels the sailors would visit before ending their journeys a mile further to the west in the commercial harbor of Charlotte Amalie on St. Thomas. The name—a riff on "love and go"—always made his inner thirteen-year-old grin.

Nia glanced over and rolled her eyes at him. "Seriously. You and Dominic. All I have to do to make you laugh is mention Lovango Island."

And laugh he did, because, well…they might have just stum bled upon a potentially terrifying new drug, but for now, it was a beautiful day, he was on a boat, and he was about to go diving with Nia. Sometimes it was pretty damn easy to look at the silver lining.

He sat back, turned his face to the sun, and left Nia to pilot the vessel. Once they rounded the west side of Tildas Island, it was more or less a straight shot north to Lovango, and it wouldn't be until they hit the waters around St. Thomas that they'd have to slow for the shoals and reefs. Until then, he'd keep an eye out for flying fish and dolphins and just enjoy the ride.

When they entered the channel between St. Thomas and St. John, Nia throttled back to a less breakneck speed. As she steered them toward Lovango, he rose and started checking the equipment. By the time they reached a small bay on the north side of the private island, he had their vests hooked up to tanks and the tanks hooked up to the dive computers they'd each carry.

"We'll tie up there," Nia said, pointing to the only floating buoy. Years ago, in order to stop people from dropping anchor and destroying coral, the government had set up several free mooring balls pretty much everywhere a boater would want to tie up. As an island-boy, Jake appreciated the concern for the natural habitat, but it did still sometimes surprise him to find them off private islands.

Using the long pole-hook, he snagged the loop at the top of the buoy, pulled it up, and tied the boat to it before dropping it back in the water. When he turned around, Nia was stripping out of her shorts, revealing the sleek one-piece bathing suit she'd changed into. He'd seen her in tank tops and, hell, he'd even seen her in more revealing suits. But there was something about the way her lithe body moved with comfort and confidence as she prepared to dive. A strange sense that he could watch her for days move around the way she was washed over him.

"Here," she said, tossing him a rash guard shirt and, thankfully, breaking his train of thought. While there'd been a time or two when they'd first started spending time together that he thought he'd recognized something more than friendship between them, he'd ruthlessly pushed that awareness into the dark recesses of his brain—she hadn't seemed to return the interest and, more to the point, he hadn't wanted to jeopardize their friendship. So why brief little hints of attraction teased at him now, he couldn't say. Nor could he say what he thought about them.

He yanked off his cotton t-shirt and raised his face to the sun, taking a moment to absorb the feel of its rays on his bare skin before pulling on the thin shirt he'd wear under his dive vest. Some people hated the heat, but he had never been one of them. Sure, there were days it was uncomfortable. But there was nothing like the first kiss of sun on your skin. Especially if it was followed by a chance to be in the ocean.

He opened his eyes to find Nia staring at him, her gaze roaming over his body, unaware that he watched. Her attention trailed up his chest then to his face. For a microsecond, when her eyes met his, he could have sworn he saw a question in them. The same question he'd asked himself at her lab—what if there *was* more between them? But then she blinked and gave him a wry smile.

"What? Do I have a glob of zinc on my nose or something?" he asked, pulling the long-sleeved rash guard over his head and glossing over that split second of awareness.

Nia chuckled and shook her head as she donned her own shirt. "You know you don't. I'm glad I know you well enough to be well acquainted with your flaws and quirks—*and* annoying habits—otherwise, you might render me speechless. You are a fine specimen of a man, Jake McMullen," she said, waving at his body.

"You like this, do you?" he said, dramatically gesturing to his chest, as he flashed her a Cheshire Cat grin. "It is a fine speci-men, I agree. You know the worst part? I don't even really work at it."

Nia shook her head and laughed as she tossed him a mask, that brief moment behind them. "Come on, Captain America," she said. "Gear up. We have some fish—or maybe drugs—to find. The day is full of possibilities."

Despite their teasing, neither took safety for granted, and they spent a few minutes checking and rechecking the gear, before lifting their vests onto their shoulders and securing them across their bodies.

"So once we're in, where to?" he asked. They'd stay close, within ten feet of each other, but Jake liked to have an idea of the direction.

"A reef is starting to take hold there," Nia said, pointing to a spot forty feet to the east. "It's naturally occurring, but because it's new, we wanted to set some beds up here to see how our coral does against what's happening on its own. Our bed is there," she said, moving her finger to point a little further to the east another twenty feet or so. "This is an unusual area," she continued as she tightened a strap around her waist. "There is a large rock formation twenty feet down. It more or less follows the curve of the island and it's about ten feet wide. After that, there's a drop off to sixty feet. The coral—both the natural and ours—is growing on the ledge on the eastern end of the rock."

As he made a final adjustment to his vest, Jake perused the waterscape, picturing in his mind's eye Nia's description. When he was ready, he turned to his friend. "Lead the way?"

In response, Nia flashed a brilliant smile then rolled over-board. Thirty seconds later, he was beside her. Then, with one last adjustment of their masks, they sank under the surface.

There was very little Nia loved more than being underwater. The noise—actual and philosophical—of the world dimmed, and nothing but nature and wonder surrounded her. She'd heard it said that scientists knew more about space than what lay beneath the ocean's surface and if it were true, she was okay with that because it meant fewer people invading her underwater sanctuary.

Twenty feet down, she reached the rock formation and, with a glance back, she assured herself Jake was with her. They'd dived together several times and she wasn't worried about his competence, but if they were diving using the buddy system, they needed to stick to the protocols. He gave her the okay sign, and she started following the ledge of the rock, letting the gentle current rock against her body.

A small school of black and yellow angelfish darted in front of her and a barracuda glided through the water below them. There wasn't a lot of food near the rocks and so not many fish, but as the coral began to grow, more fish would come, and with more fish, more coral would grow.

The new coral came into view—a few small specimens of fused staghorn and finger corals. Continuing past the fledgling beds, she led Jake to the coral nursery The Center had installed a year ago. They weren't there to check on the babies, but Nia couldn't stop herself, and she let her eyes drift over each of the tiny specimens. Some looked to be doing better than others, but overall, she was pleased with their growth.

She turned to ask Jake what he'd like to do next, but as she started to gesture, a yellow-tailed snapper bumped into her. Just like the parrotfish had a few days earlier.

She and Jake both stilled—as much as the water would let them—and after a moment, two more snapper came swimming up the rock drop off toward them. Both paused two feet away. She glanced at Jake. He was watching the two animals who appeared to be watching him. After a beat, he reached out and touched one on the nose. It bounced back an inch but didn't scuttle away.

He shot her a look that, even through his mask, she could read—he was as confused as she'd been when she'd had her first experience.

She glanced around but saw no signs of anything where a drug shipment could be left or tied to for later pick-up. And it would have to be tied to something to keep it from drifting on the currents. She considered whether the nursery—with its piping and wiring—could be used, but quickly dismissed the idea. It was simply too lightweight. If anything heavy had been anchored to it, the entire structure would pull away with even the gentlest of currents.

Jake reached out to get her attention, then gestured down. She supposed it was as good a plan as any. She couldn't see anything around where they were and down the rock wall was where the snapper had come from. She nodded and took the lead.

Slowly, they descended, following the wall. As they got closer to the bottom, the smooth, flat rock gave way to large boulders. Enough light still filtered in from the surface to create shadows in the crevices, but it was much dimmer at sixty-two feet than it had been at twenty.

Letting Jake take the lead, they began to make their way along the boulders, peeking into holes and gaps as they progressed. Jake slowed to get a look inside a particularly big gap and Nia paused to consider the area while he searched.

Taking in the somewhat bleak "landscaping" and solid rocks around them, she supposed it could be a good place to set up a drug drop. There was very little of interest here to recreational divers and it would be easy to anchor something into the heavy rocks. She glanced over her shoulder to check on Jake, and when she saw his legs poking out from behind a boulder, she turned her attention back to her surroundings.

Suddenly, a flash of silver reflected through the water about thirty feet away. The marine biologist in her refused to look away—identifying fish was as natural to her as checking for cars when she crossed the street. Another flash greeted her, then another. She frowned. There weren't a lot of food sources near where they were, so seeing more than a fish or two here and there was unusual. But sure enough, as her eyes adjusted to looking at where she'd seen the flash, she could see shadowy forms of several small fish hovering over the same area.

Which could only mean one thing—there must be a food source.

She got Jake's attention and pointed to where she wanted to go. He nodded and gestured for her to lead the way. She'd never balked at leading a dive, but the unusual gathering of fish was definitely giving her second thoughts. It was possible there was some animal that had died and was providing a feast, but somehow she couldn't bring herself to believe that.

She hesitated. This was one of those times where she could ignore her intuition and forge ahead, or she could acknowledge what she was feeling and ask Jake—as law enforcement—to take the lead. If nothing was there, she'd look foolish. But if there were...

With a metaphorical sigh—because actual sighs were hard when breathing through a regulator—she gestured Jake ahead. She'd rather look foolish than risk unexpectedly coming across something she wasn't prepared for.

His blue eyes searched hers from behind his mask, then he nodded and swam ahead, the movement of his fins causing a current of water to rush over her skin. As soon as he passed, she swung out away from the wall and came up on his left side, letting him stay a few feet ahead of her.

As they approached, the swarm of fish became clearer. What had been little more than darting shadows coalesced into distinct fish—angelfish, parrotfish, jacks, and snapper. They formed a loose ball spreading about twenty feet across, but all circling the same area.

Jake looked over his shoulder and motioned for her to stay back, clearly having picked up on the strangeness of the sight. Ignoring him, she closed the gap between them to a couple of feet. She might be okay with him taking the lead, but she wasn't okay letting him venture close to the unknown without her.

Obviously not under the influence like the others she and Jake had seen, several of the fish scattered as they approached. As they fled, the rapid movement of so many fins caused the fine sand on the ocean floor to kick up and obscure their view. In response, Jake slowed, signaling her to do the same. Together they hovered in the cloudy water accompanied by only the sounds of their regulators.

Slowly, the sand began to settle. The seconds ticked by and with each passing one, Nia's anxiety ratcheted higher. She was starting to think she needed to give herself a stern talking to about the uselessness of thinking the worst when the worst—or close to it—took shape before her eyes.

CHAPTER SIX

JAKE RECOGNIZED the shape a split second before Nia and he was already reaching for her hand, when her fingers found his.

Like some sinister version of *Weekend at Bernie's*, a man, or what was left of him, was propped against the boulders. He wore a pair of khaki shorts and a red shirt. His head lolled to the side, gently swaying with the current, and his dark hair floated around him. With the way his feet lay on the sand, and the way his hands rested on boulders beside him, if it weren't for the anchor tied to his ankles, and his mottled, fish eaten skin, he might have looked as though he was just hanging out on the ocean floor.

Jake turned to Nia and gave the gesture to surface. There was nothing he could do for the man other than to make sure his remains were raised in such a way so as to preserve any evidence of his murder.

She gave a sharp, jerky nod and they ascended slowly, stopping twice for safety checks, before breaking the surface.

"You okay?" he asked, ripping off his face mask. It wasn't his first rodeo, so to speak, but he was pretty sure it was Nia's.

Rather than respond, she removed her own mask then

inflated her vest so that she didn't have to tread water. Lying on her back, she took several deep breaths.

"Nia? Sweetheart?" he asked, getting a little concerned. He wasn't worried about water safety—her vest would keep her afloat—but her mental safety?

She held up a hand to stop him from speaking anymore. "Just give me a minute."

They had a minute. Of course they did. That man, whoever he was, had been in the water at least a few days—another few minutes wouldn't hurt. But the agent in Jake didn't accept that reasoning.

"Take as long as you need, sweetheart, but I'm towing you in so we can call for backup."

Nia was not a shrinking violet, so it was evidence of how shaken up she was when she waved her hand in a vague gesture and let him grab the top of her inflated vest and pull her toward the boat.

When they reached the ladder, he pulled her around. "Up you go," he said.

Nia shook her head. "You go. You'll be faster than me right now and you need to call whoever you need to call. I'll be fine. Go," she insisted when he looked at her doubtfully.

Heeding her last order, he yanked off his fins, tossed them on the back platform of the boat, and hauled himself up the ladder. With one last look at Nia, who was bobbing in the water, her hand wrapped around the ladder, he opened one of the small cabinets and pulled out his wallet and phone even as he started to remove his gear.

Hitting a couple of buttons, his phone dialed a familiar number. Thankfully, they were close enough to the island to pick up a signal and a few seconds later, the call connected.

"What now, McMullen?" came Beni's voice.

"You'll be happy to hear that I found a distraction. Unfortunately, it takes the form of a weird synthetic drug and a dead body lying sixty feet below the ocean's surface."

Silence met his statement. For three seconds. "What the actual fuck, McMullen. You've been gone for less than two hours. Where are you, anyway?"

It was kind of fun catching Beni unawares—it didn't happen that often—but he let the feeling slide away and filled her in on everything Nia and he had discovered. As he spoke, he could hear Beni relaying the details to Dominic and telling him to call the Coast Guard to arrange for the retrieval of the body.

A few minutes later, he hung up knowing the team was on their way—well, not all of them were actually on their way, but Dominic was going to swing by Hemmeleigh Resort and pick up Alexis then the two of them would bring the FBI boat to the scene. Jake would stay with Dominic and Alexis and oversee the recovery while Damian and Beni would begin making arrangements to open the investigation, including taking a look at the results of the blood samples Nia had sent via email. Beni hadn't opened them yet, but Jake would bet dollars to donuts that whatever drugs Nia had found in those fish, something similar would be in, or on, the man currently lying sixty feet underwater.

Placing his phone back in the cabinet, he joined Nia at the back of the boat. Her fins were beside his on the platform and she was now sitting on the edge, her feet dangling in the water. Her vest was still on, but she'd opened the buckles and it hung loose on her shoulders, the tank resting on the deck of the boat.

Gently, he removed her vest and placed it next to his. Years of training had him checking all the readings and gauges before rejoining Nia. Sitting beside her, he dropped his feet into the water as well.

"You okay?"

She waggled her head then leaned against his shoulder. "I'll be fine."

"First body?" He wrapped an arm around her shoulders and pulled her closer.

"First human body, yeah."

"I'm sorry."

"Not your fault," she said. "But thank you."

They sat in silence for nearly twenty minutes before she finally rose, removing the rest of her gear as she did. "The Coast Guard is coming?" she asked.

He glanced at his watch as he too stood. "Yes, it will take them a bit to get kitted out, but they should be here in another twenty minutes or so. Dominic and Alexis are coming, too."

"You think he's the reason those fish are ingesting the drug?" she asked, gesturing in the direction of the body as she pulled a t-shirt on over her head.

"I think it's likely, yes. Either he has it in his system, or it's somewhere on his body. We'll know more tonight or tomorrow."

She nodded, then reached for the freshwater hose and started to wash the gear down. "Once Dominic and Alexis get here, do you mind if I take this boat back? It doesn't have lights and I don't know how long the, uh, retrieval will take. I'd like to be sure to have it back long before dark."

"You okay to drive?" he asked, helping her unhook the regulator hoses from the tanks.

"Yep," she said. "Not going to lie and say everything is fine. But you know me well enough to know that I wouldn't risk one of The Center's boats if I thought I wasn't up to it."

She wouldn't. He did know that. She'd risk herself, but never anything that had to do with The Center or anyone else. He didn't like that she'd judged her current capability on how she felt about the boat, rather than *how she felt*, but at least she'd get back safely. Depending on when he returned to Tildas, maybe he'd check on her later.

When the Coast Guard showed up, she was back in her

shorts with a baseball cap shielding her face from the sun and holding her hair back. A pair of sunglasses hid her expression from the three men and two women in uniform. She stood beside him as the boat tied up to the same mooring as theirs. Etiquette would normally frown on such a thing, but nothing about this situation was normal.

"Agent McMullen?" one of the men called out as the others threw bumpers over the side of the clipper to keep the boats from causing any damage if they bumped into each other.

"That's me," Jake said, holding up his badge. They couldn't read it from where they looked down, but he suspected they didn't need to. It wasn't every day they received a call from the FBI to assist in raising a body.

"You good here?" he asked Nia as their new neighbor turned with the current and came alongside them.

Nia nodded. "I have a book on my phone. I'll let you do your thing until Dominic and Alexis get here. You'll be careful?" she asked from beside him.

He tipped his head to meet her gaze, imagining her hazel eyes looking back at him. "Of course," he said, gently.

She held still, and for a moment, Jake thought she might reach out for him.

"Permission to tie up?" one of the women called from the deck above them, breaking the moment. Both Nia and Jake looked up. The clipper was fifteen feet longer and sat a hell of a lot higher in the water than the fast, agile Marine Center boat. Jake looked to Nia, who nodded. The petty officer tossed a line down and Jake tied it up to The Center's boat.

After tying off two more lines and tethering the boats together, another petty officer unrolled a ladder, and Jake boarded the official boat.

"Will Dr. Lewis be joining us?" a lieutenant, and clearly the highest ranking member of the crew, asked.

Jake shook his head. "She'll give her formal statement to the

FBI. For now, I think it's best if we focus on how to raise the body." All five members of the Coast Guard, and Jake, glanced over at Nia. She'd taken a seat in the pilot's chair and sat with her phone in her lap. Whether or not she was actually reading, Jake couldn't tell.

"I'm Lieutenant Bates," the man said, holding out his hand. Jake shook it then Bates introduced him to the rest of the CG team. Once everyone knew each other's names, they moved to a table and a petty officer unrolled a map. Jake took a few minutes to orient the CG crew and relay what he and Nia had found. By the time they'd devised a plan to raise the body and suited up in Coast Guard issue dive gear, Dominic and Alexis had arrived.

Dominic kept their boat hovering at the opposite edge of the channel from where the body was located until Nia untied and motored toward them.

Jake kept an eye on Nia as she stopped beside his colleagues. Dominic was at the wheel, but Alexis moved the railing and the two women spoke before Nia nodded, waved, then took off. He didn't like the idea of her being on her own. Not that she couldn't handle the boat or that her reasons for leaving weren't completely logical...but still.

"This wasn't the kind of excitement I was suggesting you find, McMullen," Dominic shouted up to Jake as he brought the FBI boat alongside the Coast Guard clipper and Alexis started to tie them together using the same lines Nia had just released.

"What can I say, I'm an overachiever," Jake called down. "And it was a good thing it was me. You wouldn't have known what to do with yourself down in that water, PJ," he teased. Dominic was a former member of an elite Airforce pararescue team. Jake could jump out of a plane with the best of them, but he honestly didn't like thinking about some of the shit his good friend must have had to do in his career before joining the FBI.

In response to Jake's comment, Dominic grinned up at him then blared a ten-second clip of "Little Surfer Girl" by the Beach

Boys over the boat's sound system. With the Coasties chuckling behind him, Jake shook his head and let the ladder down.

Once Alexis and Dominic were on board with their evidence kits in hand, he updated them on the plan while the CG crew prepared the stretcher they'd use to transport the body from the site to the boat. Both of his colleagues knew how to dive, but with him and three of the petty officers going in, it made more sense for them to stay topside and manage the process once the stretcher was attached to the winch that would raise it on board. Dominic had done enough recovery work that he'd know how to treat a body that had been submerged for three days, and Alexis had an eerily good ability to read both victims and criminals, and her initial impressions would be invaluable.

Forty minutes later, he and the three Coasties had the body in the stretcher and were hooking it up to the boat's cables. With the small exception of the anchor attached to the body—it weighed more than they'd anticipated—the retrieval had gone smoothly.

Jake bobbed on the surface as the winch lifted the stretcher slowly above water, pausing right at the surface to let the rest of the water drain away as gently as possible. Once drained, the winch maneuvered the stretcher onto the deck of the boat, and as soon as Jake heard the all-clear, he was up the ladder and back with his colleagues.

Dominic studied the body and took pictures while Alexis looked on, a small frown on her face. Jake's gaze skittered around the deck as he removed his gear. He could see the curiosity on the Coasties' faces as they went about their jobs, but also some interest. He didn't think any of them would be unprofessional enough to forget their job and interfere with the investigation, but it wouldn't hurt to hurry this little show along.

"What do you think?" Jake asked, coming up alongside Alexis and keeping his voice low.

"Whoever he is, he either has money or has access to it," she said, her arms crossed across her chest. "That shirt?" His attention went to the red t-shirt with some sort of lightning design on it, and he nodded. "That's a five hundred dollar shirt," she said. "And those shoes?" His attention turned to look. "Those are nine hundred dollar shoes."

Jake blinked at the mottled, bloated body lying on the deck. Who the hell bought a five hundred dollar t-shirt?? Even if someone could afford it, it seemed like kind of a douchy thing to do.

It was hard to tell the age of the man given the state of the body, but Jake would put him no older than mid-twenties. Probably younger.

"You think he got that money from running drugs?" he asked.

Alexis tipped her head. "Too early to say."

"But you have an opinion, I can tell. You always get a little pinched right here," he said, touching the corner of her mouth, "when you have an opinion or thought you're not sharing."

She turned and her light blue eyes studied him. Then she smiled. "You are more perceptive than you get credit for, aren't you?"

He grinned. "I get exactly the kind of credit I want." While Alexis worked her ass off not to be underestimated—which a lot of people did based on her looks alone—he cultivated it. He could see how his choices wouldn't work for her—he wasn't blind to how much harder it was to be a woman in law enforcement—but they did work for him.

"So why don't you share," he said, nudging her with his elbow.

"Share what?" Dominic asked, rising from where he'd been crouched beside the body and joining the conversation.

"What she thinks, but doesn't want to say because it's too soon," Jake answered.

When he and Dominic fixed their attention on her, she sighed and conceded. "I don't think he made his money as a drug runner. For lack of a better word, he looks too soft. And no, I don't mean because his body has been sitting in water for at least three days."

Dominic made a circling gesture with his hand, urging her to continue. Alexis looked displeased at being pressed but complied. "Young men who get involved in the drug trade grow up fast. We'll have to wait for some identification or the autopsy to confirm, but I wouldn't put him any older than his early twenties. To be in your early twenties and involved in an operation like this—an operation that likely has a sophisticated network of drop sites and is dealing in designer drugs—means you would have had to put in your time. He doesn't look like a kid who has put in his time."

"Does he look like a kid who was in the wrong place at the wrong time?" Dominic asked.

Alexis shrugged. "It's possible. It's also possible that he knows—or knew—the people involved, like family or friends, and he thought it might be a kick to get involved."

"A kick?" Jake repeated.

"Believe me," Alexis said. "There are *a lot* of rich kids who are bored and entitled and think nothing can touch them. I grew up with plenty of them who would go along with a drug run just for kicks."

"That's some fucked up shit," Dominic said.

Alexis dipped her head in agreement, then asked Dominic, "Did you find anything?"

"He was shot in the right temple, but you both probably saw that," Dominic started. "Despite the decomp, his body is in pretty good shape, which might lend some credence to your thought that maybe he was just some kid out for an ill-advised adventure. I didn't want to look too closely at his hands because well…"

Because in the water, the hands and feet were first to go.

"You think we'll get prints?" Jake asked.

"Not all ten, but I think we'll get a few," Dominic answered.

"Agents," Lieutenant Bates spoke as he approached them, drawing their attention away from the body. "We're cleaned up here and ready to transport the body to Tildas Island when you're ready to go."

Jake looked at Dominic and Alexis. Over the nearly twelve months they'd worked together, they'd become pretty good at holding conversations without saying a word. After a beat, Dominic nodded.

"I'll follow behind in our boat," Dominic said.

"And you two?" Bates asked.

"We'll ride with the body," Alexis said. "Though we need to get him in a bag before we go."

Bates nodded and gestured two of his crew over. "Help Agents McMullen and Wright bag the body," he ordered. The two nodded and moved off to unroll the large, black bag. "My other crew will gather the ropes once you're untied and we can be on our way." A man of few words, Bates moved off without waiting for confirmation.

"We'll bag, you go get untied," Jake said to Dominic as he reached for the gloves Alexis held out to him.

With a nod, Dominic disappeared over the side of the Coast Guard boat as Jake and Alexis coordinated with the two crew members on how best to get the body bagged. Given that it had taken three people to lift the anchor underwater, they enlisted one more crew member who, together with his colleagues, would lift the stretcher while Jake and Alexis slid the bag underneath.

He'd just given the order to lift when, kneeling at the victim's feet, something caught his eye. "Hold up," Jake ordered. Immediately, the crew gently set the body back down.

"Jake?" Alexis said from her position at the other end of the victim.

"Can you get me some tweezers?" he asked, not taking his eyes from the victim's left shoe. "And an evidence bag," he added.

Seconds later, both appeared in his line of sight. Taking the soft-headed tweezers, Jake pinched the end of a small zipper than ran two inches along the side of the man's shoe. It hadn't been fully closed and Jake had spotted what looked like the corner of a plastic bag peeking through the small opening.

As he opened the tiny compartment, the edges of the plastic bag unrolled, and Jake knew exactly what he'd found. When the zipper was fully open, he gently reached in with his gloved fingers and freed the tiny piece of evidence.

Holding up his find for Alexis to see, he eyed the content. Water had leaked into the bag, leaving what looked to have been a white powder a sludgy consistency. Whatever tear that had allowed the water in was probably the same tear that had allowed the drugs out—the drugs Nia's fish had eventually consumed.

"Want to bet this will be the same drug Doc sampled from the fish?" he said.

Alexis's eyes flitted to his, before dropping back down to his hand. She held an evidence bag out, and he dropped the drugs inside. "You should know by now, McMullen, that I don't take a sucker's bet."

CHAPTER SEVEN

AFTER GETTING the body back to Tildas and then to the medical examiner, Dominic, Alexis, and Jake met Damian and Beni back at the office to finalize the paperwork and start the reports. There wasn't much more they could do at eight o'clock at night, so they all agreed to meet up again in the morning once they had more information from the lab on the drugs and from the medical examiner on the autopsy.

Remembering that he'd left his car parked at the Marine Center, Jake bummed a ride from Dominic, knowing that both Alexis and Damian would likely want to get home and that Beni lived just a few minutes away from the office.

They hadn't left Havensted proper when Dominic asked him if he wanted to grab a drink.

Jake hesitated. Not because he didn't know how he would answer, but because his answer would only raise more questions. Perhaps he would have been better off taking a taxi.

"Not a hard question, McMullen," Dominic said. "We're three blocks from The Queens." The Queens was one of their favorite bars in Havensted.

After another beat, Jake shook his head. "I've got some things to do. I think this case might turn out to be bigger than we think and I want to take care of a few things before we get sucked in." Like check on Nia.

"You've been antsy all day, what's going on, Jake?" Dominic asked as they stopped for a light. "And don't bother trying to bullshit me. We're the best bullshitters around and I can spot yours a mile away, so drop the act and talk to me."

"Should we go pour some wine and do facials as we talk?"

"Don't even knock a good facial," Dominic replied.

Jake raised an eyebrow at his friend, then turned to look out the window as the light turned green and they started to move. They were less than eight minutes out from The Center; maybe he could delay answering?

"I will bypass The Center and keep driving until you talk. So your choice, the easy way or the annoying way. The latter is your specialty, but it's been a long day, so I'm hoping you'll pick option one."

"You are such a pain in my ass," Jake said.

"And that's why you love me. Now talk."

Jake shifted in his seat. He *could* tell Dominic about the call from his dad. After all, that's what had initially sparked his anxiousness that morning. But if he told Dominic about his family that might lead them to other topics, topics he *really* didn't want to discuss.

So that left him with the (only) slightly less appealing option two.

Letting out a deep breath, he answered. "I didn't like getting that text from Nia Saturday night."

"Yeah, she's a friend. She was hurt and her lab was broken into. I didn't much like the situation either."

Jake cleared his throat, glad they were only four minutes away from his car now. "No, I mean, I *really* didn't like it. Like in ways I can't explain."

A beat passed, then Dominic slammed on the brakes and

pulled over. Luckily, at this time of night and on this part of the island, there was no traffic, but still, it seemed a little dramatic, even for Dominic.

"Holy shit. You have feelings for Doc, don't you?" he demanded, pinning Jake with his bright green eyes.

Jake shifted uncomfortably. "Maybe...yes...I don't know. I can't figure it out, but then maybe it doesn't matter. She seems pretty happy just having me as a friend."

Dominic stared at him for a beat, and Jake braced for more, well, more of a reaction from his best friend. But all Dominic did was let out a little chuckle and pull the car back onto the road.

"You going to say anything?" Jake asked. It would be unlike Dominic to keep his thoughts to himself and Jake wasn't sure if he hoped Dominic had more to say or that he would hold his tongue.

"Nope. I'm going to let you figure that shit out on your own."

Jake glared at his ride and fought the urge to snap back. It was a tough internal fight, but Jake had no desire to sound like a child, especially when Dominic was giving him what he wanted by not asking a gazillion questions. Or making fun of him.

Neither spoke for the last few minutes of the ride and when Dominic pulled to a stop beside Jake's car and Jake slid from his seat, Dominic leaned over to look up at him. "You gonna go check on Doc tonight?"

Jake glared down at his friend, trying to determine if he was being goaded or if Dominic was asking a simple question. Who was he kidding? There was nothing simple about Dominic's question. Not in this context. But fuck it.

"Yeah. Her car's not here, so I'll stop by her house and check on her," he answered.

One of Dominic's eyebrows went up, but he nodded. "Good. I'm sure she could use a friend. It's not every day you see a dead body."

Jake couldn't tell if Dominic's use of the word "friend" was meant to convey anything, but rather than ask, he shut the car door and pulled out his own keys. By the time he was buckled in, Dominic was gone from the parking lot. As he started the car, Jake considered texting Nia first, but knew that if he did she'd just tell him she was fine.

She might very well be fine, but he wouldn't rest easy until he saw for himself. With his decision made, he put his car in gear and started the short trip to her home.

When he arrived, her car was in her drive, but there were no lights on in the house. He had an idea where she might be, and after knocking on her door just to be sure she wasn't home, he turned and headed toward the local watering hole Nia liked. Well, "liked" was kind of a strong word—but it was close enough to walk to and had decent drink and food, though neither was anything to write home about.

Stepping through the heavy steel door and into the concrete building four blocks from Nia's, Jake paused to let his eyes adjust. To his right, the sound of a pool game starting drew his attention and he turned to find Nia surveying the table, cue in hand. Leaning against the wall behind her was a man, also holding a cue, though he looked to be surveying Nia rather than the table.

And Jake could hardly blame him. Nia hadn't dressed up— she wore a pair of cut-offs and a loose cotton tank top with tiny straps—but even so, or maybe because of her casual confidence, there was something magnetic about her. Something that drew a man's attention.

He watched as she took a shot, then another two, before finally missing and handing the table over to the man. Whoever he was winked at Nia and said something. He chuckled, she gave him a courtesy smile.

Jake moved toward her, hoping the guy wouldn't take his arrival poorly, but not really giving a shit if he did. He needed to make sure Nia was okay, and she wasn't going to talk about it here, so he'd have to get her alone.

"Nia," he said, approaching the table.

Nia's attention had been fixed on the table and when she looked up, he saw a flash of confusion in her eyes, but then she smiled at him. A real smile.

"Jake," she said, walking toward him. He leaned down and kissed her cheek as she pulled him into a hug. That was a better greeting than he expected. In fact, she seemed so genuinely glad to see him that he had to wonder if maybe the guy was giving her a hard time. Jake's gaze flickered to the man who'd stepped back against the wall again and whose eyes were bouncing between him and Nia.

"How'd it—" She cut herself off from asking anymore and glanced around the bar to see if anyone had heard.

Jake smiled. "Why don't you finish your game? I'll grab a drink, and then we can sit somewhere quiet or go for a walk or something," he suggested. Her eyes searched his, and he could see the scientist in her—the person who wanted to ask questions and learn things—struggling with the humane part of her, the part that didn't want to hear about bloated bodies and drug trafficking. Finally, she nodded.

"It won't take very long," she said with a wry smile. No doubt the game was meant to be a distraction, but judging by the man's missed first shot, she'd picked the wrong partner. Jake gave it no more than two more turns at the table before she cleaned up.

"I'll grab a beer. Need anything?"

"GnT, please. There's a table over there we can grab," she said, gesturing to a small booth in the back corner. The place wasn't crowded at all, but the table had the unique position of being tucked into a corner on the other side of the jukebox in such a way that it would be a quiet place to talk and no one else would be able to hear them.

He nodded and made his way to the bar. By the time he had his beer and Nia's GnT, she'd joined him. Grabbing their drinks, they wove around a couple of tables on their way to the corner.

"That was a quick game even for you," Jake said as he slid into the booth. Nia took the spot on his right. It was a tiny booth and a tight fit, but he didn't mind having Nia pressed against him. Not in the least. Especially when she leaned into him as she let out a low laugh.

"I knew it would be," she said. "But I was looking for a distraction. I was planning to call you later, but I wasn't sure when you'd get back in. Did everything go okay? Well, as okay as it could go?" she restated her question.

He nodded and filled her in on the events of the afternoon, including finding the little packet of drugs. Technically, he probably shouldn't have mentioned it, but he had a suspicion that Sunita Shah, his boss, would want to talk to Nia about the fish she'd discovered, so he didn't think he was crossing the line too much. Maybe by a toe, but not a full leg.

"So you won't know anything until tomorrow?" she asked when he finished.

He shook his head. "The ME promised he'd do the autopsy first thing. The fingertips were so degraded that we didn't even want to try to get prints on our own tonight. But enough about that, how are you?"

She pulled a face. "I'm fine. Was just a little surprised. The only dead human bodies I've ever seen have been on TV. They do a pretty good job of capturing the physical aspects of death, but they don't quite capture the mental gymnastics that happened in my head, so I wasn't very prepared. Sorry I kind of freaked out on you."

He bumped her shoulder—which was a poor substitute for pulling her close and kissing her, which is what he wanted to do in that moment. Actually, he wanted to do a lot more. His feelings for Nia might not be so clear in his head, but his body had no such ambivalence. Nope, it was doing a fine job of trying to convince him that what he really needed to do was to stop talking and take Nia into his arms. All of which would be swiftly followed by taking her home, laying her down on a bed, and getting lost in her for hours.

He shifted, relieving some of the pressure in his shorts, and gave a fleeting consideration as to when his body had become so decisive. In all the months they'd been hanging out, he'd never worried about having a physical reaction to her. Well, except for that time when they'd gone dancing at a new club in town. They'd had a few drinks, the music had been sensual, with a throbbing beat, and Nia's body had melded to his. He'd had to take a step back in order to not embarrass his friend.

But that had just been once...well, if he were honest with himself, there'd also been that time when they'd gone diving off of St. John. He'd known she was wearing her suit under her shorts, but even so, his eyes had trailed the motion of her hands as she'd unbuttoned her cut-offs and shimmied out of them.

He'd been glad he was already kneeling on the ground, checking their tanks, when she'd glanced up and caught his eye.

"You okay?" Nia asked, interrupting his walk down memory lane. So fine, he'd always been attracted to Nia, but now that he was contemplating it—and what, if anything to do about it—it seemed his body felt the need to lodge its vote much more adamantly.

He cleared his throat. "I'm fine. But you didn't freak out. Believe me, I've seen people freak out and your possum act wasn't even close," he said with a smile.

She laughed then took a sip of her drink. When she set it down, she leaned her head against his shoulder like she'd done a hundred times before. He should have left it at that. But once again, his body was moving before his brain caught up and he raised his arm and slipped it around her shoulders, hugging her close.

"I kind of did go possum on you, didn't I?"

"I'd much rather that than a true freak out. You even remembered our safety stops when we ascended."

He felt her smile against his shoulder. "Those are like using your blinker when making a turn in a car, it's automatic. I don't even think I think about them."

"Wait," he said, drawing back just enough to look at her. "You're supposed to use your blinker?"

Nia smiled as she and Jake headed back to her house. She lived in a quiet neighborhood and although lights were on in the houses they passed, and they could hear a few people splashing around in backyard pools, the two of them were the only people on the street.

She had her arm looped through his and when she caught sight of two teenagers having what looked like a pretty heavy goodnight make-out session on a porch, it was hard to keep her mind from picturing her and Jake on a similar porch. In a similar embrace.

She looked away from the porch and brushed her fingers over Jake's forearm, enjoying the steady, familiar strength, even as she tried to push the image that the couple had conjured out of her mind. It wasn't like that between her and Jake—they weren't make-out-together-on-a-porch kind of people. They weren't make-out-with-each-other kind of people at all, let alone on a porch. Although walking together down the quiet street as dusk was falling, she did find herself wondering if he ever read anything into how easy they were together, physically.

She'd like to say that she was, by nature, an affectionate person, perhaps a by-product of having grown up without much, but that wasn't precisely true. It wasn't *untrue*. She was definitely much more affectionate than any family she'd grown up with, but it wasn't like she walked arm and arm with all her friends.

But then again, given what Jake had told her earlier that day about his family, maybe his upbringing had shaped him similarly to hers. And having two people who'd grown up starved for affection could easily explain why they interacted together in the way they did. Couldn't it?

"Was your family very affectionate?" she asked, hoping to find some logical explanation for something she hadn't really given much thought to in the past eight months but that somehow, suddenly needed an explanation.

"My mom was, but she died when I was twelve," he answered.

The knowledge that he'd lost his mom at such a young age, pushed all other thoughts aside and imagines of Jake as a sad, lost little boy mourning his mother instantly flooded her imagination.

But no, that wasn't *quite* right.

From the few words he'd spoken, she could tell he'd been close to his mom, and she could only imagine what it would have been like to lose her. But when she really thought about Jake as a young boy, it wasn't the grieving child that was the strongest image in her mind. No, the image that was the strongest was the one most closely associated with the man she knew now. A man who was almost always playful. A man who definitely still had the sense of humor of a pre-teen boy.

"How'd she die?" Nia asked, hugging his arm a little tighter.

"Boat accident. So they say."

She let that statement sink in before speaking again. "You don't think that's what happened?"

In the dim streetlights, she saw him shake his head. "It's possible. But I'm pretty sure my dad—or someone he did business with—had her killed. She was getting ready to leave him."

Nia stumbled at his matter of fact statement. Her family was fucked up, but they didn't go around killing each other. Not physically, anyway. They were the masters of killing off any shred of hope or ambition.

"Uh, wow," she managed to say.

Jake chuckled at her reaction and tucked her closer to his side. "I probably shouldn't have dumped that on you. Not today, anyway."

"But I asked," she said, leaning into the heat of his body. "Did you suspect then?"

Jake was silent for half a block before answering. "I was twelve. I had no idea what my dad was into, but I never got along with him. I blamed him for her death. But I needed someone to blame for taking her away and he was an easy target. It wasn't until I was older that I started to put a few things together and realized that I might have had a basis for laying the blame at his feet."

"If you could have gone after him, you would have already, so I assume there's not enough evidence to do that?"

Jake shook his head slowly. "No, not yet anyway."

"But you're still looking?"

"When I can," he said as they approached her house.

She let go of his arm and pulled her keys from her pocket. She was glad when he followed her inside and continued his story.

"When I joined the FBI, I gave them everything I knew on my family and my father's associates. They're keeping an eye on them as well. When the time comes, he'll get justice. But in the meantime, I need to just try and live my life."

"But you said he calls you occasionally to get insider infor-mation?" she asked as she led him into the kitchen and pulled a couple of glasses from her cupboard. Alexis made the island's most fabulous juice that included a mix of various tropical fruits —though she refused to share the exact recipe—and she'd dropped a container by that morning.

Jake reached for a bottle of sparkling water. "He does. He thinks I joined the Bureau to help the family. The Bureau asked me to let him continue to think that. When he does call, I put him off, then get in touch with my contact at the Bureau and see if there is anything they want me to pass on."

She held out the glasses half-filled with juice, and he topped them off with the sparkling water. Then after putting both the juice and the rest of the water in the fridge, they moved to her living room.

Taking a seat in one of the upholstered chairs and curling a leg underneath her, she thought about what he'd said earlier that day as they'd walked to the marina. "You're not supposed to be telling me any of this are you?"

He grinned. "No, but it's really just my career at stake and I trust you enough not to go blabbing."

She took a sip of her drink then huffed a quiet laugh. "Now, whatever will I talk about the next time I get my nails done?"

"You don't get your nails done," he shot back. She glanced down at her fingertips. He was right, she didn't, but she was surprised he'd noticed. Looking back up, she found him staring at her legs, the one tucked under her and the one stretched out to rest on the coffee table. She wiggled her toes, and his eyes jerked back to her face. A look of confusion flashed on his face, but then he waggled his eyebrows at her. "I notice these things, what can I say?"

Before she could say anything else, her phone rang. Pulling it from her pocket, she glanced at the name and her stomach dropped. It had taken her mother twenty-four hours to decide to call after hearing her daughter had been attacked.

"Everything okay?" Jake asked.

"Yeah," she said. It wasn't, but whatever. "I have to get this," she added, rising from her seat. No way was she going to take this call in front of Jake. She wouldn't have taken it at all but since she'd been the one to text her mother, she did feel obligated to answer.

"Hey, Mom," she said as she shut her bedroom door behind her.

"Nia," her mother said.

Nia took a seat at the end of her bed. "I'm fine, Mom. I wasn't hurt too badly. The lab was trashed, and it was a little scary, but I'm fine."

Her mother hesitated. "What? Oh, well, good," she said. "I'm glad to hear that, but the reason I called is because Troy is in jail again."

Nia closed her eyes. She'd known when she'd answered the phone not to expect anything, but still...

"I'm sorry to hear that," Nia said on an exhale. Troy was her cousin. He wasn't a bad person, just someone who consistently made some bad choices.

Her mother let out a sigh. "I need you to go bail him out. I can't believe I even have to ask you."

Nia sighed. As soon as her mother had mentioned Troy, she'd known the real reason her mother had called. "We've been through this before, Mom. I'm not going to bail him out. I didn't do it last time and—"

"And now look at him. He's back in again. All he needed was a little love and support from his cousin to help him straighten out. Since you couldn't be bothered, well, I don't mean to sound, well, cruel, but really, you could have prevented this."

Of course she could have. Because everything was always her fault. "I'm not going to do it this time either," Nia continued as if her mother hadn't interrupted her.

"Jesus, Nia. You *have* the money, what's the big deal? You have that big fancy job, but what's the point if you can't even be bothered to help your family out? What kind of person are you who'd turn her back on her family?"

The kind of person who'd more or less offered to help all of her cousins and nieces and nephews get an education and some kind of job. The kind of person who tried to encourage her younger family members to think beyond the limitations their parents had not just accepted but also enforced. But because that was *different*—different from the life of generational poverty her family embraced like a cause—she was the one in the wrong. Always in the wrong, and never quite good enough.

Nia took a breath and dug deep for some empathy. She was well aware of how hard it was to end the cycle of poverty—she'd worked her ass off to get to where she was. But what she couldn't accept was how her family demonized her for daring to —and succeeding in—breaking that cycle.

A part of her had hoped that in taking the job on the island where she'd grown up, that she'd be able to reconnect with her family as an individual and not as one more mouth to feed. She'd hoped to grow close to her nieces and nephews and maybe have the chance to show them that there was a world out there that was different from the one they lived in—that they had choices, that they had options.

But none of that had happened. Instead, she'd been shunned, ridiculed, and judged. Not just by her parents, but by most of the family as well. She was smart enough now to recognize that she was in that in-between phase of growth—she had to cut ties with them; her relationship with them would never be healthy. But she wasn't quite able to do it yet. A small part of the little girl she'd been, the little girl who'd wanted her parents to *care,* to be excited about her science project or winning the spelling bee, was still stuffed inside her—as evidenced by her text the night before. And until she could come to terms with that little girl, there was always a niggling of hope that maybe *this* call would be different.

And always the bitter disappointment when it wasn't.

"Troy will be fine. It's been a long few days, Mom. I need to get some sleep."

"You can't be serious? You can't take a little bit of your precious time to help your cousin? Your aunt Noreen asked me to call you, what am I going to tell her?"

Nia let out a long breath. "Tell her whatever you want, Mom. Troy is thirty-two years old, well past the time when he should know good decisions from bad ones."

"It wasn't his fault," her mom all but shrieked. Because of course it wasn't. It was always someone else's fault—usually Nia's in some way.

"Look, Mom, he figured it out last time, he'll figure it out this time. I need to get some sleep." She heard her mom sputter and start to speak, but Nia ended the call, then silenced her phone and tossed it on the bedside table. Lying back, she stared at her ceiling, the fan circling round and round.

She wanted to go back to her living room and recapture the easy feeling she'd had when chatting with Jake. She wanted to have normal friends and normal relationships.

A knock sounded at her door, and she raised herself up on her elbows. "Come in."

The door swung open, and Jake stood there. His black t-shirt was tight enough to show his lean body but not so tight as to be cheesy. His sun-streaked brown hair curled at the edges and was a little longer than usual. His dark blue eyes traced the line of her body—from her toes to her head—before they fixed on her face.

"You okay?" he asked.

She wasn't. Talking with her family always threw her. But she would be. She glanced outside. It was too late to go for a run and she wasn't about to go back to her lab alone—those were her usual go-to activities to distract her after such a call. Neither was an option at the moment.

She turned her attention back to Jake, who stood watching her. Suddenly, she became aware of her surroundings. How easy

81

would it be to open her knees and invite him to join her on her bed? But they were friends and friends didn't do that. Did they?

She let her gaze drift over his body, remembering the feel of his arms around her the night before and the heat that poured from his body. It wasn't a far leap for her to imagine what it would feel like to be skin to skin with him. The call with her mother had messed with her head, but that didn't explain why she was suddenly craving Jake—craving the feel of his hands on her skin, craving his attention, craving the way he always made her feel like she was more than enough.

"Nia?"

Had his voice dropped? Nia let her eyes take a leisurely stroll back up his body toward his face, pausing only when she noticed evidence that her mind wasn't the only one imagining what she was imagining.

She tore her gaze away from his arousal and lifted her eyes to his face. His jaw clenched and she could see the tension in his body. Slowly she rose, then, holding his gaze, she pulled her tank top over her head and slipped out of her shorts. His nostrils flared and his breathing changed as she stood before him in her strapless bra and panties.

She let the moment drag on, reveling in his perusal and letting his restraint edge the tension up between them. She reached up and unhooked her bra, letting it fall from her fingers before sliding her underwear down. His body physically jerked when her thong hit the floor, but still, he didn't move.

She smiled and took four steps, bringing her to less than a foot away from him. She raised her hands and cupped his face. "You are my friend. You will always be my friend. But tonight, and for as many nights as we want, will you be more?"

Jake inhaled sharply and his hands closed around her waist, pulling her against him. The feel of his clothes against her bare skin and one of his hot palms flat across her back was more erotic than she would have imagined. She might have surprised him, but his body was telling hers that it wasn't an unwelcome one.

He lowered his head and brushed his lips against the skin just below her ear. She was melting into him as his lips traveled down her neck and his hands crept up, wrapping around her ribs, his thumbs brushing the underside of her breasts.

"Jake?" she asked. She knew his answer, it was in the touch of his fingers, the beat of his heart, and the brush of his lips. But she wanted to hear it. She wanted to hear that she hadn't just made a mistake.

He pulled back and rested his forehead against hers. His eyes locked on hers, and after a beat, he spoke. "I don't think I realized until now just how long I've been hoping you'd ask that question." And then he bent his head and captured her lips.

CHAPTER EIGHT

JAKE LIKED that Nia's bedside tables didn't hold a clock. They had their phones, of course, and he'd even set the alarm, but without a clock glaring the time at them, he didn't have to think about how few hours they had left until he had to leave. When the sun came up tomorrow, he'd only be leaving to go to work—because he was not allowing this to be a one-night thing—but their time together was limited, and he didn't want to be reminded of that.

"Jake," Nia said. They were both curled on their sides, facing each other, naked as the day they were born. The room was dark, but in the ambient light from the street lights, her sleepy eyes watched him.

"Yes?" he said, leaning forward to brush her lips with his.

She wrapped one of her hands around his and pulled it close to her heart. "You said you'd been waiting for me to ask you for more than friendship. Why didn't you ever ask?"

The answer to that question had come to him in blinding clarity when he'd been buried deep inside her. It was kind of an odd, and not particularly comfortable, moment to have such an epiphany, but there it was.

He brought her hand to his lips and dropped a kiss there before returning both of them to rest against her heart. "Two reasons. The first is that I'm a coward. I've never done the friends-to-lovers thing before. I've been friends with women I dated, but we usually started with the dating part then became friends along the way. I *like* spending time with you. You're one of my favorite people on the island and I didn't want to risk that if you didn't feel the same."

"Cliché, McMullen. You can do better than that." Nia smiled as she teased him. But she wasn't wrong. It was so cliché as to be cringe-worthy.

"I'll give you that, but my second reason is better," he said.

She laughed softly and propped herself up on her elbow before leaning over to kiss him. He slipped one hand behind her neck and the other around her waist and pulled her against him. He liked having them skin-to-skin.

Slowly, she ended the kiss and drew back enough to see him, though she stayed pressed against him.

"I never wanted you to think I thought of you as an extended vacation fling," he said.

She frowned. "You're not on vacation," she pointed out.

"I know," he said, stroking her bare back as he spoke. "But that doesn't change the fact that you live here and have an important job here. And despite what's happened in the past few days, it's a job you love."

He saw understanding dawn in her eyes. "And your task force ends in May," she said.

He nodded. "We'll probably be here until June. But once it's wrapped up, there is literally no job on the island for me. Not if I want to stay with the Bureau."

"And you didn't want me to think that you thought of me as just a spot of fun you could have while on the island. Which is how it might have seemed if you'd proposed, well, this," she said waving at their entwined bodies. He nodded. He didn't know *what* they were, but it was more than a "spot of fun." And he would rather have cut off his own arm than let her think it was *just* anything.

"Hmph," she said, then rolled onto her back. Oh no, she wasn't going to get away with a response like that. He followed her over and pinned her body to the bed with his.

"What does *that* mean?" he asked, trailing kisses down her neck.

She shifted her head against the pillow to give him better access. "It means that I'm kind of annoyed that you didn't trust me enough to know that you wouldn't treat me like that."

He reared back at that. That was *not* what he'd expected her to say. Giving her words a quick consideration, he could see her point. Nia was smart, and she was particularly smart about seeing through his bullshit. But at the end of the day—or more precisely, the end of May—he would be the one leaving Tildas Island, and it hadn't seemed right to be the one to start something when he'd also be the one ending it as soon as the task force disbanded in just over seven months.

She wiggled her legs from under his and wrapped them around the back of his thighs as she smiled at him. "But another part of me," she said, sliding her fingers through his hair, "feels all warm and fuzzy knowing that I mean enough to you that you didn't even want to risk making me feel like just a spot of fun, that you didn't want to make me feel like that's what I was worth to you. You couldn't know this, because we've never talked about it, but my family does a bang-up job of making me feel inadequate—there is not a world that exists where I am good enough for them, where I am worthy enough of their care. The fact that you were conscientious enough about it without even knowing it's one of my triggers, well, like I said, it gives me the warm fuzzies. You are a good man, Jake McMullen."

Her words filtered into his mind and had he not heard the raw edge of pain in her voice, he would have doubted her—

because in his mind, there was not a planet in their solar system on which Nia Lewis would ever *not* be the amazing, smart, fun person she was. But rather than let them dwell in the darkness that she'd shared, she pulled him down into a heated kiss and did an excellent job of distracting him.

Slowly, sinuously, they started rocking against each other. When the sheet slipped off his body and the cool breeze from the fan struck his backside, he pulled back. He wanted her—all of her. He wanted her more this second time than he had the first.

"Nia?" he asked, needing to be sure she was ready.

She smiled at him. "You're a good man, Jake McMullen. But you'd be even better if you'd grab a condom and make me come a time or two."

"Demanding wench," he said on a chuckle. She laughed as he grabbed the foil packet from her bedside table, though he had other plans for her first.

"You're just jealous that I can have more orgasms than you in a single go," she said as he placed a kiss on the spot between her breasts.

He kissed his way down her stomach then paused below her belly button. Looking up, he met her gaze as her fingers trailed gently over his face. "There you're wrong, woman," he said. "I'm not jealous at all. In fact, you have no idea how grateful I am for that particular biological inequity." Then he dipped his lips back to her bare skin and spent the next hour proving to her how grateful he was.

Nia reached for her phone and glanced at the time, then at the empty spot in the bed beside her. Earlier that morning, she'd awoken with Jake's head between her thighs. Then once he'd given her one very satisfactory good morning kiss, he'd kissed her forehead, told her he'd call her later, and slipped out.

She'd drifted back to sleep after he'd left, but now that the sun was up, she had a decision to make. She'd had enough physical activity the night before that if she skipped her run today, it wouldn't be the end of the world. Then again, she'd already skipped it two days in a row.

With a groan, she pulled herself from bed, threw on her workout clothes, and headed out. Even at six-thirty in the morning, it was eighty degrees and humid. She considered pushing herself to make up for her two days off, but after three miles, she decided enough was enough—she'd gotten her cardio for the day and now she just wanted to spend some time pondering the events of the previous night before she started work for the day.

They were good events to ponder.

She smiled as she let herself back into her house. Now that she and Jake had crossed that line, it seemed it was all she could think about. Oh, she'd have her head in the game when it came time for work, but for now, as she puttered around her house, made her coffee, and got ready for work, she enjoyed remembering the feel of his hands on her, of his skin against hers, and yes, the many times he'd shown her that their biological inequity—as he called it—was something to celebrate.

By the time she made it to work, her mind was firmly back on her schedule. She had two school tours that day—one in the morning and one in the afternoon—and Detective Anderson had called to see if she could come into the police station to go through mug shots. She'd gotten a pretty good look at the man who'd broken into her lab, so if he had a record and the police had his mug shot, chances were she'd be able to identify him.

Several hours later, she was saying goodbye to the teacher of the first tour group and watching the chaperones herd the second graders onto the bus when Jake called. Excusing herself, she stepped away.

"Good morning. Or almost afternoon," she corrected, glancing at her watch. It was ten minutes to twelve and she'd told Detective Anderson she'd be in by twelve-fifteen. That gave her ten minutes to grab her purse and sign out before she needed to leave. If she was going to be on time, she needed to walk and talk.

"So, first things first," Jake said as she pushed through the door back into the Marine Center. "I'm calling for professional reasons, but I want to acknowledge the sexy time we had together last night—"

"And this morning," she interjected with a smile. It was so like Jake to make sure she knew that last night wasn't something he'd blow off—especially after what she'd told him about her family.

"And this morning," he acknowledged. "And I sincerely hope that I can bring take-out over tonight and we can do it again because I'd like nothing better than spend several hours with your legs wrapped around me and hearing you screaming my name."

"Such a smooth talker, you," she teased as she entered her lab. Grabbing her purse from its usual spot, she turned right back around and left again, locking the door on her way out.

"I am a smooth talker, and you love it," he said.

"Turns out that I've discovered something I like more about your mouth than talking."

He chuckled. "So that's how's it's going to be?"

She pushed back out into the October noon heat and started toward her car. "If you're lucky, yes."

He barked out a laugh that made her smile. She'd been pretty sure that she and Jake could stay friends if they started sleeping together, but in the back of her mind, there had always been a risk. Hearing him laugh allayed any lingering fears. He was still

Jake, and she was still Nia, and there was just a new dimension to their relationship.

"To answer your question, yes, bring take-out. I'll be home by six. Now, what's the professional reason for your call Agent McMullen?" she asked, sliding into her car. She turned it on and let the air blast for a moment before closing the door.

"Have you made it into the police station to look at mug shots yet?"

"Actually, I'm on my way now. I have an appointment for a quarter after twelve."

"Good," he said. "Any chance you can pop over to our office after? Director Shah has a few questions about what you observed in the fish and also the results of the blood work you did."

She did a quick calculation as she pulled out of the parking lot. "That should work provided it doesn't take me too long to go through the photos at the police station. I have a tour I need to give for an after school program at three-thirty, so I need to be back by three to get ready."

"Ah, yes, that's right. You do all the school tours, don't you?"

"How do you know that?" she asked. She did do all the tours —at least all the ones she could. She liked the kids on the island to see her—someone like them, someone who'd grown up on Tildas—in a professional way. There were lots of directions these kids' lives could take and she liked showing them at least one possibility.

"I had a beer with Roger one night. He mentioned it to me." Roger was her right-hand man and assistant director. He'd been with The Center almost as long as she'd been alive and though he had no desire to run it, he was an excellent researcher and facilities manager. Much of the success of their labs was due to his attention.

"Anyway," Nia said, as she reached the western edge of Havensted. "I should be able to make it. But if things run long at the police station, I'll text you. If they do, I can come in tomorrow morning. Will that work?"

"You're doing us a favor, so yes, it will work."

They ended the call as she hit her favorite intersection, the one that had both a light and a stop sign, and she focused on crossing. With two cruise ships docked in the harbor, all the tourists meandering around town made driving that much more interesting.

Parking in the lot across the street from the police station, Nia locked her little hatchback, dodged a few cars, then walked into the lobby of the three-story building. Dumping her bag on the x-ray belt, her eyes strayed to the television hanging on the wall behind the guard. Her pulse hitched at what she saw—a map of the Atlantic with two tropical storms forming over it. It was a little late in the year, but even so, it wasn't unusual, and she paused to watch the closed caption text.

"Tropical storms Othello and Penelope," the guard said, drawing her attention back to the security gate.

"What are they saying?" Nia asked, walking through the metal detector.

"Othello looks like it might dissipate, but Penelope is the one they are keeping their eye on."

"And its trajectory?" she asked, picking up her purse and glancing back at the screen. The news had moved onto the next story, so she looked back to the guard.

"Right now? Just north of the island, but it's about three days out, so you know how those things go," he said.

She did. Between now and then, there were dozens of changes that could happen to the tropical storm, ranging from weakening altogether to changing course to strengthening into a full-blown hurricane. The chances of it growing into a hurricane *and* changing course to hit the island were slim, but her mind was already making preparedness plans as she stepped into the elevator.

By the time she stepped out of the lift onto the third floor, she'd determined what to do with two of the Marine Center's three boats if Penelope became a threat. The third boat was their largest and she had her own enclosed berth, so Nia didn't worry too much about her, although she made a note to run some scenarios with Roger before finalizing any plans. That was something that would have to wait as Anika Anderson was walking toward her.

"Thanks for coming in, Dr. Lewis," Detective Anderson said.

"Please, call me Nia," she said, shaking the woman's hand.

"Since protocol won't let me extend the same courtesy while I'm on duty, I'll stick with Dr. Lewis for now, but I appreciate the offer." As Anderson spoke, she led Nia through a door and into a small, windowless room.

"It's a bit dreary in here," the policewoman said. "But at least it has the best ventilation. Being anywhere near our bullpen is something you'd want to take a pass on, especially this close to lunch."

Nia smiled and took a seat as another officer popped in with a laptop that he handed to the detective.

"Did you see the news?" Nia asked as Anderson booted up the computer.

"Penelope?"

Nia nodded. "At least it explains the heavy air we've been having." When tropical storms brewed, the air changed, especially this time of year when the humidity tended to be a little bit lower than in the summer.

"Did you see the thunderheads last night?"

Nia thought about what she'd been doing last night. Escaping from her day, then getting lost in Jake. She shook her head.

"Here," Detective Anderson said, sliding the computer over. "I've set a filter for male, blond hair, less than five foot ten. I know you said he was probably closer to five foot seven, but I wanted to give you a broader pool, just in case."

Nia glanced down at the first image staring back at her. He had blond hair cut the same as the man she'd seen in her lab, but it definitely wasn't the man she'd seen.

"How do I move to the next one?" she asked.

Anderson gave her directions, then sat back and let Nia focus on the task. Given that there wasn't a lot of crime on the island in general, there were a surprising number of men who met the basic criteria. She continued to click through, and it wasn't until the thirty-seventh photo that she recognized a face.

"Did you find him?" Detective Anderson asked, straightening in her seat.

Nia's gaze flickered up, then back down the screen. She shook her head. "No, but it did surprise me to find my cousin in the line-up. I hadn't given him much thought, but I guess he does fit the criteria."

Troy's face was staring back at her. They'd been close as kids but had grown apart by the time she'd turned twelve. Occasionally, they had a drink together, but she hadn't seen him since she'd refused to bail him out of jail that first time.

Nia flipped the computer around for Anderson to see.

"Troy Beaufort is your cousin?" she asked.

Nia nodded. "On my mother's side. Is this from his first arrest or from the one last night?"

"Must be from the first," Anderson said, sliding the computer back to Nia. "If he was brought in last night, his details wouldn't be in the system yet. You close?"

She shook her head. "I haven't seen him since before I refused to bail him out from this," Nia answered, waving to the screen. He'd been arrested for attempted grand theft after trying to rob a jewelry store in Havensted. Robbery itself was a bad choice, but picking a jewelry store on Main Street was beyond comprehension. There were several along the main drag and everyone on the island knew that street was the most surveilled street on this rock they all called home.

"That's tough, but probably a good choice since it sounds like he's in again."

Wanting to drop the subject of Troy, Nia gave a vague nod and turned back to the photos. In her heart, she believed she had made the right choice—both the first time he'd been arrested and then again last night. But that didn't mean she didn't see his toothless, grinning, sweet seven-year-old smiling face when his mug shot stared back at her.

The room fell into silence as she clicked through a few more photos. Most were obviously not the man she'd seen, but she forced herself to look at each image methodically, not wanting to risk missing something.

When she clicked over to the forty-second picture, she drew back, sucking in a quick breath through her nose.

Anderson looked up but didn't say anything.

Nia forced herself to breathe and focus on the image. Eyewitness accounts were notoriously unreliable and she didn't want to play any part of the statistics that sent the wrong person to jail based on her identification. When her mind confirmed what her instinct had first told her, she turned the computer around.

"This is him," she said.

Officer Anderson's eyes scanned the image. "You sure?"

Nia nodded. "One-hundred percent sure."

"That's all I need then," Anderson replied. "Well, that's not technically all I need. I still need you to sign a statement about that night and an affidavit of your identification. But with your confirmation, I can get all the paperwork started. Do you have thirty minutes or so?"

Nia pulled out her phone and glanced at the time. It wasn't even one o'clock yet. "I do. Do I stay here, or do you need me to do something else?"

"If you wouldn't mind staying here. Based on our conversation Saturday night, we typed up a statement for you that we'd like you to go over. You may want to edit it to include anything you might have found missing between when we talked on Saturday and today, but I'll bring it up on this computer, and you can do that while I prepare the affidavit. That work?"

"Of course," Nia said as a text dinged on her phone. She picked the device up to read the text message as Detective Anderson clicked away on the keyboard, presumably bringing up the statement.

"*You nail the bastard yet?*" Jake asked.

"*I've always thought that phrase was a bit ambiguous. Are you really asking me if I nailed another guy?*" she answered. A few seconds passed before the little bubbles appeared, letting her know Jake had figured out what she'd meant.

"*There will be no nailing of any men but me.*"

She chuckled, and Anderson looked up, but then went back to her work when Nia didn't meet her gaze.

"*On that, we can agree. But if you want to know if I identified him, I did. But I don't know his name. They only showed me pictures, no names.*"

"*Standard operating procedure. They don't want you to be influenced by any names you might recognize. Still, I can find out later today if you want to know. One of the perks of sleeping with a federal agent.*"

"*Believe me, that perk is WAY down on the list of perks I took into consideration when deciding to sleep with said federal agent, but thanks for the offer. I should be done in thirty minutes. I'll walk over after that.*"

"*Great, see you then. And tonight, I want to know all about the perks you did take into consideration.*"

She chuckled again but didn't respond. She didn't mind getting a little risqué on text, but she wasn't going to get graphic.

"Here's the statement," Detective Anderson said, handing the computer back to Nia. "Have a look while I'm pulling together the affidavit, and we can go over everything when I get back."

Nia nodded and dutifully started reading as Anderson stepped from the room. Fifteen minutes later, she was electronically signing the document when Anderson walked back into the room. They went through the affidavit, confirming that the picture Nia had identified was the one listed in the document, and as they did, she caught a glimpse of his name, Carl Westoff.

"I have an appointment around the corner that I need to get to, but if you have a few minutes, can you tell me why he's in your system? What did he do?" Nia asked, after signing the document and handing it back to Anderson.

The detective closed the folder and rose. "We can walk and talk. I wouldn't mind a bit of air," she said with a smile.

Nia stood, and, grabbing her purse, she followed Anderson out. When they stepped into the elevator, Anderson started speaking.

"The files you went through cover most of the Caribbean region. Kind of like the national database for the US, but combined with Interpol for the Caribbean. All the islands are so close together, relatively speaking, that all but a few of the countries have agreed to participate."

"Is that your way of telling me this is his first crime on Tildas?" Nia asked.

Anderson snorted. "That we've identified him as being a part of, yes," she said as the elevator opened and they stepped out into the lobby. "He was convicted of possession on St. Thomas a little over a year ago. But it was a small amount, so his sentence was minor. Before that, he was convicted of assault in the British Virgin Islands and robbery in the Dominican Republic."

"So, really, an overall great guy," Nia said, her dry tone juxtaposed with the damp air they stepped into as they exited the building.

"The kind I'd like to bring home," Anderson quipped. Then she took a deep breath and everything about her relaxed, from the tenseness in her shoulders to the straightness of her back.

"You okay?" Nia asked.

Anderson smiled. "Now that we're outside and I no longer have to cling to authority with my fingertips, you can call me Anika. And to answer your question, I'm fine. It was just a bit of a rough morning on the force."

Nia recognized Anderson's tone. "Not a lot of women?" she asked. While her current job was a great place to work, she'd experienced her fair share of struggles as a female scientist.

"There are thirty-six officers in the Havensted department and only three are women. I'm the only detective. It's not bad, I love the work, but being barely five foot two and with this," she pointed to her nearly white-blond hair that was pulled up into a bun. "My physical presence doesn't command a lot of respect."

"And sometimes it's exhausting when they think your mind is as petite as you are," Nia finished.

Anika offered her a wry smile. "Something like that, yeah."

"Yo, Doc!"

Nia and Anika turned to see Dominic walking down the street toward them.

"Hey, Dom," she called back as he jogged up the stairs to greet her.

Placing a kiss on her cheek, he then turned to Anika. "We didn't officially meet on Saturday. I'm Dominic Burel," he said, holding out his hand.

To her credit, Anika didn't appear as awed by Dominic's looks as she had on Saturday and she eyed his hand warily before reaching out to take it.

"Anika Anderson," she said.

"Nice to meet you, Anika," he said, flashing her his trademark smile.

Nia recognized that smile and that tone. Over the months

she'd known Dominic, she'd seen him deploy it on any number of women. Based on her calculations—because she loved stats—it had a 97.6% rate of it leading to a night in said woman's bed for her friend.

"What are you doing out here?" Nia asked, dragging Dominic's attention back to her. Anika looked like she might fall into that scant 2.4% that wasn't impressed with Dominic, but even so, Nia didn't think the woman really needed to deal with Dominic's special kind of charm at this moment.

"Just coming from the medical examiner's office," he said, holding up a file. "He sent preliminaries over this morning, but Shah wanted me to go over and get some additional details."

"That for the body that was brought in yesterday?" Anika asked.

Dominic's eyes flickered to the detective before landing back on Nia, leaving it up to her what she wanted to say.

"Yeah, it is. Jake McMullen, the other agent you met Saturday night, and I were out diving and found it," Nia said.

Anika stared at her, then a small smile flirted on her lips. "You've had a rough couple of days, Dr. Lewis. First, a lab break-in then a dead body that you happened to come across. I assume they're related." It wasn't a question.

Nia nodded, but Dominic answered.

"The body was found with drugs on it. We think the fish Nia collected last week ingested those same drugs."

"Which is why someone wanted to steal them back," Anika said.

"That's our theory, yes," Dominic said.

"What kind of drugs?" Anika asked.

"We can't say," Dominic answered. "For a few reasons, but the main one being we don't know yet. We haven't identified it," he added when Anika looked to protest.

"Well, Carl Westoff, the thief that broke into Nia's lab, has prior drug, robbery, and assault convictions. I'm sure you'll want to look into him," Anika said.

Dominic nodded. "We will, thanks."

"I assume you have access to all the files I do, but if you need anything, let me know," she said.

"Thanks, we will. Or rather Dominic and his team will," Nia said, looping her arm through Dominic's and pinching him to stay quiet. Once again, the expression on his face was transparent. He'd been about to ask Anika for her email or contact information and Nia knew exactly what Dominic intended to do with it. She wasn't opposed to her friend pursuing Anika Anderson—Anika seemed like a woman who could take care of herself—but she wasn't going to let him do it under the guise of professional cooperation. Her new detective friend deserved more than that.

Anika's gaze went between the two of them, then she nodded. "Thanks for coming in today. If we catch him or find anything else you should know, we'll reach out."

Nia thanked her, then both she and Dominic shook Anika's hand before turning and heading toward the FBI office. When they were around the corner, Nia pinched Dominic again.

"Ow, woman. Stop that," he said, disentangling himself from her arm and dramatically rubbing his side.

"Are you having policewoman fantasies, Dominic Burel?"

He chuckled. "As a Black man, that seems a bit sadistic. But yes, I am. Hard not to with a woman like Anika Anderson."

Nia tried to scowl at her friend. She didn't want Anika to be judged by her looks. But in the end, the scowl turned into a resigned shake of her head. Even she could see how attractive Anika was. The detective might be petite, but she had curves Nia envied, flawless skin, and a face that was reminiscent of Elle McPherson, the supermodel. She also had a big ol' "don't fuck with me," vibe that Nia respected and Dominic would see as a challenge.

Really, he was so predictable.

They'd reached the FBI office, but before entering the building, she pulled Dominic to a stop. He shot her a questioning look, but he halted.

"Look, Dom. I get it. She's beautiful and seems unimpressed by you, which together is probably irresistible. But she's one of three women on the force, and I get the sense that it's not an easy position to be in. Pursue her if you want, she's an adult and will make whatever decisions she wants to, but don't use her job to get to her. Respect her position and her career and don't treat them as a means to an end. If you're interested, just ask her out without any pretense."

Rarely did she and Dominic talk about anything serious, but she could see him taking in what she'd said, weighing it. Finally, he gave a little dip of his head in acknowledgment. "Fair enough. Her job is one I respect, and you're right, using it as a means to an end would be a pretty shitty thing to do."

"Thank you," she said, then she leaned up and gave him another peck on the cheek. "You may be a manwhore, but you're my favorite manwhore."

Dominic laughed then gestured toward the door. "Ready to meet with Shah?"

She hesitated. "Give me a minute?" she asked. "I need to make a quick run to the store. I'll be in right after." She pointed to the catch-all drug store across the street.

He eyed her, then nodded. "I'll let everyone know you're on your way."

"You're the best," she said as she turned to cross the street.

"That's what she said," Dominic called after her.

"Such a manwhore," she muttered just loud enough for him to hear, and the sound of his laughter followed her across the street.

CHAPTER NINE

JAKE'S IM dinged with a message from Steven, the FBI receptionist, telling him that Nia had arrived. But before he could rise
from his desk, Alexis, who was nearer to the door, let her in.
Jake paused and watched the interaction. The two women
hugged, then Alexis, with her hand lingering on Nia's arm,
nodded in response to something Nia said. As a friend and a
psychologist, Alexis was probably checking in to see how Nia
was holding up.

As the two women conversed, Beni walked out of a side
office, where she'd gone to take a call, and joined them. Beni
wasn't overly demonstrative in the best of times, but she, too,
hugged Nia. Nia smiled as she pulled back, and an entirely too
strong emotion—something that felt like a combination of jeal-
ousy and frustration—gripped him.

He, too, wanted to hug her. But he also wanted to slide his
arm around her waist, pull her to him, and let her lean into him.
They hadn't discussed whether or not they'd share what had
happened between them—what *was* happening—with anyone,
and his desires were at war with his uncertainty. Did Nia want
people to know their relationship had changed? Did he?

Just as he rose from his seat, Damian and Charlotte stepped out of Director Shah's office. As a renowned economist, Charlotte was acting as a consultant to the task force on the upcoming World Summit being held on Tildas Island in seven months. She was part of the steering committee responsible for the conference, but she also had tremendous insight into most, if not all, of the participants—something Director Shah and the team appreciated.

With her hand in Damian's, Charlotte approached the women and when she reached Nia, the two gave each other a kiss on the cheek. Charlotte's free hand lingered on Nia's arm, much the same way Alexis's had, as the two talked. When they finished speaking, Damian accompanied his fiancée to the door, where he tugged Charlotte to a stop. She turned and placed her hands on Damian's chest as he slid his around her waist, then Damian lowered his head and placed a lingering kiss on her lips. Not an inappropriate one—there was no tonsil hockey going on —but definitely an intimate one.

And as he watched the couple, an emotion that Jake was afraid might be *longing*, sucked the breath from his lungs.

This was exactly why he didn't combine friendship—deep friendship—with sex. In the span of less than three minutes, he'd been gripped by jealously, frustration, and longing. And he didn't know what to do about—or with—any of those feelings.

His gaze flitted to the exit as his muscles bunched and his heart rate accelerated with the urge to run. Maybe he could sneak out and spend the next twenty-four hours in his warehouse, escaping from the world in a way that always soothed him. The idea held appeal, he could work himself into exhaustion and then maybe these *feelings* would go away.

"Jake?" Nia called from across the open office. He glanced over to see her watching him, Director Shah at her side.

His fingers twitched and his leg started to jiggle under his desk. He glanced at the exit again.

Nia paused and waited until he turned his attention back to her. "Director Shah wants us all to gather in the conference room to go over the tox report on the body we found yesterday. She also has something else to share that she hasn't told us yet," Nia continued. He could see the questions in her eyes, and the concern. She searched his face, then turned her back on his colleagues. Cocking a flirtatious eyebrow at him, she threw him a small, but sultry smile, and winked. "Coming anytime soon?" she asked.

His breath left his lungs as he laughed at the double entendre he was sure no one else picked up on. He might want to run from all the feels he was experiencing, but he didn't want to run from *her*.

"Right. Just woolgathering. On it," he said, grabbing a notebook and pen as he rose.

Less than a minute later, everyone was sitting around a large conference table staring at four sets of data projected on a large screen.

Director Shah stood at the front of the room and started walking them through the information. "What you see on the top right are the results of the bloodwork Dr. Lewis did on the two fish that were taken from her lab. Below are the results from the two fish that weren't tested until a few days later. In the upper left is the tox screen for Angela Rosen, and below is the screen for the body we found yesterday—Mr. Robin Spencer, age twenty-two, and a resident of London, England."

Nia's results were charted in graphs with spikes and valleys, whereas Rosen and Spencer's results were in text with numbers indicating the concentration.

"It's clear that the four fish ingested the same drug," Jake said. "And it also looks like Rosen and Spencer had similar—but not the same—tox screens, but what's the correlation between the tox screens and the spectrometer results from Nia?"

While Beni was a trained medic and Alexis a doctor of

psychology, Nia was the only scientist in the room, so all eyes, including his, turned to her. She was studying the four images, her eyes darting between them, her head cocked to the side.

After a beat, she frowned then rose as she started speaking. "Assuming the fish we found ingested the drug from the bag Spencer had on him, I think it's safe to say that these results," she said, pointing to Spencer's, "are the same as what I found in the fish, but it's a less detailed description. My results show the specific chemical breakdown, whereas Spencer's tox screen is a little more generic. Can you have the lab run his blood through a mass-spec?" she asked, turning to Shah, who nodded.

"Good. I think it will confirm what I said, but it's always good to have that actually confirmed." Nia paused and turned her back on the group to better study the images. "This is interesting though," she said, pointing to Rosen's results. "Any chance we can get mass-spec tests done on this sample?"

"Unfortunately, no," Shah said. "I can double-check with the lab, but I'm not sure they will still have her sample."

"This is that CIA agent who died last June, right?" she asked.

"It is," Shah confirmed.

"You can see that her results are similar to Spencer's except for here and here," she said, pointing at two different lines in the reports. One was for barbiturate and the other for Rohypnol. "If I didn't know any better, I'd think that whoever is developing this drug is refining it and Rosen's was a more primitive, or earlier version. I don't know what their ultimate goal is, so I'm not sure what they are fine-tuning it for, but I would wager that that is exactly what they are doing, and that's what accounts for the difference between Rosen's and Spencer's results."

"Based on how they've fine-tuned it, can you hazard a guess as to what they were trying to accomplish?" Jake asked.

Again, she turned her back on them and studied the images. "There's a little more barbiturate and amphetamine in Spencer's than in Rosen's and a little more Rohypnol in Rosen's than in Spencer's. I'd say they are trying to balance keeping a person mobile and physically capable—which a reduction in Rohypnol would do—but still dull their mind—which is what the barbiturate would do."

"Make them more robotic," Alexis said.

Nia turned. "Unfortunately, that would be my guess, too."

Jake's focus returned to the images as his teammates started to toss around theories. The potential uses of such a drug were staggering and horrendous—from rape to terrorism—but with such a broad spectrum, he wondered what the creator's true goal was. Was it something he or she intended to sell to a military power as a way to control people, or was it something to be released on the streets? Both would net massive financial gains, though the former would result in a single, big payout and the latter would likely come in as more of a steady stream.

"I know barbiturates can be addictive, but is there anything in there that would give someone a high?" Jake asked.

The room silenced, and everyone turned to him. The sudden attention wasn't unusual; he tended to surprise his colleagues on a fairly regular basis. "I'm trying to figure out if this is supposed to be a street drug or something more for the industrial-military complex. If it were meant to be a street drug, if there was something in it to make someone feel good, that would ensure its uptake. Then, of course, the addictive qualities would take over after that."

Nia shook her head. "Nothing like what you're talking about. A barbiturate is a sedative, like an opioid. But like an opioid, it won't really make you feel high, but it will make you feel numb, which can be just as alluring."

"What about the amphetamine and the scopolamine?" he asked.

Nia tipped her head to the side in thought. "The

amphetamine amounts in Spencer's system would be enough to counteract some of the sedative effects, but probably not enough to make him feel high—though on its own, and not in combination with the other chemicals, it might. As for the scopolamine, I don't know much about it as a chemical, but if you look at history, Devil's Breath, which is what I found in my sample and which is naturally occurring, has often been used to stimulate hallucinations. I suppose that could be a draw for certain recreational drug users, but that kind of experience is easy to get in so many other ways from mushrooms to LSD, that it's almost overkill to take something as designer as what we're looking at just to have a hallucination."

"I think we need a little more research into how all the components of this drug work together," Damian said.

"I agree," Dominic weighed in.

"In addition to figuring out who is behind this and what—as Jake mentioned—is their purpose," Beni concluded.

Nia smiled. "I think you're right. But I also think that's not something I can help much with and I have a tour I need to give back at The Center. I'm happy to help more if needed, but I work with sea life, not human life. You may want to bring in an MD or someone who specializes in human drugs."

"I think that's an excellent idea, and thank you for coming in today, Dr. Lewis," Shah said. "Jake can escort you out, and I hope the tour goes well."

Nia gathered her purse that she'd hung from her seat. "Always happy to help, and please, don't hesitate to reach out if you need me again. No need to walk me out, though. You should stay and sort through whatever it is you all are going to sort through," she said, placing a hand on his shoulder as he started to rise.

She gave a little squeeze, and while he had no idea what she was up to, that tiny little movement told him everything he needed to know—they were fine, she'd see him in a few hours, and he better bring take-out. He sank back into his chair and tried to hide his smile.

Dominic raised an eyebrow at him. Jake ignored him and turned his attention back to the images, knowing that if he looked at his friend, everything between him and Nia would be written on his face.

An hour later, he and the team walked out of the conference room, each with an assignment. Dominic would start looking at the possibility of drugs being transferred via no-contact drop-offs and pick-ups. Alexis and Damian were assigned to researching where the drugs might be being manufactured, and Beni was assigned to pulling up recent drug deaths and hospitalizations to see if there might have been signs of the drug that had gone unnoticed because it had been unknown.

As for him, well, he was tasked with combing through the lives of Robin Spencer and Carl Westoff. He was contemplating his best approach as he rounded his desk and saw a folded note taped to his screen.

Frowning, he reached for it.

"What's that?" Dominic said.

Jake shrugged, unfolded the note, then smiled when he recognized the handwriting.

"See you tonight. I should be home by six. I hear that new tapas place in Spanish Town has excellent paella. I'll make sangria."

"Just a note from Nia," Jake said, refolding it and sliding it into his pocket.

"I know that smile," Dominic persisted. "Did you and Doc…?"

"I'm smiling because she's funny," Jake said.

Dominic gave him a hard stare, and Jake had no illusions that his friend was coming to the right conclusion, but he wasn't going to confirm or deny anything until he talked to Nia first.

Dominic finally relented and, accepting that Jake wasn't going to say anything, his gaze flitted over Jake's desk. Then he frowned. "Why didn't she just text you. And where did she get the tape?"

At five minutes after seven, Jake walked into Nia's house with an overnight bag and a couple of boxes of take-out from the tapas place. He set his bag down on the floor and the boxes on the table, but it wasn't until forty-five minutes later that they got around to opening one.

Standing in Nia's kitchen in his boxer briefs, Jake watched Nia's food go round and round on the microwave plate as she poured the sangria. It was kind of mesmerizing, and as he watched it make turn after turn, his mind turned back to the afternoon.

"Are we keeping this thing a secret?" he asked. He heard Nia set the pitcher down, but he didn't look over. "I don't want to, so you know," he continued. "But, as the saying goes, it takes two to tango and if you want to, I'll respect that."

Nia came up behind him and put one hand on his back as the other snaked around his torso and handed him a glass of sangria. She pressed her body against his and laid a kiss on his bare shoulder.

"I have no need to keep this a secret from anyone, but I do have one condition," she said.

The microwave beeped, but he ignored it and turned around. "What's that?" he asked, sliding one hand around her waist while holding his drink in the other.

She smiled up at him. "I think we both know it's going to be awkward. At least initially. Can we come up with some really big, maybe even crazy way to tell everyone, so that the awkwardness is overrun by the humor?"

He grinned. Damn, he loved how this woman thought. "Any ideas?"

She winked at him and stepped out of his arms. Opening the microwave and reaching in for her food, she looked over her shoulder. "Oh, I have a few. Most of which involve Dominic and a certain detective I know."

CHAPTER TEN

"What happened to you? You look like hell," Jake said to Dominic as he set a coffee down on his friend's desk.

"Been here most of the night," Dominic said. "I can't believe we haven't been covering this angle of island security before."

"What angle?" Jake asked, coming around the desk to look at the papers spread across the surface.

"The drug drop angle," Dominic answered. "It's probably been going on under our noses all this time and we've never looked into it."

Jake frowned as he tried to absorb the amount of information staring back at him. "We have been following the drug trade, just not this part of it. We know there are recreational users on the island and we have an idea of several of the major players. We've never gone after them though because we don't have enough evidence; and, as you well know, it's not *that* big of a problem on the island."

"Not yet anyway," Dominic replied, picking up his coffee and leaning back in his chair. "But this drug could change things."

Jake picked up the ocean map of the US Virgin Islands and

studied the red dots Dominic had drawn on it. "What are the dots?" he asked.

"Those are areas that share similarities with where we found Robin Spencer—including currents, reefs, accessibility, visibility, and general location."

"Potential spots where someone could drop-off and pick-up drugs?"

Dominic nodded.

"Do you think the drug is meant to be distributed here? For recreational purposes?" Most, but not all, of the dots were relatively close to islands with significant tourist populations.

"I don't know," Dominic answered. "But I do know that this kind of drug is in an entirely different ballpark than what we usually see on the island. It's a different game altogether. I'm concerned about it getting out onto the streets, of course, but what I'm most concerned about is who's making it and who has control over its distribution. The kind of money, and the power that comes with that control, is what's giving me the heebie-jeebies. Whoever it is, we need to know, because I do not want a drug kingpin gaining power right under our noses just as a couple of hundred world leaders descend on the island."

Jake's gaze lingered on the maps, "You have a fair point. And these *would* be good drop spots," he said, pointing to the red dots. "They are accessible enough by a small boat, but out of the way of the major boating channels. They are also good fishing spots so if someone used a lobster pot or something with a similar line and float—"

"It would look like every other fishing gear," Dominic finished.

Jake nodded. "So, what's the plan?"

"I'd like to get out on the water and check out some of the floats to see if we can find any that look, well, pun intended, fishy. If we do find any, then maybe take a little dive or two. What do you think? We can get Damian to join us."

Jake scanned the papers and though it was unlikely they'd find anything, they were even less likely to find anything if they didn't at least look. Besides, Dominic had said Jake's favorite words—well, now that he was with Nia and Nia said all sorts of interesting things in the heat of the moment, maybe they were his second favorite words, but they were still favorites.

He grinned at his friend. "You had me at 'out on the water.'"

"Did you and Alexis find anything yesterday?" Dominic asked Damian as the three of them studied the map laid out on the console of the FBI boat.

"Nothing concrete. We're waiting for some more satellite images to come in today on some of the smaller, privately owned islands," he answered. "But these are interesting," he added, pointing to a cluster of dots on the southwest side of Little Hans Lollik, a small island off of another small island off the north shore of St. Thomas.

"Why's that?" Jake asked.

"The waters around those two islands, Hans Lollik and Little Hans Lollik, aren't visited regularly by any tourists as it's kind of tricky getting to them. Little Hans Lollik is also fairly hidden from view if you're on St. Thomas. Not entirely, of course, but if you're on St. Thomas and can see Little Hans Lollik, you're probably too far away to see much of anything else except maybe a dot of a boat."

"But they aren't near any of the islands you're looking at that could be the place of manufacture, are they?" Jake asked.

"Not that close, no. St. Thomas is too populated to hide the kind of lab we think we're looking for, so we're not focusing much attention there. But, there are a few smaller islands around St. Thomas and St. John—or even on St. John itself—that could sustain the lab. As you said, they aren't that close to

Little Hans, but they aren't that far either." As he spoke, he pointed to four different, privately owned islands, all within an hour's boat ride from Little Hans Lollik.

Jake glanced at Dominic then to Damian. "Anyone have a better plan?" Both men shook their heads. "Then I guess it's to Little Hans Lollik we go."

A little over an hour later, they zipped through the channel between two cays to the west of Lovango Island and turned westward on their final approach to Little Hans Lollik. It was still a bit of a way, but once they cleared the two cays, it was more or less a straight northwesterly shot through open waters to the Lolliks.

Dominic opened the throttle as they cleared Thatch Cay, and Jake glanced over at Damian, who hadn't put his phone down since they'd left Tildas Island.

"What's up with that?" Jake asked. Damian looked up, and Jake nodded to the phone. "You've been on it for the past hour non-stop."

Damian lifted a shoulder. "I like being on the water, but I'm not a water rat like you. I've got other things I'm trying to do." Their boat had a satellite connection that allowed them to use their phones wherever they were, but Jake couldn't imagine keeping his head buried in his device while on the water.

"Such as?" Jake prodded.

"Stuff."

Jake swung his legs around and faced Damian. "You would think by now that you'd know better than to wave a flag like that at me. Now tell your friend, Jakey, what's going on."

Damian held his gaze, then shook his head. "You are such a pain in the ass."

Jake grinned. "It's been at least two days since you told me that. I was beginning to think you didn't love me anymore. Now, what's going on?"

Damian ignored him for thirty seconds, but Jake didn't

relent in his one-man staring contest. "Fine," Damian huffed. "You want to know what's going on?"

Jake nodded. "I do, especially since you're the most share-iest of all share-ers I know, and the fact that you aren't sharing is *very* interesting."

Damian stared at him. "You know," he said after a beat. "That actually makes sense."

"Of course it does," Jake said, swinging his legs back around and leaning against his seat. "I may be a pain in the ass, but I notice these things. Now, what's going on?"

Damian started to answer, but Jake cut him off with a gesture as he sat up. "Dom, avoid that area there," he said, pointing to a small patch of water. It was churning in a way that made his water rat senses tingle, and though things like whirlpools weren't common in the Caribbean, he didn't like the look of it.

"That spot at our one o'clock?" Dom called back even as he changed the direction of the boat a little more westward and a little less north.

"Yeah, give it a wide berth. I don't know what it is, but with the changing air pressure and Penelope and Othello on their way, I don't want to take any chances," he answered.

"You think there's going to be a problem?" Damian asked once Dominic was on a new course.

"Today? No. But give it a day or two and I think at least one of those storms is going to make its presence known."

"The weather app says Othello will likely die out and Pene-lope will veer north," Damian said, holding up his phone.

Jake shot his friend a look though Damian probably couldn't really grasp the full effect since they all wore aviator-style sunglasses. "Tell me you weren't looking at the weather app this entire time. Please."

Damian turned his head and looked at him. Hmm, interesting, it seemed that emotions *could* be communicated through mirrored sunglasses.

"I wasn't looking at the weather app this entire time, but Charlotte's mother texted me and is keeping an eye on it," Damian said.

"Well, you can tell Charlotte's mother that she should keep an eye on it. I don't care what the weather app says, I'll bet you a night out at Lola's that Penelope will hit the island. She might be a tropical storm, but I'm guessing a category one hurricane."

"You're shitting me," Damian said.

"Wish I was, but I'm not. Call it the sixth sense of a water rat or whatever you want, but she's going to pay us an unwanted visit. It's the reason I wanted to come out today. It might be a wild goose chase, but I bet this is the last day this week that we'll be able to be out on the water at all in this boat."

The FBI boat was a sweet little ride, but she was built for law enforcement—fast enough to discourage someone from trying to outrun her, but big enough to carry the team. She was nowhere near big enough to withstand a hurricane in open waters and he'd already planned to suggest to Shah that they dry-dock her tomorrow.

"Shit, I'm not taking that bet," Damian said, sliding his phone into his pocket.

"Wise choice, Rodriguez. Now let's get back to the issue at hand. What's going on? Other than Charlotte's mother worrying about the weather."

Damian sighed as he leaned his head back against the seat. "Some texts were with Alexis, letting her know what we're doing. She was on duty today at Hemmeleigh and was a little put out that she couldn't join us." As part of the work the task force was engaged in to prepare the island for The Summit, once a week, each member spent either a day or a night shift at the resort working with the security and event planning departments. Of all the tasks the team engaged with—including running security exercises, updating security systems on a near daily basis, weekly meetings with the security teams of each attendee, and coordinating with the rest of the island's agencies on the logistics of flying in world leaders and transporting them to Hemmeleigh from the airport—the once weekly security shift was everyone's least favorite activity because it tended to be deadly dull.

"Based on the scant info we have, she agrees that where we're headed is as good a place to check as any," Damian added.

"Of course she does, Alexis is a smart woman. Now, what else?"

"Just catching up with a couple of people. That's all," Damian said as he turned his gaze away from Jake.

"I'm sensing something personal. And not just that, something personal you don't want to share. And since we've established that you're a sharer, I think whatever it is is...Oh my god! You're going to propose to Charlotte, aren't you?" Damian's head whipped around, but Jake kept talking. "I mean, of course you already sort of unofficially did. We all know that you two are getting married, which is why we always refer to her as your fiancée, even though she may not 'officially' be your fiancée. But you're going to make it official, aren't you? And you're going to do it soon, aren't you? And you're planning it? What are you going to do? Sky write it? Fancy dinner with the ring in the champagne? Although that one always seemed a little gross to me, but to each their own. Who's helping you? You should really ask Alexis. I mean, I don't think any of us can compete with her when it comes to class, and Charlotte is also a very classy lady. Don't get me wrong—"

"Could you shut up," Damian shouted over the wind.

"What?" Dominic called back, hearing Damian.

"Rodriguez is going to officially propose to Charlotte," Jake called back.

"You are such an asshole, McMullen," Damian grumbled.

"No shit!" Dominic said with a grin. "It's about time you get those wedding plans going. Can I be your best man? I look damn fine in a tux. You are going formal, right? I mean, you're not going to do one of those casual things on the beach, are you? Those are nice and all, but Charlotte strikes me as someone who'd like a nice formal ceremony and then a kick-ass reception."

"Fuck off, both of you. And no, you can't be my best man. And since I haven't officially asked her yet, I have no idea what kind of wedding we'll have."

"I call bullshit," Jake said with a laugh. "I bet you've been thinking about it since the day you met her, haven't you?" Jake was all jests, but in his heart of hearts, he was kind of jealous that Damian had never doubted that he and Charlotte were meant to be together. Yes, they'd had their ups and downs, including a year of separation, but Damian had never backed down or denied his love for Charlotte, even when it wasn't clear if she felt the same. She had, of course, but Damian hadn't always known that. Thankfully, they'd found their way back to each other.

To have such certainty and, more to the point, to be so open to the kind of love that existed between Damian and Charlotte was a bit of a mystery to Jake. But then again, Damian had always been the best amongst the team at processing emotions. It was a skill Jake respected, but now that Nia was in his life, in the way she was, he had to admit to being a little bit awed by Damian. What would it be like to be so grounded in *feelings*?

"So have you been imagining your wedding?" Dominic pressed.

Damian rolled his eyes and muttered something that sounded suspiciously like "fuckers," but then he answered. "I have not been picturing a wedding since we first met. But," he said, cutting off both Jake's and Dominic's protests. "I have pictured spending the rest of my life with her. That was easy to imagine; even from the first day I met her standing on the porch of her friend's house putting me in my place. But the wedding," he shrugged. "I don't really care. I'd like it to be a memorable way to celebrate this next step in our relationship, but beyond that, I haven't given it much thought. I doubt Charlotte has either."

In an odd way, Jake could see that. Charlotte hadn't grown up in the best of circumstances, but with a lot of hard work and some unexpected good luck that had hit at the age of thirteen, she'd made a one-hundred-eighty-degree turn from the life she'd been born into. But what she hadn't lost was her grounding in family and friends—they'd helped her survive her first thirteen years in the projects outside of New York, and they'd stuck by her when everything changed. No, whatever wedding Charlotte wanted, it would be grounded in what mattered to her, family and friends.

For a fleeting moment, Jake wondered what kind of wedding Nia would want or if she even wanted a wedding to begin with. As the thought danced in his mind, Jake recognized the oddity of it—never before had he wondered whether a woman wanted to have a wedding or, if so, what kind. But what struck him most was that his knowledge of Nia's family consisted only of what she'd told him their first night together. Unlike Charlotte, he couldn't say whether or not Nia would want them at the fictional wedding he was imagining for her—he thought probably not, but he wasn't certain of that. Which was kind of messed up in more ways than one. Why did he know more about his friend's fiancée's family than he knew about Nia's?

"There's our first fishing float," Dominic said, interrupting Jake's train of thought. He glanced over to see Dominic pointing toward something bobbing in the water two hundred yards away and slightly to their right.

Jake frowned and stood up to get a better look. The water was a deep blue and the float was a dark green. An unusual color to choose when wanting something that can easily be seen. At least when used legitimately. Not to mention the location was off.

"Slow up," he said, walking around the console. Dominic throttled back, and Jake joined him at the controls.

"What's up?" Damian asked, joining them, all talk of his upcoming nuptials pushed to the back burner.

"That isn't right," Jake said.

"What isn't?" Dominic asked.

"The color and location of that float," he answered.

All three of them looked up, their eyes trained on the small, green tube-like float bobbing in the water.

"Shall we check it out?" Damian asked.

"I think we shall," Dominic answered, before turning the boat in that direction and slowly motoring toward it.

"Get the mooring hook," Damian called as they neared.

Releasing the long pole with a hook on its end from its secured position, Jake leaned over the side of the boat as Dominic maneuvered close to the float. When he was the right distance away, Jake swung the pole down, letting the hook end fall under the waterline. Bringing it alongside the float, he pulled up. It was a textbook catch and what should have happened was that both the float and the rope it was attached to would snag on the hook. But that wasn't what happened.

"What the hell?" Damian asked as he leaned overboard when Jake came away with nothing. "That was a good hook."

Dominic reversed the engine and brought them back alongside the float.

"It was a good hook, but the float's not attached to anything. It's been cut. Get the net," Jake said to Damian. He'd almost just dived in, but he didn't have a change of clothes and as much as he liked the water, he didn't like the way saltwater dried on clothes. They got itchy and stiff, and it offended his delicate sensibilities.

TAMSEN SCHULTZ

Without a word, Damian scooped up the float using the net they kept on board, but he paused before dumping it on the deck.

"Anything I need to think about before I set this down?" he asked.

Jake grinned. "Feeling a little skittish?"

"Fuck off. You are not the one that's almost been blown up three times in the last eight months," Damian shot back.

"Here," Jake said, stepping forward and lifting the float out of the netting. "It feels like a regular float." He turned it over in his hands and it did, indeed, look and feel like an off-the-shelf version.

But then a little splotch of white caught his attention. He turned the float upright and held it up. "It looks like something was painted here," he said, pointing to the splotch.

Damian reached out, and Jake handed it over. He held it up, catching it in a different light. "It looks like it might have been an 'X' at one point, but it's worn off."

"And it was obviously cut from the rope," Dominic said. "I don't know about down here, but in Louisiana when folks are out crawfishing or dropping crab pots, they don't tend to cut their floats unless there's a problem pulling up the rope."

"City boy, here," Damian said. "What does that mean?" He handed the float back to Jake.

"There are two expensive pieces involved in pot fishing, the pot itself and the float," Jake said. "You don't want to lose either, but if a pot gets caught and can't be pulled up—"

"Then you cut your losses, so to speak, and save the float," Damian finished. "Then what's this one doing here? If someone cut it to save it, why didn't they take it?"

"I have no idea," Jake answered. "It could have fallen off the boat for all we know. But it's an odd color for a legit fisherman, too. It doesn't stand out at all."

"It could be nothing," Damian said. "I mean, what are the

chances of us picking this random spot to come have a look and then actually finding something?"

"Maybe the research you and Alexis started was better than you give yourself credit—"

Jake smashed the float down on the deck, cutting off the rest of Dominic's sentence.

"What the hell!" both men shouted as they jumped back.

Jake didn't answer right away. Instead, he eyed the two halves of the float that had broken apart with the force of the impact. Then he knelt, his colleagues following.

"That," he said, pointing to a small device attached to the inside wall of the float.

"What the hell?" Dominic muttered again.

"It looks like a tracking device to me," Damian said.

"It is," Jake confirmed. "We used to use similar ones when I worked in the LA office."

"Is that common for fishermen to add those?" Damian asked.

"No, it's not common. Not unheard of, but not uncommon, although you usually only see it in areas where commercial fishing is big and it's worth it to invest in this kind of technology. That device isn't cheap," Jake answered. "But why would they cut the rope and leave this, though?" He pondered that question as he studied the tracker.

"Like you said, maybe it fell from the boat?" Damian suggested.

"If they had to cut the rope, I'm wondering what it was tied to? Do we have a drug shipment floating somewhere on the ocean floor around here?" Dominic asked.

The channel was a hundred fifty feet deep where they were, definitely within diving depth. But the float could have drifted from anywhere. So while the urge to suit up and take a dive held some appeal, Jake didn't think that was the wisest course.

Just then, a swell hit the side of the boat and all three men scrambled to stay upright at the unexpected shift. Rising, Jake glanced up.

"Penelope is giving us a heads up that she's on her way," he said. In the few minutes they'd been studying the float, the seas had changed. They weren't dangerous yet, but they were darkening from blue to grey and beginning to churn. "We should head back. We could make it to Little Hans, but based on the maps, I think the reefs around there are a little trickier than we might want to take on with the changing weather."

Dominic and Damian turned their attention to the original destination. The island wasn't far away, maybe a little over a half mile, and it was frustrating to be so close and not be able to finish what they came out to do. But Jake had a feeling about the float. There were still a lot of open questions, and it could mean absolutely nothing, but he didn't think so. However, those questions could be answered back at the office as easily as they could be answered on the water.

"Is that tracker on?" Dominic asked.

Jake nodded. He'd used them often enough in LA to be familiar with how they worked.

"We should turn it off," Damian said. "On the off chance this has anything to do with drug drops, we don't want anyone tracking it to our offices. It would be better if they thought it was lost at sea and its power had just run out."

Jake knelt and squeezed two prongs together then depressed a button twice. "My prints will be on it now, but at least no one will know we have it." He rose and the three men looked down at the device, each had their hands jammed on their hips.

"Why does this feel creepy as fuck?" Dominic asked.

"I don't know, but I'm with you," Damian answered.

"Because if that is what we think it is," Jake said, pointing to the parts split open on the deck, "then whoever is manufacturing this drug already knows the value of it."

"Which means it's less likely to be designed to trickle out for recreational use," Dominic said.

"And more likely being bankrolled for military or political reasons," Damian added.

"And the idea of that drug being used to control masses of people is scary as fuck," Jake finished.

"Shit," Dominic muttered.

"I'm with you again," Damian concurred.

"I was thinking something a little stronger than that, but we can go with that," Jake added quietly as the full weight of what they might be up against sank in.

CHAPTER ELEVEN

ALEXIS, Beni, and Director Shah were waiting for them when they arrived back at the FBI offices, carrying the parts of the float in a big evidence bag. After being in the seawater, it was unlikely to have any prints on it that weren't theirs, but protocol was protocol, and if nothing else, it would preserve the chain of evidence.

"Conference room," Shah said without preamble, and the five of them followed after her like a row of ducklings.

"Before we get to that," she said, pointing to the bag, "I want Beni to update us on anything she found today."

Beni dropped a stack of files on the table then divided them into two piles. "These are drug-related deaths or deaths with an unidentified cause that occurred on the islands in the past six months," she said, pointing to one stack. Then she pointed to the other. "And these are just weird crimes that I decided to look into when I found that four of the twelve deaths were men who had been committing crimes at the time they died."

"Died or were killed?" Dominic asked.

"One died on the scene and was found the next morning, but two were killed by the property owners when the perpetrators attacked them. The last one charged a responding officer and was shot by the officer's partner," she answered.

"It's hardly unusual that someone on drugs would commit a crime, so there's got to be something more," Damian said.

"There is. Look at the locations of the crimes," she said as she brought up a map of the islands on the large screen. There had been one each on four separate US Virgin Islands, St. Croix, St. Thomas, St. John, and Tildas, but all four had taken place in a night club in a touristy part of the main town on each island. "And then there's this," she said, displaying the names and records of each of the deceased. All four were young men. Two were white and two were West Indian.

"No real priors?" Jake asked.

"One had a speeding ticket," Beni answered.

"That's it? Just a speeding ticket," Jake clarified.

"Yep," Beni said with a nod. "Just a speeding ticket. Hardly the types to go from living clean lives to robbing popular night clubs."

"What about the drugs?" Alexis asked.

"All of them had weird tox screens. None matched Angela Rosen's or Robin Spencer's exactly, but there was a similar combination of drugs in their systems," Beni answered.

"Whoever has been making this drug has been taking it out for test runs," Jake said, feeling a little nauseated at the thought.

"Probably on unknowing victims, if the lack of priors is anything to go on," Damian said.

"That's what we're thinking," Shah said. "We've put out a call to the local law enforcement and the clubs to see if they have any CCTV from the nights in question."

"I wonder if we'll see Carl Westoff in any of the videos," Jake mused. Yeah, he was being judgmental as hell, but the guy who'd broken into Nia's lab looked to be the kind of guy who might supply unsuspecting partiers with drugs just for the hell of it.

"The videos should start coming in tomorrow. We'll know

more then," Shah said. "Now, tell us about the treasure you three found today."

Dominic and Damian looked at him, so Jake answered. "It might not be much of a treasure, but it was weird enough to catch our attention," he said, then proceeded to tell them where they'd found it and what they'd found inside.

"Is there any way to know where it was transmitting to without turning it on?" Beni asked.

Jake paused before answering, his mind quickly sifting through his experience with the device. "I was going to say no, but I don't know that for certain. Anyone know if it's possible to track where a device is transmitting to without turning it on? I would think not, but if it has any memory stored inside it, maybe there's something there?"

"Didn't you say you worked with that brand before?" Damian asked.

"Same brand, different model," Jake answered. "We were live-tracking the device, so didn't need it to store anything."

"Anyone know anyone who might know?" Alexis asked. "I could ask my security, but this might be a little out of their wheelhouse."

Yes, Alexis had her own personal security. It was weird when they'd first learned about it. What kind of FBI agent had her own personal security? But after the initial weirdness had worn off and they'd all learned the reason behind it, it had just been yet another thing that Alexis Emelia Wright, daughter of an R&B megastar and Swedish supermodel, had access to that mere mortals did not. Along with her private plane and the mansion she lived in with Isiah.

"Rodriguez," Shah said, cutting into Jake's thoughts.

Jake glanced at his friend, who was studying Shah. Shah was studying Rodriguez right back. Since when did Shah learn to communicate silently with Damian? Jake had to admit he was kind of jealous that she'd singled Damian out for some reason. But then again, as she continued staring at Damian, maybe not.

Jake shifted in his chair. "Do you have super-secret skills you haven't told anyone about, Rodriguez?" Jake asked, mostly to break up the awkward tension building between his friend and their boss.

"I don't," Damian said, breaking eye contact with Shah and flicking a glance at Jake.

"Then why that...?" he wagged his finger between Shah and Damian. "Because I gotta say, it was a little uncomfortable to watch."

"You're such an ass," Beni said.

"Love you too, babe," Jake shot back.

"Don't call me 'babe,' and my guess is that Damian has connections we don't know about and Shah would like him to bring them in."

"Only if you're comfortable and only for this," Shah said, confirming Beni's read on the situation.

"Why wouldn't you be comfortable?" Jake asked.

"Yeah, are they like mafia guys or something, and if you ask you're going to owe them a favor?" Dominic jumped in.

Jake couldn't help but wince at that comment, but thankfully no one noticed because Damian responded quickly.

"No, dick, they aren't mafia," he said. Leaving Jake with no illusion of how Damian felt about the mafia. Of course, Jake felt the same, it was just unfortunate that some of them happened to be his family.

"Then who are they?" Alexis asked.

"They're friends," Damian said. "I try not to ask too many favors because both are married, and Naomi is pregnant with twins, and I think her brother Brian and his wife are trying to start a family, too. I don't like dragging them into things if I don't absolutely need to."

"Wait, is it those twins you always talk about? Not the in

utero ones, but the other ones? The ones that are crazy smart?" Jake asked. Damian nodded. "If they're that smart then, wouldn't this be a simple question? Whether or not we can find where the device is transmitting to?"

"If one of your really good friends called you and asked you whether they should take up surfing, would you answer with a simple yes or no?" Damian countered.

Uh, Damian had a point, because no, he would not. He would want to know why they were asking and what they were looking to accomplish, and then he'd probably walk them through the pros and cons of different boards and different ways of learning.

"Okay, fair point. Your call. We can always send it to the lab for analysis," Jake said.

Damian remained silent for a moment. "I'll ask them," he finally answered. "Brian and Naomi, the twins—and Lucy, Brian's wife—would be pissed if I didn't. Then, of course, if Naomi is pissed, Jay, her husband, will get upset, and since he's in the middle of his second World Series in a row and the Rebels are ahead three-to-one, I don't want to upset the balance."

"You do know that if you decide not to ask them, you don't have to tell them you didn't ask them," Alexis pointed out. "No one would get pissed that way."

Damian arched an eyebrow. "Let's just say the DeMarco grapevine would put Hollywood to shame. And since my best friend—a friend I'm supposed to catch up with tonight—is married to a member of that extensive family, once he senses something is on my mind, his wife, who is eerily prescient, will hound me until I tell her and then all the DeMarcos will know. Their saving grace is that all of them have some sort of security clearance, so while I don't share everything, if I do share, I don't have to worry too much."

"Sounds like my kind of family," Beni said with a grin.

"Thank you, Damian," Shah said, cutting off any further discussion. "So tomorrow is a big day, ladies and gentlemen. By now, we've all heard about Penelope and Othello. I believe the latest is that Othello is dissipating, but Penelope appears to be changing course again and heading for the island. There will be no boat trips or water-based activities, and I've pulled all of you from duty at Hemmeleigh for the rest of the week. Tomorrow, and maybe the day after if the weather allows, will be office days. We've got more research to do than we normally have the time for, so I'm making the time."

Everyone in the room nodded, though they each had varying degrees of interest in research. It was an inevitable part of the job and they'd all do it, but if Jake had his way, he'd be out on the streets, so to speak, rather than in front of a computer.

"Now," Shah said. "Don't you all have some sort of waffles and wings tradition on Wednesdays that you need to get to?"

That elicited smiles, partly because Jake was certain no one had ever told Shah, but she knew anyway, and partly because the thought of their waffles and wings night at The Shack was smile-worthy. About two months after Isiah and Alexis had started dating, Dominic had convinced Isiah to try his hand at making chicken and waffles, a southern specialty he missed from his home state of Louisiana. True to form, Isiah had surpassed even Dominic's high standards, which said a lot as his mama was a professional chef.

"I'll see you all bright and early tomorrow," Shah said, dismissing them.

They all filed out, and Jake walked over to his desk to grab his computer bag.

"Want to ride up to The Shack together tonight?" Dominic asked as he gathered his own things.

Jake nodded. "I've got a couple of things to do, but pick me up at seven?"

"And by 'do' do you mean—"

"Do not finish that sentence, Burel," Beni cut in.

Dominic grinned but didn't finish.

"See you at seven," Jake said, slinging his bag over his shoulder. He was almost out the door when Alexis spoke loudly enough to get his attention.

"Just a heads up, everyone. Penelope is gaining strength. They don't know if she's going to stay a tropical storm or turn into a category one hurricane, but either way, if anyone needs shelter—and yes, I'm looking at you Jake, since you live on a boat—my house is open. You know I have the room."

"Thanks, Lex. I'll keep that in mind," Jake answered as Shah walked out of her office. "Oh, and Director Shah? I made arrangements to have our boat dry-docked tomorrow. The warehouse is sturdier than the marina, and though it will put her out of commission for a few days, I'd rather just a few days than a few weeks—or more—if she were to get tossed around."

Shah nodded. "Good call, McMullen. Now all of you, go enjoy your evening."

Jake didn't need a third reminder of what awaited him—his mouth was already watering at the thought of Isiah's cooking. But before he could partake, he had a couple of things to prepare for, including a little surprise he and Nia had planned.

Pulling out his phone as he rode the elevator to the parking garage, he texted Nia.

"Everything set for tonight?" he asked.

A few minutes later, her response popped up. *"She's onboard, we're a go. See you at seven-thirty, Baby."* Then she added a laughing and a winking emoji.

With a grin, he slipped his phone into his pocket. He had one more errand to run before the fun would begin.

Two hours later, he was sipping a beer on the veranda at The Shack, surrounded by his teammates and their significant others. Well, Charlotte was sitting with them, Isiah was going back and forth between the table and kitchen.

Damian had given both him and Dominic a hard look when they'd greeted Charlotte, making it quite clear that the former Army Ranger would happily disembowel them if they so much as hinted at the conversation they'd had on the boat earlier. Normally, Jake might weigh the risks against the fun he might have, but two things stopped him. First, there was a line even he wouldn't cross when it came to razzing his friend, and ruining whatever Damian might be planning would definitely cross that line. Second, if he started in on Damian and Charlotte, Dominic would then start in on him and Nia. He'd tried in the car, but Jake had shut him down. Now he just had to hold him off for another fifteen minutes, and turning the conversation to anything relationship-y would definitely make that harder.

Isiah had just set down another round of beers and promised to be back with the platters of waffles and fried chicken when they heard the door of the bar open with such force that it banged against the opposite wall. Conversation stopped, and Alexis and Beni craned their heads to see what had caused the noise. Jake sat back in his corner and took a sip of his beer.

"Oh my god, thank god you guys are here," Nia said, rushing to the table.

In an instant, everyone was sitting straighter. "What's wrong, Doc?" Dominic asked as he stood and put a comforting hand on her arm. "Is everything okay?"

She dashed a furtive look over her shoulder. "No, I don't think it is. I don't know what's going on—"

"There you are," Detective Anika Anderson said as she strode into the bar. "Running to your little FBI friends isn't going to help you. I told you back in Havensted that this is a police matter. There's nothing they can do." As she spoke, she unhooked her handcuffs.

"Whoa," Dominic said. Damian rose, and so did Jake. "What's going on here?" Dominic demanded. "And there's nothing little about us," he added, glaring at Anika.

"Your little friend here was spotted by an eyewitness last night paying a visit to Carl Westoff," Anika said, reaching for Nia. Dominic stepped in between them.

"There's got to be a reasonable explanation," Damian said. "Did you even ask her before you decided to chase her down? And if you were serious about arresting her, what's she doing here?"

Anika made to move around Dominic, but he blocked her way. Taking a step back, Anika eyed the man with all the disdain a five foot two woman with rage issues could muster. "I wasn't planning on arresting her until she made a run for it. Lucky for me, she ran here, where she's cornered, and despite being friends and all, none of you can stop me from doing my job."

"Doc, what's going on?" Dominic said, half-turning toward Nia but not taking his eyes off Anika. Probably a wise move since she appeared to have the tenacity of a Chihuahua.

"I don't know what she's talking about," Nia said.

Anika let out a sigh. "You do know. I told you exactly what we found. If it's not true, then give me a reason not to believe it. Were you, or were you not at the Taphouse last night at nine PM?"

Nia's head darted around as she looked at each of her friends. "I wasn't. I told you I was at home."

"Can anyone validate that?" Anika asked, jiggling her handcuffs.

"No," Nia drew out her answer. "But it's true."

"If it's true, then you have nothing to worry about and shouldn't have run. Unfortunately, because I have an eyewitness and you have neither an alibi nor the good sense to stay and talk things through, I have to take you in," Anika said. "Hand her over, Burel. You know you have to."

Dominic didn't answer, but he didn't move either. No one at the table did. Jake glanced at each person and it was clear no one believed Nia had done anything wrong, but it was just as clear that they weren't sure what they could do about it.

"I have an alibi," Nia blurted out. "I just can't say who it is."

Anika snorted. "Right, hand her over, Burel."

"I know Nia wasn't at the Taphouse last night," Jake said, breaking the building tension. All eyes turned on him.

"Jake," Nia whispered.

He took a deep breath. "I know she was in her house all night. And the reason I know is because I was with her. All night."

Dominic stared at him for a beat. Then his eyes narrowed. "Did you just quote *Dirty Dancing*?"

Jake gave him his best guileless look. Dominic swiveled his head to Nia. She held his gaze for a minute, then grinned. "No one puts my baby in a corner," she said, then she stepped over to Jake and pulled him down into a kiss that would leave no room for anyone to misinterpret where he and Nia stood.

When she loosened her grip a little bit, he pulled back and grinned at her. "That was masterful," he murmured, then dropped another kiss on her lips before looking up to see the varied expressions looking back at them.

"What the actual fuck?" Dominic exploded. "Was that your way of telling all of us that you two are a couple? If so, then jesus, I'd hate to see what you do for a wedding or birth announcement. And as for you," he said, swiveling around to face Anika, thankfully not giving anyone any time to absorb, let alone respond to the wedding or baby comment. "You have no idea what you've just stepped into."

Anika quirked a brow at him. "Bring it," she shot back. "I have five older brothers. I can guarantee you can't bring anything I haven't seen before."

But before Dominic could respond, Damian started laughing. Soon the rest of the table joined him while Jake and Nia, still holding hands, smiled at them all. When everyone finally quieted, Nia stepped away from him and moved to Anika's side. Slipping her arm through the detective's, she made introductions.

"Everyone, this is my new best friend, Detective Anika Anderson of the Havensted police force. Anika, this is Damian, Charlotte, Beni, Alexis, and—"

"Anika, good to see you. Brody's going to get a kick out of this one," Isiah said, dropping a kiss on her cheek. "Her brothers aren't strangers here," he said to the group. "But I don't see your face often enough," he added, turning back to Anika.

She lifted a shoulder. "I got enough of them growing up. Now I prefer to only take on one at a time." Everyone stood or leaned across the table to shake her hand.

"Now, you going to join us for drinks and dinner?" Isiah asked.

Anika grinned. "If you don't mind. But even if you do mind, Nia promised me the best fried chicken and waffles on the island—which, to be fair, probably isn't hard since I think you're the only person who serves them—so you're stuck with me. Once I change out of this uniform that I had to dig out of my closet," she added.

"I've got some stuff upstairs," Alexis offered. "A dress or two that will be a little long, but would fit."

Anika shook her head. "Thanks, but I've got clothes in the car. I just need a place to change, any suggestions?"

Alexis glanced up at Isiah. "Your office, babe?"

He shrugged. "You know where the key is, go ahead and let her in while I finish up in the kitchen."

"Perfect," Alexis said as she rose gracefully from her seat. Then, after raising her face for a kiss, which Isiah happily obliged, she gestured for Anika to follow her.

"That was dirty," Dominic said when they were out of earshot.

Nia grinned and went on her toes to place a kiss on

Dominic's cheek. "It was, but just think, I could have asked her partner instead of Anika. Now, poor you, you have to sit beside her all night and have a few drinks. I'm so sorry we subjected you to this." Nia gave him a dramatic frown that had Jake chuckling.

"You're both assholes, you know that," Dominic grumbled, before swiping his drink from the table and retaking his seat. Jake followed suit as soon as Nia was seated.

"While all that was amusing," Beni said. "Can we talk about the elephant in the room?"

All eyes turned to her. "What's that, Beni?" Charlotte asked.

Beni pinned Charlotte and Damian with a look. "I didn't miss that little bomb you dropped this afternoon, Rodriguez. You know the one about your friend being pregnant with twins and 'Jay' being in the middle of his second World Series. How is it that both of you know Jason Even Greene, the star pitcher of the Rebels and quite possibly one of the best pitchers of all time, and you never told me about it?"

"Actually," Charlotte said, picking up her drink. "I think the real elephant in the room is why Dominic apparently knows all the lines to *Dirty Dancing*."

CHAPTER TWELVE

JAKE STEPPED onto the back deck of his boat then turned to offer Nia a hand. She smiled—she didn't need help boarding a boat, but she took his hand anyway.

"I'll grab an overnight bag, and then we can head to your place," he said, leading them up the stairs to the main deck of the boat he called home. He'd bought the ninety-five footer with money he'd saved from his time as a pro surfer when he'd been assigned to the LA offices of the FBI. Ever since then, he'd called it home. Yeah, it was kind of unusual, but he'd learned long ago that he got twitchy if he was far away from the sea for too long so this was his way of ensuring it would always be there for him.

"Help yourself to something to drink, if you like," he added, after unlocking the door and walking into the galley.

"I'll just grab some water," Nia said. "Want anything?"

"I'm good. Just give me five minutes." He jogged down the stairs leaving Nia on her own. She'd been over before—many times—but still, he hurried.

He was throwing his running shoes in his bag when she popped her head into his cabin.

"You know, for as many times as I've been here, I don't think I've ever seen your room," she said, stepping into the space as he zipped his bag. "Oh, you have a Broussard!" she said before he could respond. He looked up to see her pointing at a painting hanging on his wall.

"I do," he said. "Two, actually."

"I love her paintings," Nia said. "I have one, too, did you know that?"

"I did not," Jake said, coming to stand beside her as they faced the painting that had caught her attention. It was a seascape. Sort of. It reminded him of home.

"It's in my office," she said. "I thought about putting it in my living room or my bedroom, but I'm rarely in the former and it's usually dark when I'm in the latter, so I figured I'd put it in my office where I spend most of my time. I love how they are landscapes at first glance, but then as you look more, they sort of morph into not the actual landscape, but one your imagination might conjure."

"I think that's probably what the artist hopes, you know? Something beautiful, but also something hidden, some depth to the surface that each person sees differently," he said.

She turned and looked up at him. "I didn't know you were an art aficionado."

He grinned down at her, then dropped a kiss on her lips. "I'm not," he said, shuffling her out of his bedroom because if they didn't get out in the next thirty seconds, they weren't going to get out until tomorrow morning. "But I do like it. How'd you come by yours?"

She threw him a smile over her shoulder as she walked back through the main cabin. "Can't afford one on my own, but I won it at a fundraising auction I attended in grad school. You know, one of those things where there are 200 tickets and each is $200? I bought two, and no one was more surprised than I when I won."

"Lady luck was with you," Jake said, locking the door behind them.

"The one and only time, and if you even think about making a comment about me getting lucky tonight, you will regret it, McMullen."

He chuckled. "You're no fun, sugar."

"Ha," she said, tossing him a wink. "That's not what he said."

Jake pulled on his running shoes, checked the laces, then leaned over and kissed Nia. She was a runner, too, at least a recreational one, but she'd made it very clear when he'd awoken her in the middle of the night that he could either have her company during his morning run or he could keep her up for a little longer. He'd chosen the latter, of course—what man wouldn't—and so he was headed off on his own this morning.

"The door will lock behind you. I'll be awake by the time you get back," she grumbled, then rolled over and pulled the cotton blanket around her shoulders.

With a smile, he let her be and headed out into the dawn light, double-checking that the door did indeed lock behind him before setting off. He didn't know the area that well, generally just having driven to and from her place, but it was a quiet neighborhood, so he decided to target his run for a specific time rather than route. Glancing at his watch, he gave himself thirty minutes out and thirty minutes back. That would give Nia an hour of sleep.

As he jogged, he tried to clear his mind, but the thoughts of Robin Spencer, Carl Westoff, and the potential impact of the drug they'd found, refused to be quiet. Robin Spencer was British. The island Angela Rosen was being taken to just before she'd died, was in the British Virgin Islands—was there a connection? He'd be surprised if there wasn't, and that was something he could look into when he got to the office in a few hours.

Also, how would a drug like the one they'd found work? It wasn't too hard to see it as some sort of mind control substance, but to what extent was the mind truly controlled? Did someone have to stand over the user's shoulder and tell them what to do? That didn't seem likely given the crimes Beni had been looking into—there'd been no evidence of anyone being involved other than the perpetrators.

But was a simple suggestion enough to exert control? That option seemed more akin to a hypnotic trance and it aligned with what they were seeing, but was it possible for a drug to induce that kind of behavior?

Hitting his thirty-minute target, Jake turned back toward Nia's and continued to ponder ways the drug might work. There was a lot of room for chance if a simple suggestion could result in such a drastic change of behavior—what if someone gave a counter suggestion before the drug wore off? Which would control? And given the compound of the drug, could the creator even guarantee that once a suggestion was given, that the person who'd consumed it would remember?

He turned the corner down the block from Nia's and filed that last thought away as something to ask Alexis—she'd studied mind-altering substances as part of her Ph.D. and would likely have some opinions.

As his legs covered the remaining distance, thoughts of the case didn't flee his mind, but thoughts of Nia definitely started to take over. Maybe he could convince her to jump into the shower with him? In fact, he was pretty sure he could.

Picking up his pace in anticipation, he neared the house to see the door open and Nia standing on her porch in a pair of boxers and a tank top. The smile that started to form quickly turned to a frown when he saw a man on the walkway at the base of her stairs.

Nia shook her head at something he must have said, and made to move back inside. An early morning visit from a man Nia obviously didn't want to see raised the hairs on the back of Jake's neck, and he picked up his pace even more.

The man said something more, his voice now audible yet still indistinguishable, and Nia turned back to respond. She raised her hand and shook her head, as if telling her visitor she was done talking with him. Jake was one house away when she caught sight of him and a smile spread across her face.

Panic burst through Jake as his eyes dropped from Nia's beautiful expression back to the man. Whoever he was that stood before Nia, was there to cause trouble. He shook his head angrily, then, in a motion Jake was all too familiar with, his hand reached for something behind his back and under his shirt.

Now it wasn't just panic taking over his body, fear and adrenaline lanced through Jake as he shouted for Nia to move. She looked at him in confusion and her hesitation was just long enough for the man to draw his weapon and point it directly at her.

With his heart pounding at the horror unfolding before him, Jake sprinted the last ten yards, shouting at Nia to get down. The last thing he saw before tackling the man and taking him to the ground was the look of shock on her face.

And the last thing he heard was the sound of the gun firing.

CHAPTER THIRTEEN

JAKE PACED the hospital waiting room. He'd flashed his badge and forced his way onto the ambulance for the ride, but they'd whisked Nia away the second they'd arrived, and he hadn't heard any news since. Not that it had been that long, but he was pretty sure he'd aged ten years in the last thirty minutes.

He spun on his heels and all but ran into Anika Anderson. Dressed in plain clothes, she reached out and placed a hand on his arm.

"I heard it on the scanner. How is she?" she asked.

He shook his head. "I don't know. They haven't told me anything yet," he managed to say. The image of Nia lying on her porch, unconscious and blood pooling beneath her, was one he'd never forget. And the longer he waited for information, the stronger that image seemed to imprint on his mind.

"What can I do?" Anika asked.

He started to shake his head again, then stopped. "The guy, the one who shot her? His name is Troy Beaufort. According to the arresting officer, he's her cousin. When I was restraining him, he kept mumbling something about someone telling him he had to kill her. It's weird as fuck that it was her cousin, but all that aside, he was acting strange. Can you have them order a full tox on him and get a sample to our lab? Also, if he was acting on someone's orders, and he failed, he needs a guard on him. I think the police are there already, but they aren't there for his protection."

Anika nodded, but before she could answer, Alexis and Dominic walked in.

"What do you need us to do?" Dominic asked.

Other than what he'd asked of Anika, he didn't know what else could be done. That's what was killing him. He'd never felt so helpless.

"Come with me, Burel," Anika said. "Jake asked me to help with a few things, you can help me make them happen."

Dominic looked at him. Jake appreciated how his friend clearly struggled with leaving him, but Anika was right, and he'd feel better if his friend was out there doing something rather than sitting around with him.

Jake gestured with his head to Anika. "Go help and keep us posted."

Dominic studied him, gave a single, sharp nod, then, following Anika's lead, the two started down the hospital hallway.

"Talk to me, Jake," Alexis said.

She was doing her shrink-psychologist thing, but at this point, he didn't care. Seeing any friend shot was an agent's worse nightmare, but when he'd heard that gunshot and seen Nia fall, it had been so much...

"I can't," he said, then started to pace again, which he'd found helped him to remember to breathe.

Alexis stopped him and, much as Nia had done a few days earlier, she cupped his face in her hands and forced him to look at her. "Whatever you're feeling, let it happen, Jake. You just watched someone you care about a great deal get shot. Be scared, be angry, be everything you're feeling."

He looked into her blue eyes and his stomach squeezed. "I can't," he said.

She said nothing, just held his gaze. He knew what she was doing, he knew she was waiting for him to fill the silence with his own story—not a recitation of the facts, but his feelings, his fears, his pain. Even as he shied away from talking—they weren't important right now, only Nia was—he found himself talking, anyway.

"I don't ever want to be that terrified again, Alexis," he managed to say. "You can't—" he cut himself off because of course she could understand what he was feeling. Maybe not exactly, but Alexis was no stranger to terror.

"It's awful," he said. Nothing could capture the true depth of what he was experiencing, and those two words were a paltry effort, but it was all he could manage.

"I know," she said quietly. Then she pulled him into a hug, and damn if that wasn't what he needed. He rested his head on her shoulder and let her hold him up, if only for a moment.

When he pulled back, he tried to blink the tears away, but Alexis wouldn't let him hide from her and just handed him a tissue.

"This fucking sucks," he said, crumpling the damp tissue in his hand and shoving it into his pocket.

"Yeah, it does," Alexis concurred.

He was about to comment that the least she could do was try to make him feel better when two women walked into the waiting room and approached the front desk. He'd never met anyone from Nia's family, but he'd bet dollars to donuts that the taller of the two was her mother—with the exception of the woman's pinched expression, her likeness to Nia was uncanny. He glanced over at Alexis, who was watching the women as well, a small frown playing on her lips.

"I'm Jackie Lewis, this my sister Noreen Beaufort. We're here to see Troy Beaufort," the woman who had to be Nia's mother said.

Jake waited for them to ask about Nia, but the two stood there as the nurse looked up the information.

"I'm sorry, he can't have any visitors," the nurse said.

"I'm his mother," Noreen said. "Why can't he have any visitors?"

The nurse's eyes darted to him and Alexis and, in tandem, the two women turned. "Who are you?" Jackie asked.

"I'm Agent Jake McMullen. Your daughter's boyfriend," he answered. "She's in surgery, by the way. You must know Troy shot her."

Jackie frowned. "Her boyfriend?"

Jake blinked and glanced at Alexis, whose tiny frown had turned into a much more pronounced one.

"I just told you that your daughter has been shot, and what you take away from my comment is a question about me being her boyfriend?" The question wasn't really a question, but he didn't know much about Nia's relationship with her mother— other than it was strained—and so he didn't want to unleash the full scorn that was starting to bubble within him.

Isiah walked in at that moment, and though Alexis took his hand, he must have sensed something going on and he remained silent. The three of them stood there, united, for Nia.

"You all here for Nia," Jackie said, wagging a finger between them.

"Yes," Alexis answered.

Jackie shot her sister a knowing look and sniffed. "Then she hardly needs us, does she? Doesn't need us and doesn't want us. Never has."

An urge to shake the woman—something that had never happened to Jake before—gripped him fiercely, and he stepped forward. But Alexis's hand on his arm stopped him.

"Don't, Jake," Isiah said, lending his support.

Alexis cleared her throat, drawing the attention of the two women. "Perhaps the reason Nia doesn't need you is because you've taught her not to."

Jackie blinked at Alexis's words and, for a split second, seemed to consider them. Then she turned to her sister. "Let's go see if we can find someone else who can get us any information."

"Let them go, Jake," Alexis said as the sisters left. "We don't all get the family we deserve, but Nia's chosen us as hers and we're here. That's what matters."

Jake wasn't sure about that. Despite everything Alexis had gone through as a child, she had a loving and supportive family. She'd never known the doubts and conflicts both he and Nia experienced when it came to their biological families.

But what would he say? He wasn't about to get into the story of his family while Nia was in surgery, and he didn't know enough about Nia's family to speak of it—not that he would have even if he *had* known, as it wasn't his story to tell.

The door to the emergency room opened, and a doctor strode out. "Are you Jake McMullen?" she asked.

Jake gave a hesitant nod.

"Good. Dr. Lewis is in recovery and asking for you. As far as getting shot goes, it was a pretty clean one. The bullet grazed her just beneath her shoulder blade and bumped up against a couple of her ribs—both of which are bruised, but neither is broken. I assume she must have turned away just in time, otherwise, it's likely the bullet would have pierced her lung. While we're lucky that didn't happened, I don't want to downplay her injury. The graze was a deep one and she has fifteen stitches running from just under her arm to along the lower part of her shoulder blade. She lost a lot of blood, so between that and the sedative we gave her for the surgery, she'll be a little groggy. But she wants to see you."

Relief swamped him, and the only thing that kept him from

collapsing into a chair was knowing that if he did, it would delay him seeing Nia.

"We'll be here when you get done," Alexis said. "And in case she asks, Beni and Damian are already back at the offices looking into Troy and what he might have been involved in."

He nodded.

Alexis smiled. "Now go say hi to Nia for us. Tell her we'll bring her some good food tonight."

"I know she's partial to my chicken," Isiah said.

For the second time, Jake found himself blinking away tears. "Thanks," he said, giving each a quick hug. "I'll definitely let her know. Keep me posted," he said over his shoulder as he followed the doctor back down the hall.

"Of course," Alexis responded, as the doors shut behind him.

Nia opened her eyes at the sound of the door opening. Jake walked in, still in the shorts and t-shirt he'd gone running in that morning. Only there was blood, her blood, all over him. Her stomach roiled at the sight, but she willed it to calm when she took in Jake's expression.

Striding into the room, he reached her side in seconds. Then he hesitated. She held out her hand for his. "I won't break, Jake. I'm going to be fine," she said as he wrapped his fingers around hers.

He closed his eyes for a moment and when he opened them, they were so dark blue as to be almost black.

He leaned over and, brushing her hair from her face, he kissed her forehead before sitting down and pulling her hand to his cheek.

"I don't ever want to fucking go through something like this again," he said.

She turned her hand around and cupped his cheek. "You can't stop all the bad things in the world, Jake."

"I don't want to stop them all. Just the bad things that happen to you. Maybe a few for work, too if I have to," he grumbled, making her chuckle. Which quickly turned into a wince from the pain.

"I can't believe my cousin shot me," she said. The words were inadequate. Intellectually, she understood that Troy had pulled the trigger, but it was still so hard to believe. The stitches along the right side of her back, and her bruised ribs, wouldn't let her, though.

"I don't really want to talk about it," Jake said.

She pulled his hand to her lips, then let go and brushed a lock of hair from his forehead. His fingers lingered, tracing the line of her cheek.

"Not talking about it isn't going to make it go away," she said. "And I have so many questions. Why? Where'd he get the gun? I didn't even know he could shoot."

A text dinged on his phone and he pulled it out, read the message, then slipped the device back into his pocket.

"I know you have questions, we all do. And this is what I know so far," he said, then proceeded to tell her what Anika and Dominic were doing with regards to Troy and the drug testing, what Damian and Beni were looking into back in the office, and that Alexis and Isiah had stopped by as well and were planning to bring dinner. By the time he was done, she was almost in tears. Yes, they were law enforcement, and it was their job to look into crimes, but they were going the extra mile for her. They *cared*. Not that she'd doubted it, but times of crises always revealed people's true nature, and, even though the task force would disband once The Summit was over, those people, those five people—seven if she included Charlotte and Isiah, which she most definitely did—were her people.

"Now, none of that," Jake said, brushing a tear from her cheek with his thumb.

She took a deep breath and gave him a wobbly smile. He smiled back, then leaned in and kissed her. Pulling back a little bit, he looked her in the eye. "I don't know what motivated your cousin, but I promise you, we'll find out."

She nodded. She believed him. She believed *in* him and the team. "Thank you," she said. "And I didn't say it before, but thank you for saving my life."

Shadows danced across his eyes. "If I'd been a minute faster, it wouldn't have happened."

"If you'd been a minute slower, I wouldn't be here at all, and neither of those thoughts bear any consideration."

"There you are," a familiar voice said as the door to her room flew open.

Nia looked up to see her mother standing inside the room. She glanced at Jake and saw the disdain written on his face. Her heart sank. Jake must have had a run-in with her earlier and, if his expression was anything to go by, it hadn't gone well.

"Mother," Nia said. The tone in her voice drew her mom up short, and Jackie cocked her head and looked at her.

"I hear you're fine," her mom said.

"I was shot. 'Fine' isn't the word I'd use, but I will be okay. Thanks for asking," she added.

One of her mother's overly constructed eyebrows went up. "Well, that's good," she said.

"Yes, we like to think so," Jake said, sarcasm heavy in his voice. Nia almost smiled.

"Well, since you're going to be fine, can you talk to someone about Troy? They aren't letting us see him, but they said he's conscious," Jackie said.

"Yeah, the cops don't usually like to let someone who has just attempted to murder another catch up with their family," Jake said.

Jackie's eyes flickered to the man sitting beside Nia, and Nia knew her mother was trying to figure him out. As Jackie watched him, he raised Nia's hand to his lips and placed a kiss on the back. It was a very subtle sign, but he had clearly just told Jackie that Nia wasn't on her own anymore.

Jackie's brow furrowed and she turned her attention back to Nia. "You're obviously fine. Can't you talk to them about not charging him with anything? It will ruin his life."

Jake's hand twitched in hers, but she gave him a squeeze and he remained silent. "I have no say in what the police charge him with," Nia replied.

"But couldn't you put in a good word?" Jackie asked.

"And what would that be? That he didn't mean to? Because he did. Or that he's a good guy? Because I'm pretty sure 'good guys' don't go around shooting people," she answered.

"The only reason he did it was because you didn't bail him out, and Noreen had to put their house up for...what's that word? You know, so the bail bond people would give her the money?"

"Collateral?" Jake suggested.

Jackie nodded. "Yeah, that. And he was pissed at you for making her do that and putting her at risk. Which, quite frankly, I can understand. I mean shooting you is, I'll admit, a little overboard—"

"Gee, thanks, Mom," Nia interjected.

"But he was angry with you. That's the only reason he did it."

Nia wasn't so sure, not after what Jake had told her about his behavior, but she wasn't going to say anything to her mom. No, instead, she stared for a good long while at the woman who'd given birth to her. As she did, her situation sank in, really sank in. Her family by blood was doing everything they could to get the man who'd tried to kill her out of trouble whereas Jake and her friends—her family by choice—were doing everything they could to protect her and make sure that didn't happen.

And just like that, those last little feelings of wanting to be accepted by her family, of wanting to be wanted and liked by them, died. She *had* a family, it just wasn't the one she'd been born into. The one she'd been born into was, in truth, just a bunch of grasping strangers.

"Goodbye, mother," Nia said. Jake's head jerked around to look at her.

"So you'll do it?" Jackie said.

"I won't. I also won't be calling you or reaching out to anyone in the family in any way. Go ahead and think of me whatever you want to, your opinion of me no longer matters."

Jackie stared, then her mouth opened and closed. Then opened and closed again. Finally, she turned and, without a word, left.

Both she and Jake stared at the door as it closed after her. After a beat, he looked at her. "You okay?" he asked.

She rolled her head on her pillow and smiled at him. "Yeah, I think I am. I really think I am."

Despite what she'd told Jake, Nia wasn't altogether sure she *was* okay. She would be. There was not a doubt in her mind that she'd made the right decision. Her family was toxic and cared for no one but themselves. If they hadn't been her family, there was no way she ever would have given them a second thought and certainly wouldn't have given their opinion any hold over her.

But she also knew that a visit or two—or twenty—to a therapist might be a good option for her.

She mulled this over throughout the day, as doctors came and went, as Jake came and went, and as members of his team came and went. Maybe she'd ask Alexis for a good recommendation.

"What are you thinking?" Jake asked from her bedside later that evening. Other than going home to shower and change, and a few calls that had taken him out of the room, he'd stayed by her side most of the day. Night had fallen and they were now passing the time playing Cards Against Humanity. Only it was hard to play with two people, so really, all they were doing was having a competition to see who could come up with the most outrageous combination. It was both the best and worst idea they'd collectively had, since laughing hurt like hell, even though it felt good to laugh.

"That mine is going to beat yours, of course," she said, pulling her cards closer to her chest. Jake was not above cheating, and there was a window behind her bed that, if the light were right, he'd be able to see a reflection of her cards.

"That's what you said the last three times, sugar. I think I'm on a streak."

"You want the good news or the not so good news?" Dominic asked, striding into the room and startling them both.

"Jesus, Burel, announce yourself next time, will you?" Jake grumbled, picking up the card he'd dropped. Nia glance over at it.

"I was so going to beat you," she murmured.

"In your dreams, sugar. Now, what's the news, Dom?" Jake asked.

"They are going to let you break out of this joint tomorrow morning. I talked to the nurse at the nurses' station, you know the one with long hair and the hips that don't quit." He flashed them his trademark smile.

"Ninety-seven-point-six percent chance she'll end up going home with him after her shift," she said.

"Bet?" Jake asked.

"Drinks at Lola's once I get out of here?" she suggested.

"Deal. Now, what's the bad news?" Jake asked.

Dominic stared at Jake for a beat. "Did you just bet against me?"

"I did," Jake said, handing over his card combination to her. Nia glanced at the cards and laughter burst from her.

"Oh shit, that hurts," she said, trying to rein it back in.

"Sorry, sugar. I had to. I couldn't waste the opportunity." Jake leaned over and kissed her forehead.

When she got her breathing under control, she shot him a look. "Fine, okay, I admit, that was worth it. Now, are you going to tell us anything, Dominic?"

"If you two would shut up for ten seconds, maybe I could get a word in?" Dutifully, both Nia and Jake set their cards down and looked at him. "The only reason you're getting out is because Penelope has picked up speed. She's a category one hurricane now and is expected to hit the island within thirty-six hours. They want all non-life threatened patients out of the hospital before that happens."

"Called it, didn't I? About Penelope," Jake clarified, sitting back in his chair, though he reached for her hand.

"Yes, you did, cocky bastard," Dominic said, grabbing a chair at the end of the bed and taking a seat. "Alexis has invited us all to her place."

"I've what?" Alexis said, walking into the room with Isiah following her. They both carried a couple of bags and, judging by the smell, the content of those bags was going to make Nia a very happy woman.

"You brought me chicken," she said, sitting up. In an instant, Jake was standing and helping her get pillows adjusted and the bed raised.

"Fried and wings," Isiah said.

"Any drinks in there?" Dominic asked, taking the bag Alexis carried and starting to rummage through it.

"No, but there is in here," Alexis said, pulling a large flask from her bag. "Go grab some sodas from the vending machine. Nia, unfortunately, my conscience won't let me give you any, but I'll make it up to you when you're not doped up."

Nia waved her off. She'd had enough painkillers that any alcohol probably wasn't a good idea.

"I was saying you've invited everyone over. You have like a hundred generators and all sorts of things to protect your house during a hurricane, right?" Dominic said.

"Six, I have six generators. Three for the house, two for the security systems, and one for the gatehouse," she said. "Now go get the sodas before you annoy me and I decide not to share."

"You are one tough dude, Clarke," Dominic said to Isiah as he started to leave. "I'm glad she's your handful to deal with."

Isiah rolled his eyes, then pulled Alexis into a kiss. "Alexis isn't anyone's to deal with, but she is more than a handful and that's the way I like it," he said when he pulled back.

"Oh good, food," Beni said, walking into the room as Dominic walked out. "I'd heard you were bringing stuff, glad I didn't miss it."

The door had barely closed behind Beni when Damian and Charlotte opened it again and walked in. "Hey guys," Damian said as he dropped a laptop on the table at the far end of the room. "We brought you some entertainment for later."

"And I picked it," Charlotte said, giving Nia a look. "You would not have been amused by what Damian wanted to download for you to watch."

"I don't know," Damian said, wrapping his arms around Charlotte from behind and dropping a kiss on her bare shoulder. "You seemed interested in—"

Charlotte elbowed him. "Why do I always feel like I have to remind you that some things are best kept private?" Charlotte said, though her smile told Nia that she kind of liked it.

"I don't even want to know," Beni muttered as she started pulling out food and setting it on the table at the foot of the bed.

"Look who I found, everyone," Dominic said, walking back into the room with Anika on his heels. She was carrying a file and had a look on her face like she wasn't quite sure if she should be there or not.

"I can come back," Anika said, holding the file behind her back.

"No, stay," Nia said. "We're about to eat, and Isiah always makes enough for an army. Besides, I think we might want to know what's in that file you're trying to hide."

All five agents in the room turned and looked at the detective.

The look Anika shot her told Nia she was not happy with being the center of attention, but regardless she held out the file, and Beni, being the closest, took it.

"What is it?" Jake asked.

"We got the lab to fast track the blood sample from Nia's cousin," Anika said. "Burel filled me in on Robin Spencer earlier today and while we're still waiting on the breakdown, at a high level, it looks like Troy's blood sample matches that of Spencer."

The room stayed silent as Beni read the report. When she looked up, she nodded at everyone.

"Any idea what your cousin was into?" Damian asked Nia.

Nia shook her head as she accepted the plate of food Isiah had made for her. "Anika can tell you about his arrest the other night. But I haven't seen him in months, maybe close to a year."

"His behavior aligns with what you found yesterday, Beni," Jake said, all traces of her fun-loving Jake gone, to be replaced by FBI-Jake. Until the last few days, she hadn't really seen this side of him. And until the last few days, she'd had no idea that she apparently had a thing for FBI-Jake.

"Wait, what? What did you find yesterday, Beni?" she asked.

Beni glanced around the room, most notably at Isiah and Charlotte. The group was like family, but even so, the agents did have confidentiality obligations.

"The arrests are public record, Beni," Damian said. "It's only our theory that's sensitive, and it's your call."

Beni's gaze held Damian's, then she sighed and filled Nia, Charlotte, Isiah, and Anika in on what the team had discussed the day before about the unusual crimes. When she finished, the room was silent before Isiah spoke.

"This could have massive repercussions for political warfare," he said.

"That's our biggest nightmare," Alexis said. Nia had to admit, she was a little surprised that neither Charlotte nor Isiah had heard the theory before—that their partners hadn't told them. She supposed that knowing when Jake could share things, and when he couldn't, was something she'd have to learn to navigate.

"So you think my cousin was another test dummy, so to speak?" Nia asked, the plate in her hand all but forgotten.

Jake held her gaze. "It aligns with his behavior after I subdued him. He kept saying he had to kill you. Like he was just repeating orders. I know he has two priors…"

"But he hadn't been in trouble before six months ago," Nia said. "And that attempted robbery of a jewelry store on Main Street always seemed so bizarre to me. What was he arrested for a few days ago?"

All eyes went to Anika, who let out a deep breath and answered. "He tried to steal a police boat from the marina. From the well-lit, well-monitored marina."

Yet one more crime that didn't make sense. Maybe if he'd been drunk and acting stupid, but Anika hadn't mentioned him being under the influence, and she would have if it had been a factor.

"We need to find out where this drug is being manufactured and by whom," Nia said, stating the obvious.

"Any updates on the tracker?" Dominic asked.

"Tracker?" Nia asked.

Damian took a few minutes to fill in the non-agents in the room on the float and tracker they'd found the day before, then answered Dominic's question. "Lucy and Brian texted just before we got here. The float was delivered this evening, and they'll be working on it tonight."

Nia didn't know who Lucy and Brian were but figured they were specialists Damian knew. "So, what now?"

"Now, I suggest we eat," Charlotte said.

Alexis nodded. "And maybe have a drink, too. Except you, Nia."

"Shouldn't someone go talk to Troy?" Nia asked.

"He became agitated when we started questioning him," Anika said. "The doctor sedated him an hour ago."

Nia glanced over at Jake. Troy's shoulder had been dislocated when Jake had tackled him and he'd needed surgery. Although once they'd realized he'd been drugged, they'd had to wait, and so he hadn't gone in until late that afternoon.

"When can you talk to him?" Nia asked.

"We'll question him tomorrow," Jake said, brushing a hand gently over her hair. "Now that we have the tox breakdown, and we can tie his attempt on your life to our case, the FBI will probably take over."

Her eyes searched Jake's and though she saw nothing but steady reassurance there, she had so many questions bouncing around her mind. What had Troy gotten involved in? Who had he been hanging out with? What would that kind of drug do if let loose on the street?

"Eat, sugar," Jake said, his voice quiet but firm. "Eat now, and tomorrow we'll figure everything else out."

Slowly, she nodded, and Dominic let out a dramatic sigh. "Finally, can I have my rum now?"

CHAPTER FOURTEEN

"I'd like to go with you," Nia said as she tried to sit up in bed.

Jake eyed her. To be fair, the full night's sleep had helped and she looked a lot better than she had the day before. But still, she'd been shot. He could understand why she'd want to talk to her cousin, but she was going to be released that afternoon and Jake wasn't so sure that two outings in a day would be good for her.

"Do not get all overprotective of me now, Jake. It's too late for that. You lost that right that night at Lola's. You know, the night you encouraged me to streak naked down the beach where that wedding of a senator's son was taking place?"

"It would have made for a good story for them, don't you think?" He grinned though he didn't feel particularly happy. She was right, and he didn't like it. He had always trusted her to take care of herself—that didn't mean they didn't look out for each other, or that he didn't worry about her, but it did mean that he trusted her to tell him when enough was enough. Apparently, now was not enough.

"I thought you promised never to bring up that night at Lola's again," he added.

She flashed him a mirror of the grin he'd just given her. "Nice try. I will *always* bring up that night when it suits my needs."

"Anyone ever tell you you're mercenary?" he grumbled, helping her out of bed.

"I'm a youngish, fairly attractive woman in academia. I don't need anyone to tell me I'm mercenary. It's practically a requirement of the job."

"Fair point. But you're more than just fairly attractive," he said, making sure she was steady on her feet before he reached for the yoga pants Alexis had brought by that morning. The rest of his colleagues were at the office, downloading everything they could before Penelope hit. She was on schedule to move right over the island in less than twenty-four hours, and everyone had agreed to stay at Alexis's that night. As soon as he and Anika were done questioning Troy, and Nia was discharged from the hospital, they were going to meet everyone at the house. Hopefully, they could start putting together the pieces of the puzzle and figure out who was behind this new drug and to what purpose.

"You ready to—" Anika said, walking in. "Oh, sorry," she mumbled, turning her back as Jake helped Nia pull on a lightweight, button-up tank top.

"They're boobs, not like you haven't seen them before," Nia called, and behind him, Anika laughed.

"Every day since I was ten," Anika said.

"Ten?" Nia half-asked, half-exclaimed. Jake eased her down into the wheelchair that a nurse had brought by.

"My family is cursed with early blooming. What can I say? It's like I stopped growing up and everything went into the girls."

"You're gorgeous and all, but that must have sucked," Nia said as Jake slid her flip flops on. "Are you really going to make me ride in the wheelchair?"

"It did suck," Anika answered. "And yes, he is going to make you ride in the wheelchair. It would take you ages to walk, and we'd like to make it to Troy's room before Penelope hits."

Jake hid his snicker.

"I was shot yesterday, you don't have to be so mean," Nia said, clearly not really offended.

Anika shrugged as she turned around. "You look like you can take it. Are we ready?"

Jake wisely held his tongue as Nia answered with a gesture, and the three of them made their way to the elevator and up to the fourth floor. Anika checked them in with the nurse and greeted the two policemen standing guard outside Troy's room before pushing the door open and holding it for him and Nia to enter.

As the door swung shut behind them, Jake got his first real look at Troy Beaufort. His attention had been focused on Nia the prior morning, and as he looked at Nia's cousin, he considered whether it would have been better if he'd let one of his teammates have the honor of questioning Troy. Because as hard as he'd try, he wasn't sure he'd be able to give the guy a fair shake. He'd tried to kill Nia, and though Jake wasn't a violent person by nature, he was seriously contemplating hitting the guy who was stretched out on the bed before them smiling. Yes, smiling. The smarmy son of a bitch.

"Watch it, McMullen," Anika said, obviously sensing his train of thought.

"Jake," Nia said, reaching her hand up for his. He let go of her chair and came to stand at her side. He took a deep breath and focused on the feel of Nia's hand in his because she was the real —the only—reason he was here.

"Sorry, Nia. Glad my aim was off," Troy said.

"Your aim wasn't off," Jake said, barely restraining himself from adding "Asshole" onto the end of his sentence. "I tackled you."

Troy switched his gaze to Jake, then frowned. "Thanks, I guess? I mean, I did have to have surgery and all."

Jake had never thought of himself as the growly type, but sure enough, one rumbled out of his throat. Nia's hand tightened in his, and Anika cast him a wary glance. He took a deep breath and gestured for the women to continue. Anika flashed him another look, then nodded to the phone Jake held in his free hand. Once he started the recording app, Anika turned to Troy and reminded him that he'd already been given his Miranda warning.

"Why did you do it, Troy?" Nia asked, kicking off the conversation.

Her cousin frowned and his eyes went a little distant. "You know, I don't actually know. It just seemed like something I needed to do."

"My mom said you were upset about me not bailing you out," Nia continued.

Troy scrunched his face. "No, that's not right. I mean, I was pissed. But not surprised. You didn't bail me out the first time, why would I think you'd come through the second time?"

Nia glanced up at him. As disconcerting as Troy's confusion was, it did give them more insight into how the drug worked and it appeared that memory loss was one of the side effects.

"I didn't think you even owned a gun," Nia said.

Troy stared at the ceiling, but shook his head. "I don't. You know how hard it is to get a gun on this island."

It was Nia's turn to frown. "Where'd the gun come from?"

"I don't..." Troy's expression shifted and Jake recognized the signs. The man was balancing that thin line between confusion and panic as he started to realize just how many hours of his life he couldn't recall or explain.

"Troy, why don't you walk us through the events leading up to your arrival at Nia Lewis's home," Anika said, stepping into the fray.

Troy's eyes bounced between all three of them, then finally landed on Anika. "I don't remember much. I mean, I remember holding the gun and I remember getting tackled, but not much more than that."

"Where were you last night?" Nia asked.

Troy's brows dipped. "At The Taphouse," he said. Nia's hand jerked in Jake's. "Wait, no, not The Taphouse. I mean, I was there, earlier in the night, but later I was at that place around the corner, you know the one that, uh..." his eyes darted to Anika.

"The one that what?" Jake pressed.

"Nothing," Troy mumbled. "I don't remember."

"You are so full of shit," Nia said. "Were you at The Rye Barrel?"

Troy's eyes widened. "How do you know about The Rye?"

"The Rye?" Jake asked.

"Illegal distillery," Nia answered. "It's been around for years. Makes a lot of bootleg rum and some whiskey."

"We've tried shutting it down a couple of times," Anika said. "But every time we raid, they've been tipped off. Makes a girl wonder," she added.

Jake wasn't a stranger to corruption and he wasn't all that surprised to hear Anika suggesting that Tildas' finest might have a rat or two in their midst.

"Look, Troy," Anika said, moving closer to the bed and drawing the younger man's attention. "We're not interested in The Rye right now. But can you walk us through your night?"

"And what if I want a lawyer?"

Anika started to answer, but Nia jumped in. "You can't afford a good one and do you really want Neville or Stanwood Parker defending you? Remember how you used to torment Neville? And how you made fun of their little sister, Janine?"

Troy's face went a little pale. Jake didn't know who Neville and Stanwood Parker were but assumed they must be public defenders.

"We might be able to get the charges reduced if you talk to us," Anika said.

Once again, Troy's attention bounced between the three of them. When they flitted over Jake, Jake narrowed his gaze and shot Troy a look to let him know he didn't really have a choice, so he better make the right one.

Troy's face scrunched, but then he let out a long breath. "I don't remember much," he started. "I met a few friends at The Taphouse for a drink."

"At what time?" Jake asked, at the same time Anika asked, "What friends?"

Troy looked unsure as to which question to answer first, so Nia stepped in. "What time?"

"Nine or so, maybe a little after."

"And who did you meet?" Nia followed up.

Troy gave three names that Jake didn't recognize but Anika wrote down.

"Then what?" Nia pressed.

Troy frowned. "We went to The Rye around two or so when The Taphouse closed down. There were a couple of other guys there that I've talked to a few times before but don't really know."

"Is this one of them?" Anika said, bringing up an image on her phone and holding it up for Troy to see.

Troy squinted at the picture then nodded. "Yeah, that's one of them. He's usually there with a couple of others. They're cool. Work with the boat charters or something."

"And this guy?" she asked, flipping to another photo and showing it to Troy.

He shook his head. "He wasn't there. I've seen him before, but he wasn't there that night."

Anika walked back to where Jake and Nia had planted themselves at the end of Troy's bed. She held up her phone and on it was a picture of Carl Westoff's face. The second picture she showed them was one of Robin Spencer. Yeah, Spencer had been long dead before Troy's latest adventure, but it was interesting that they now had a solid connection between Westoff and Spencer.

"What can you tell us about Carl Westoff?" Jake asked.

"Who?" Troy countered.

"Westoff, the blond guy," Jake answered.

"That's not his name. His name is something like Weston or Carlton or..."

The wheels inside Troy's head were practically grinding as they watched. Jake didn't know the rest of Nia's family, but it was clear she definitely got the brain gene that seemed to have skipped her cousin.

"Oh, he probably wasn't giving us his real name, was he?" Troy asked.

It was all Jake could do to hold in his snort. Thankfully, after a beat, Anika answered. "No, he wasn't. Now, what can you tell us about him?"

Troy shrugged with his good shoulder. "Like I said, seems like a cool guy. Good pool player. But kind of, I don't know, maybe a little stuck up?" It came out like a question.

"In what way?" Nia asked.

"In some ways, he reminded me a little of you, Nia," Troy said. Nia's hand gripped Jake's, and Anika placed her hand on his other arm. It wasn't like Jake was going to go after the guy, but it was tempting to consider. Maybe even fantasize about.

"In what way?" Anika asked.

Troy shrugged again. "He always acted like he was better than the rest of us. Like he was doing us a favor hanging out with us, you know?"

No, Jake did not know. At least not when it came to Nia,

because that description was *nothing* like Nia—she was one of the most down to earth people he'd ever met.

"Jake," Nia said, drawing his attention down to where she sat…in a wheelchair because that asshat had shot her. "Breathe," she commanded.

His jaw clenched, but she held his gaze. He took one breath, then another, and as he did, he suddenly understood that his attitude was adding to the burden Nia was already carrying. With that guilty realization, the tension he'd been holding in his body at confronting the man who'd nearly killed Nia, washed away. Because the last thing he wanted to do was make anything harder for her.

"I'm good," he said.

Her eyes searched his. "Yeah?"

"Yeah," he said with a nod.

"So how long have you known Carl?" Anika asked.

And so it went for another thirty minutes. Jake remained mostly silent as Anika and Nia asked most of the questions. Anika took notes, and Jake recorded the interview as he did his best to lend Nia whatever support she needed. Though truth be told, she didn't need much, and yes, it was humbling, and somewhat annoying, that she seemed to have weathered her near-death experience better than he had.

When they walked out of the room, Jake pushing Nia, they still had a few lingering questions, but there was one certainty. Westoff was definitely involved. Based on what Troy had told them, they were fairly sure Westoff had drugged Troy on each of the three occasions—the first being the night of the attempted robbery on the jewelry store, the second being the night he'd attempted to steal the boat, and the last being just before he'd shot Nia. They didn't have proof, but Troy swore up and down that he didn't do drugs, and despite the guy being a grade-A douche, Jake believed him on that score. So if he didn't take them on his own accord, someone must have given them to him, and Westoff was the prime suspect.

This possibility terrified Jake—the idea of Westoff randomly conducting lab tests with the new drug was a nightmare—but it also provided a small bit of relief when he considered Nia. Yes, her cousin had tried to kill her, but it hadn't been *personal*. She hadn't seemed overly surprised that Troy had committed the crime, but Jake had to believe that she took some comfort in knowing that drugs—drugs Troy hadn't willingly ingested—had been a significant factor in his actions.

"I'll take this information back to the station and type up my report," Anika said as they walked toward the elevator.

"I've got the interview recorded. I'll go through it with my team, but I'll send you the voice file as well," Jake said.

"They are going to let us out of here before you start any of that, right?" Nia interjected.

Anika shot him a look at the fatigued irritation in Nia's voice, then, telling them she wanted to take the stairs, she left them alone, waiting for the slowest elevator on the planet. Seriously, was that thing run by squirrels? Only they didn't have squirrels on the island. So maybe chickens?

"Jake?" Nia asked.

"Hm?"

"Can we go home now?"

He liked the sound of "we" and "home" being used in the same sentence. But that was mostly because "home" meant "bed," and now "Nia" and "bed" had taken on a whole new level of importance in his life. But she'd been shot just over twenty-four hours ago, so maybe his mind shouldn't be going there.

"Of all days, why do you have to have the attention span of a gnat today?" she grumbled, bringing him back to the here and now as the elevator door opened.

He pushed inside, and as the door closed, he answered.

"Because you said 'home' and that means bed and I was debating whether or not I was a horrible boyfriend—a word I hate by the way, because I'm thirty-five, not a boy, but whatever—for thinking about getting you back into bed. Then I was feeling guilty for even thinking about it. But it's hard *not* to think about it, because well, it's my new favorite pastime. It was wreaking hell on my brain."

She blinked at him. "You were thinking all of that in the last three seconds?"

"Hell, no," he said. "That's just the start of it. I was also remembering that freckle you have on your lower back, then thinking about how we need to get to Alexis's, then wondering if the guest room she's going to set us up in has a queen or a king-size bed. I even wondered how Red and Howdy, Alexis and Isiah's dogs, were going to handle having everyone in the house. I know Howdy will be fine because she loves everyone, but Red? I'm not sure what she'll think. Then again, as long as she can stay with Isiah, she'll probably be fine."

For a moment, Nia stared at him. He considered retracting some—or all—of what he'd said, but then reminded himself that this was Nia. He'd never held anything back from her.

Finally, she nodded, just as the elevator brought them to the second floor, her floor. "Okay, how about we get me checked out, then back to my place to pick up some clothes, then to your boat so you can grab your own clothes, then we head to Alexis's? Once we're there, I'd encourage you to unleash that somewhat wild, but bizarrely fascinating brain of yours for the greater good and figure out how Troy's statement might help you all get this mess sorted out?"

"That's very practical of you," Jake said, pushing her toward her room and signaling the nurse as they passed the nurses' station. She nodded in understanding, knowing he was asking for the discharge papers.

"I'm a very practical person," she said. He snorted at that, drawing a low laugh from her. "Fine, maybe I'm not that practical outside of work, but I know something you don't know. Two things, actually." As she spoke, he'd wheeled her into the room, and the door closed behind them.

"What's that?"

"The first is that the sooner we get to Alexis's, the sooner I can really rest."

Guilt lanced through him—how much had the trip to talk to Troy tired her out? Was she in pain? He started to ask, but she stopped him by hooking her fingers into his belt loops and pulling him close. Ever obliging, he lowered his head and brushed his lips against hers.

"And the second thing I know is that the guestroom where Alexis is planning to put us has a king bed. A very nice, big king-sized bed."

And in that moment, with Nia giving him a ghost of a smile, he was pretty sure he fell in love.

CHAPTER FIFTEEN

Jake walked into Alexis's house a few hours later and, after giving Howdy—one of her dogs—a good greeting, he made his way up from the entry-level to the main living area. He'd adjusted Nia's plans a little bit, and, after swinging by her house to pick up some clothes, he'd dropped her off earlier. After he'd made sure she was resting, he'd headed back out to run a few errands, including stopping by his boat to pick up his own overnight bag.

"She's still resting," Alexis said, as he looked around the living room. The agents and their significant others were scattered around the big, open space.

"I closed the hurricane shutters in the room shortly after you left," said Yael. She was Alexis's head of security and the one who'd let him in earlier.

"The room is dark," Yael added. "She fell right to sleep and is probably still sleeping."

He debated whether or not to check on Nia, and though he knew she'd make her presence known if she were awake, he couldn't stop himself. Dropping his computer bag beside the couch where Damian was sitting with his feet propped up on a coffee table and Charlotte beside him, he jogged back downstairs and quietly cracked the door open. The room was dark, as Yael said it would be, but light from the hall filtered in and Jake was relieved to see Nia curled up on her good side, fast asleep. Letting out a breath, some of the tension left his body and he gently closed the door and jogged back upstairs.

"So you two seemed to have gone from zero to sixty in a heartbeat," Beni commented, not looking up from her computer. In anticipation of Penelope, the team had downloaded more information than they could possibly cull through onto both their laptops and the private server Alexis had in her home.

He considered saying something flippant, but in the end, he grabbed his computer and an empty seat and ignored her. Unfortunately, not saying anything said more than he'd intended and out of the corner of his eye, he saw everyone in the room raise their heads and look at him. Isiah was the only one not staring, but that was because he'd gone to the kitchen.

"We're a thing. You know that," he said, hoping to get away with just saying that, but knowing it wasn't likely.

"Seems like a little more than a thing," Dominic said.

Jake glared at his friend as his computer booted up. "Don't you have something to do? After all, we do have a crazy new drug that someone is test driving on the street, which, once perfected, could be used to basically brainwash entire populations. And we don't know who is developing it or to what end."

"We've got all night," Dominic countered.

"Yeah, Penelope isn't supposed to hit until around dawn, so we should have power for several more hours," Damian added.

Jake looked to Charlotte to see if she'd at least rein Damian in. In response, she grinned at him. "You know I'd really like to help you, Jake. But you were *so* understanding when Damian and I were getting back together, that I find it hard to intervene."

He tried to glare at her, he did, but damn if she wasn't right. He *had* given Damian a hard time when Charlotte had shown back up in his life.

"Seriously, can we concentrate on figuring this shit out?" he said, nodding to his computer as he logged into the FBI server. Alexis's generators would keep them with power, but the internet was a whole different ball game—they had no idea how long it would stay live, and so his plan was to use it as long as he could. Once it went down, and it would go down once Penelope swept in, then he'd switch to culling through the files the team had backed-up.

"We could, but where's the fun in that?" Damian asked.

"You all are assholes," he muttered, drawing chuckles.

"I think that's usually our line," Alexis said, taking a drink Isiah brought over to her. "That's amazing, babe," she said after taking a sip.

Jake glanced up to see Isiah smiling down at Alexis. "It's alcohol-free, so you all can drink as much as you like. Anyone else want any?"

"Yes," everyone said at the same time. The group response startled Isiah, then made him laugh. But no one would ever accuse anyone in the room of being dumb, and refusing something created by Isiah definitely fell into that category. Ten minutes later they each held a drink and their attention was back on their computers.

"I've been so caught up in researching Robin Spencer—and tormenting you about Nia—that I didn't ask how the interview went," Beni said. "Anika sent her report over just now, but what was your take?"

Jake pulled his eyes from his computer and stared at Beni. He'd already dipped his toe into the dark web to see if he could find any rumors about their mystery drug.

"The interview you did," she prompted.

He frowned. He'd gone over it in his head so many times as

he'd run his errands that he'd forgotten no one else was privy to what Nia's cousin had told them. Pressing play on the recording app, he set the phone down and let them listen to the thirty-minute interview.

When the recording ended, he glanced around, and every one of his teammates wore a thoughtful expression.

"I think I'm going to change focus and start looking into Carl Westoff rather than Robin Spencer," Damian said. "Anyone object?"

There was a round of "nos" and headshakes.

"The composition of the drug itself bothers me," Alexis said. "I know we've had the breakdown of the compounds in the mix for a few days, but other than a general knowledge of each, I haven't really looked into them. When Beni presented her theory about the drug being tested, it seemed an interesting option, but now that we have Troy as a potential first-hand report of being a lab rat, I'm going to switch my focus and take a much closer look into the chemical make-up and affect of the drug."

"And I'm going to look into those cases I pulled," Beni said. "I'll look for more and see if we can find a pattern. I don't know that any of the parties arrested will have much to offer, but if we can link them to places that Carl Westoff hangs out at, then that might be an interesting line of inquiry to pursue."

Jake nodded then turned his attention to Dominic. He was relieved to have the focus off him and Nia. He understood why they felt the need to bring it up—he was just about the nosiest person in the group and turnabout was fair play—but they *did* have a case to solve.

"What about you, Dom?" Jake asked.

"I'll pick up Damian's research into Robin Spencer. Based on what Alexis said, he probably didn't run in the same circles as Westoff, but he got those drugs somewhere. And you?"

"I'll go back to looking at the islands and potential places where a lab might be set up," Jake answered.

Yael and Isiah walked back into the room and Isiah dropped a kiss on Alexis's head. "I'm making a final run to The Shack to help Huck get the shutters in place and get some things in storage. Anyone need anything while I'm out?" Huck was a former SEAL teammate of Isiah's who had decided, after seeing some shady shit in his subsequent role with the CIA, that he'd rather retire and tend bar with Isiah. He lived in the apartment above The Shack now that Isiah had moved in with Alexis, and was kind of an all-around go-to guy for anything from fixing a sink to tracking an international terrorist. Although these days, he much preferred the former to the latter.

"The guys are set up at the gatehouse," Yael said, referring to the two onsite security that worked for the Wright family. "I'll leave with Isiah and head home. You have the two-way radio?" she asked Alexis, who nodded. "Good, use it if you need me and can't call, but I think everything is buttoned-up tight here. Or will be once you drop the shutters tonight."

Penelope had announced her upcoming arrival during the afternoon with heavy rain and blustery winds. But she wasn't scheduled to hit landfall until around six-thirty in the morning and so the metal shutters that would protect the windows of Alexis's house hadn't yet been lowered.

"We'll do that after dinner," Alexis answered. Yael nodded, then after admonitions for everyone to stay safe, she and Isiah left the group to their work.

Dusk was falling when Nia made an appearance at the top of the stairs. Jake started to jump up to help her, but she waved him back into his seat. He eyed her, then sank back into his chair. She was moving gingerly, but she looked better.

When she reached the landing, she paused and answered a few questions from Charlotte and Damian about how she was feeling, then her gaze went to the huge glass wall and door that led out onto the patio and pool. The patio was covered, but even so, the wind had picked up enough that rain was being hurled against the glass, and in the dim light, they could see trees swaying and bending.

"Huh," Dominic said, drawing everyone's attention to him. "Guess who Robin Spencer's mom is?"

"Mrs. Spencer?" Nia said, moving toward the kitchen rather than the living room.

"Very funny, Doc. Now, why don't you sit down so Jake can relax? He looks like he wants to jump out of his chair," Dominic said. Nia glanced back at him but kept walking.

"Alexis, I'm going to grab some fruit or something," she said. "I'm starving."

Charlotte hopped up, then set her laptop down on the coffee table. "Eric left some of his homemade pizzas that we just need to throw in the oven. Why don't Nia and I get dinner ready and you guys can do your FBI-thing." Second to Isiah, Eric, who was Yael's husband and Alexis's personal chef, was one of Jake's favorite cooks.

"FBI-thing," Damian said on a chuckle. "So much respect for the badge, babe."

Charlotte rolled her eyes. "Right," she said, bending over to place a kiss on the top of Damian's head. "Because when you call my work 'fun with numbers' it's spoken with such awe." Damian grinned and Charlotte shook her head before adding, "If you need anything, Nia and I will be in the kitchen. We'll have dinner ready in thirty minutes or so."

"So who's Robin Spencer's mom?" Beni asked after Charlotte had left.

"Madeline Carruthers," Dominic answered.

"And why is that interesting?" Alexis asked.

"Because of this," Dominic said, turning the screen of his computer around. Everyone leaned forward to look at the picture of a couple. She was glossy and beautiful with blond hair piled on her head, an ice blue gown with a deep 'v,' and a huge diamond hanging right in the center of that 'V.' But it was the man who caught everyone's attention. His blond hair showed signs of greying at the temples, but in his tux, the man could have stepped out of an Armani ad.

"Duncan Calloway," Jake said, sitting back in his chair.

"This is one of several pictures I found," Dominic said. "She's a British heiress, and it appears Madeline and Duncan dated for a little over a year."

"Past tense?" Damian asked.

Dominic nodded. "Broke up a little more than nine months ago. She's with some oil sheik now. But it looks like Robin and Calloway stayed friends." He flipped to another picture of Robin and Calloway at the British Open the prior July, less than three months ago.

"Do you think Duncan Calloway is an overall shitty person and is involved in whatever sketchy things come his way, or do you think there's a plan to what he's involved with here in the Caribbean?" Jake asked. This was the third investigation they'd been involved in that Calloway's name had come up. While they only had clear evidence of wrongdoing in one of the three— though not enough to charge, let alone convict him—having his name crop up three times seemed too much of a coincidence to ignore. So now, in Jake's mind, the question was whether or not Calloway had some sort of overall plan for what he got involved with, or if he was just an opportunist and as things fell into his lap, he took the opportunity.

"Hard to say at this point," Damian said. "But I definitely think he bears looking into more. I know he's been on our radar —especially after last July—but with his name cropping up again, I think we need to do a forensic analysis of his life."

Jake agreed, but there was a problem with that approach. After last July, when they'd discovered that Calloway had been involved in compromising the identities of at least one CIA asset, they'd kept their eye on him, but at Shah's orders, hadn't done a deep dive into his life.

"So is this one of those situations where we act first and ask for forgiveness later, or we go to Shah?" Jake asked. Shah had never said why she'd put a damper on the Calloway investigation, and though none of them had argued with her outright, he knew he wasn't the only one harboring questions about that order.

The group was silent for a long moment, then Dominic spoke. But what he said wasn't what Jake was expecting. "Well hot damn, y'all are going to love this."

Everyone looked over. He still had his laptop on his lap and was staring intently at the screen. "Anyone want to take a guess as to who owns the island where Mariston was killed in July?"

Philip Mariston had all but kidnapped Alexis and was the errand boy for Calloway. And it had been Calloway who'd been the broker between the buyer of the CIA asset's identity and the agent who was selling that asset out. Unfortunately, Mariston hadn't learned not to tangle with the big boys, and he'd ended up in countless pieces scattered across the ocean's surface when a bomb had torn his boat apart.

"We know who owns it," Alexis said. "The Wainwright Holding company. They're legit, we looked into them."

"They are," Dominic said. "But any guesses who the chair of the board is?"

"Don't even say Duncan Calloway," Jake grumbled.

"I won't. But I will say Georgina Grace," Dominic responded.

"And she is?" Beni asked.

"She's a British socialite," Alexis answered. "Her mother and my mom modeled together a few times. Her father is Raymond Greene, Viscount something-or-other."

"Actually," Dominic said. "Greene is her step-father. Her real father is…drumroll please."

Jake shot his friend a flat look, and Beni threw a pillow at him.

Dominic glared back at all of them. "Fine, be that way. Her real father is Stuart Calloway."

Jake blinked. *That* was a surprise. "Duncan Calloway's father? So the chair of the board that owns the island where Calloway's lackey was killed is Calloway's half-sister?"

Dominic nodded. "I don't know about you all, but that's a surprise twist I wasn't expecting."

"And one worth looking into," Alexis added.

"Dinner's ready," Charlotte announced, standing in the doorway to the room. "Pizza, salad, beer, and Eric even made us a cake."

Food was the magic word, and everyone rose at the same time, setting laptops down and stretching. Jake was the first one out, but Charlotte stopped him as he passed.

"Nia is already at the table. I know you'll take good care of her, but she's exhausted and I think what happened is really sinking in now."

Jake nodded his thanks at Charlotte's concern and proceeded to the dining area. He had anticipated that it would take a while for Nia to really absorb the fact that she'd been shot and that she'd, literally, been inches away from death. He hated that it had happened while they were working a case—he'd like nothing more than to take her away for a few days to work through, or at least start to work through, how fucked up the past two days had been. But with the case, and Penelope, the best he could do was to make sure she was comfortable, well-rested, and well aware that he was steps away if needed.

The wind picked up as they gathered in the kitchen, and the rain lashed against the windows in deafening waves.

Jake took a seat beside Nia. "Can I get you anything?"

She gave him a wan smile. "I'd like a beer, but Charlotte said no. At least Eric made me this delicious juice," she said, holding up a tall glass. "It's supposed to have all sorts of things that will help me heal."

"I don't know what it is with this house and juice, but they could go into business selling whatever it is Eric and Alexis come up with in that kitchen," he said.

"Oh good, you have the juice Eric made," Alexis said, taking a seat on the other side of Nia, her dog Howdy at her feet.

Charlotte set a big salad on the table, and Dominic, Damian, and Beni followed, each carrying a large pizza.

"Whether it helps or not, who knows, but the taste makes me happy, so I guess there is at least that." Nia smiled at Alexis then startled as Howdy leaped to her feet, started barking, then ran downstairs.

"I guess Isiah's back," Alexis said with a smile.

"Where's Red?" Dominic asked, referring to Alexis and Isiah's other dog—though everyone knew that she was really more Isiah's than Alexis's.

Alexis reached for a piece of pizza. "She waits by the door for him. We finally moved a bed down there for her."

As she finished, Isiah came into view and stepped into the room, the two dogs on his heels. "Looks like I have good timing," he said.

Alexis gestured to the empty seat beside her. "Everything locked up at The Shack?"

Isiah nodded as he sat, then he half rose to snag a couple pieces of pizza. "Huck's tucked in, the shutters are on. Now, all we do is wait."

All eyes went to the massive glass wall. It was too dark to see anything anymore, but the wind was definitely getting louder.

"What did the road look like?" Damian asked.

"Not bad, not yet."

Jake glanced out the window again. He'd been in his fair share of hurricanes over the years and while they were never to be taken lightly, a category one hurricane didn't give him too much anxiety.

"Anyone check-in with Anika?" Beni asked. "Not sure what we can do, but it might be worth offering our help if needed."

"Already done," Dominic said as he picked up his beer. "She said she'd call if they need anything. Assuming cell reception works in the morning."

That was always the problem with hurricanes—it was unpredictable how they'd impact both the electrical grid and the cell reception. But those weren't things they could do anything to fix, so instead of lingering on what they couldn't control, Jake brought the conversation back around to the question he'd asked before Charlotte had called them to dinner.

"So, do we tell Shah or just do our thing?"

No one spoke for a while, then, to Jake's surprise, Isiah was the one who answered. "I don't know what you all are talking about, but knowing Shah, I'd recommend staying on her good side." Back when Isiah had been a SEAL, he and his team had benefited from intel Shah had provided. No one but the two of them knew the details, but it was no secret Isiah held the woman in the utmost respect.

"He's probably right," Alexis said as she set her beer down. "I don't know why she had us stand down last summer, but with what we found tonight, I don't think she'd be able to decline our request."

"Like Isiah, I don't know what you all are talking about," Nia interjected. "But have you considered that there's something else at play with Shah? I just find it weird that she specifically formed this team—picked each of you individually for the strengths she thought you'd bring—and then she has you stand down?" Nia shrugged then lifted her pizza. "I like her, you know I do. But you have to admit, it's weird."

And of course, leave it to Nia to put out in the open the question Jake was sure he wasn't the only one pondering. His gaze swept the table and the expressions that met his mirrored the unease teasing at his body. He didn't think Shah was dirty, but he wouldn't put it past her to be keeping something from them.

Beni let out a long sigh. "Do we need to finally discuss the elephant in the room?"

Jake didn't like the way this conversation was going. But, Beni was right, it was past time they had it. "Why don't you spell it out?"

Beni shot him a look, then took a sip of her drink. After she set the bottle on the table, she looked around the table. "I know I'm not the only one who has wondered how we all got here. Why us? I know we're good agents, but the Bureau is filled with good agents. Why, out of everyone, did Shah pick us?"

Beni paused then let her gaze go to the darkened windows. "I have a chip on my shoulder the size of Colorado, Damian was a hair's breadth away from losing his job because of a deal he'd made with a reporter, Dominic had been suspended twice in his first year, Alexis kept more secrets than teenager's diary, and Jake was little more than a pretty boy with a bad driving record. We're all good agents, damn good agents..."

"But we're all loners," Alexis finished.

"Or we were," Damian said.

"We have each other now," Dominic said. "But even so, I don't know that I'd call any of us team players outside this group."

Jake sighed. "So the question isn't just *why* did Shah pick us, but also *how* did she even know about us? None of us were or are interested in climbing the ladder. We've all worked high profile cases, but none of us ever had any interest in calling attention to ourselves. So why and how did we end up here?"

No one spoke for a moment, though the sounds of beer bottles being moved around the table and the scrape of forks on plates could be heard over the wind.

"Did I cause an existential identity crisis with my question?" Nia asked, no doubt hoping to lighten the mood. There were a few quiet chuckles, but no one laughed.

Nia sighed and set her fork down. "Look, I didn't mean to imply that Shah was up to something shady. But it's possible she is up to something that she hasn't shared with you yet. I've only ever known you all as a team, so seeing you as loners is hard for me. But even if that's true, maybe that's exactly why she picked you—not because you're isolated and alone, but because you've insulated yourselves."

Everyone looked up and locked their eyes on Nia. Her brow furrowed as she took in the scrutiny.

"She's right," Isiah said. "If what Beni said about what each of you was like before coming here, and if Shah is up to something she wants to keep to herself for the moment, what better than to surround yourself with good agents who haven't, for lack of a better phrase, drunk the Kool-Aid? None of you are going to go running back to old colleagues and gossip about what's going on down here."

Isiah and Nia were right, but Jake wasn't sure if he just wanted to believe them because it was a much better way to think about their role on the task force than the alternative. Finally, after a long silence, he spoke. "Whatever the reason was that Shah brought us all together, we still need to figure out if we're going to ask for the green light to dig into Calloway."

"Ask," Isiah said. All eyes landed on him. He wasn't part of the task force, but he'd been around the block more than once. His opinion wasn't one they should dismiss even if he didn't know the specifics.

"If you're going to place your trust in anyone other than who is at this table, Shah is who I would place it in," he continued. "Ask and if she says 'no' then trust her and shut it down. I know it will be hard, I can see how much you all want this. It's written on your faces. But you have to trust someone and she's someone I would, and have, trusted with my life."

Alexis reached over and took his hand in hers. He turned and held her gaze. After a moment, she nodded. "We all have questions," she said. "But we all also came to work for Shah for a reason. We don't just need to trust her, we need to trust ourselves, trust whatever it was that had each of us agreeing to join this task force."

Jake shifted in his seat, and Nia's hand came up to rest along his back. The steady warmth of her palm against his spine centered him. He had no idea what Shah would say, nor what her answer might be, but at least they'd have a direction.

Finally, he looked up and met Alexis's gaze. "I agree. Why don't you make the call?"

Alexis nodded, then in silent agreement, she dialed the number, put her phone on speaker, and set the device down on the table.

"Alexis," Shah said, answering. "How is everyone faring?"

Alexis updated her on their condition then succinctly filled their director in on what they'd found about Calloway.

When she finished, Shah was silent for a beat. "That's good work, agents," she said. "And in the middle of a hurricane, too. I suppose you want permission to look into Calloway now?"

"Yes, we do," Alexis confirmed, her eyes darting to each of her colleagues as she spoke. "I know you asked us to pull back last summer, but with this new information..."

"There is a time and a place for everything," Shah said. "I had my reasons for slowing the investigation down over the summer, but we're closing in on The Summit now. The timing is still a little early, but better."

Jake looked around the table. Judging by his teammates expressions, no one had a clue what that cryptic comment meant.

"Director?" Alexis asked.

Shah didn't answer right away, but they could hear her tapping away on a laptop. "You're cleared to investigate Calloway," she finally said. "I don't want to lose focus on the drugs, but to the extent you think he's part of that investigation, you have clearance to dig."

"And the timing?" Alexis asked. Alexis was digging, hoping to get some light shined on that vague reference.

"We'll discuss that once we've closed this investigation."

No one misunderstood the finality of Shah's statement, and Alexis thanked her then ended the call.

"What do you think that was about?" Damian asked.

Jake shook his head. "I have no idea, but at least it doesn't sound like she's keeping us out."

"Just keeping us out for now," Beni interjected.

"Trust," Isiah reminded them. "Trust her and yourselves."

"I do," Dominic said. "I think we do trust her. It's just…"

"Uncomfortable," Jake said and everyone nodded. "But there's not a lot we can do about it right now," he continued. "So, maybe we finish eating, then go do what she's just given us the green light to do."

Alexis and Beni shook their heads, but the guys chuckled and started to dig back into what was left of the pizza. Beside him, Nia's laugh was soft enough that only he heard.

"Always with the food, McMullen," she said, as she reached for her glass of juice.

"Well, Captain America has to keep up this fine physique, you know," he shot back, gesturing to his body.

"It is a fine physique, I'll give you that," she agreed. At the lightness in her voice, a wave of warmth swept through him, and he leaned over and kissed her.

"If you're lucky, I'll let you explore it later," he whispered to her.

Nia snorted. "If I'm lucky, you'll grab me that last piece of pizza."

Jake barked a laugh and, because making her happy made him happy, he handed her the last slice.

After dinner, they divided the work, with Damian and Dominic taking point on Calloway, while Jake, Beni, and Alexis continued their research into Westoff and the drugs. But at just after two in the morning, they decided to close the shutters and call it a day. None of them knew what the hurricane, or its aftermath, would bring, and they wanted to be at least a little rested in case their presence was needed.

While they still had power, Jake grabbed a quick shower then brushed his teeth before sliding between the covers and scooting up behind Nia, who'd gone to bed long ago. She murmured something and snuggled back into him, but didn't fully wake up.

Focusing on the feel of her heart beating beneath his hand and the steady rise and fall of her chest, he let his mind drift over what they'd uncovered in the past few hours. Dominic and Damian had discovered that the half-siblings—Duncan and Georgina—weren't strangers to each other. They didn't pal around together, but based on their respective business dealings, several of which overlapped, it was clear they had some sort of relationship.

Damian had also heard from his contacts in Boston about the tracker they'd found on the float. They assured Damian they could find where it was transmitting to, but they needed more time to make sure they could do it without alerting anyone as to what they were doing. The info would have been nice to have sooner rather than later since it would help him narrow down where they should look for the manufacturing facility, but the truth was, even if they found a likely location, it would be at least a few days before they could get out there. Penelope would primarily pass by mid-morning, and likely the trailing wind and rain would pass within forty-eight hours. But that was when the clean-up would start, and, of course, it would take some time to get the FBI boat out of dry-dock.

He let out a long breath and placed a kiss on Nia's neck, letting his lips linger against her skin. She smelled of the same soap and shampoo that he'd used in the en suite bath, which meant that she, too, had taken a shower. The nurse had given Nia a waterproof bandage so that she could bathe, but he didn't like the idea of her doing it alone...she might be mentally tougher than nails, but physically, it was a different story.

"I'm fine," she murmured as if hearing his thoughts. "I didn't want to smell like the hospital anymore."

Her words pulled to the surface all the panic and fear he'd felt the day before—from watching her fall to waiting for news from the doctor in the hospital. He didn't want to think of all that right now, he didn't want to experience that terror ever again, not even through his own memories. But even as he tried to stuff them down, he knew he'd failed when Nia let out a long breath.

She wrapped her fingers around his and pulled him closer against her back. Curling a leg behind her, she slipped it between his and twined their bodies together even more. "Just breathe, Jake. Tomorrow is going to be another day. We're here now, so just breathe and let it be."

He didn't think he could, but for Nia, he'd try. Focusing again on her heart beating under his palm, he took one breath, then another, then slowly drifted off to sleep.

CHAPTER SIXTEEN

"OH, SHIT," Nia said, jerking in surprise. Behind her, Jake pulled her tighter against him. She didn't have to ask if he was awake, aside from his movement, no one could have slept through what sounded like a tree coming down on the house. Nia wasn't worried about the house—much—it was built of cement and all the windows had been covered by metal shutters, but if the wind was powerful enough to fell one of the old, and big, palm trees around the house, then she'd bet that Penelope had upgraded to a category two hurricane at some time in the early morning hours.

She glanced at the bedside clock, but it just blinked at her. The power was on, thanks to the generators, but none of the clocks had been reset. Stretching across the bed—because somehow she'd managed to slide to the opposite side and into Jake's arms—she grabbed her phone.

"How long?" Jake asked.

"If she didn't change course over the night, she should be hitting Tildas in fifteen minutes," she answered.

"You know we're not going back to sleep, don't you?"

She considered rolling over and snuggling in next to Jake,

but there was no way the stitches in her back or her bruised ribs would let her do what she really wanted to. So instead, she nodded then swung her legs from the bed. They might as well get up and see if any of the others were awake.

"How do you feel?" Jake asked as he pulled on his shorts. For a moment, he stood before her, holding his shirt in his hands as he waited for her answer. "Nia?"

She blinked. "Sorry, just lost in all..." she waved in the general direction of his chest. "That." Jake grinned at her. "But to answer your question, it's more of a tugging than a consistent pain. It seems like it should hurt more, doesn't it? I'm not about to head out on a hike or a dive anytime soon, but getting around the house shouldn't be a problem."

"Maybe Eric's juice really did help." Jake pulled on his shirt as he spoke, which allowed her to focus on his words.

She shrugged. "It definitely didn't hurt. Maybe I'll go pour myself another glass while you make coffee?"

He laughed, then wrapped an arm around her as they left their room. "Happy to, but don't think I'll need to." He pointed to the door of the other guestroom on the ground floor—the one beside theirs where Damian and Charlotte were staying. The door was open, and as they walked up the flight of stairs to the main living area, they could hear voices.

"You think we're late to the party?" she asked.

He leaned over and tipped her head up for a kiss. "Sugar, we *are* the party."

She was laughing when they hit the landing, and everyone in the kitchen looked over. And by everyone, it was everyone. They really were the last ones to the party.

"How are you feeling?" Charlotte asked from where she sat at the breakfast bar, cradling a cup of coffee. Something whipped against one of the shutters, and everyone winced.

"Much better, thank you," she said. "Any of that juice left?"

Alexis, who was leaning against Isiah, nodded and waved

Nia over to the fridge. "Help yourself, you know where everything is. Jake, help yourself to coffee."

Nia walked to the fridge while Jake made his way to the coffee machine. "Any news?" Nia asked as she pulled the bottle of juice out.

"She's not quite a category two, but she is gaining strength," Beni said. "When she hits Tildas that might slow her down—"

"Hopefully not too much," Dominic interjected from his seat at the table.

"Yeah, hopefully not too much," Jake said, punching a set of buttons and bringing the coffee machine to life. Having a hurricane stall out over the island was everyone's nightmare.

"If Penelope's gaining strength, the only thing that will happen when she hits Tildas is she might drop back down to what she was before. Our island isn't big enough to get her to stop," Nia said. She took a sip of the juice and savored the sweet spiciness. She didn't know everything in it—Eric and Alexis were weirdly protective of their juice recipes—but she could taste ginger and turmeric and maybe even a little bit of guava and pineapple.

Nia looked up to see all eyes on her—some were more awake than others, but all seemed to be contemplating what she'd said. Jake was the only other one who'd grown up on an island, and she glanced in his direction. He was looking at her but seemed to be mulling over her words. Then he nodded.

"You're right. And as the only one who's grown up on this island, I suspect you know better than any of us," he said.

"So, what now?" Damian asked, sliding onto a stool beside Charlotte. Nia was pretty sure he was the only one who hadn't experienced a hurricane before.

"Now we wait," she said, sinking into a chair. "It will get worse before it gets better—"

As if on cue, a tsunami of wind slammed into the house. It shook on its foundation and the shutters rattled, and everyone held their breath. The lights flickered but didn't go off, then the sound faded to a consistent roar—a roar that would stay with them until she passed over.

"Now we wait," Nia repeated, speaking loudly to be heard over the wind and generator. "Penelope is going to do whatever she's going to do and there's nothing we can do about it until she passes."

"I did get an interesting text from Brian and Lucy before cell service went out," Damian said. "They needed a little more time to triangulate a precise location, but they did get a general location of where the float was transmitting to. I haven't had a chance to look since we only got up a few minutes before you all did, but we could pull up the maps we downloaded. You know, pass the time looking for drug dealers."

Nia snorted a laugh—how she'd ended up hanging out with people who passed their time looking for drug dealers was beyond her, but she wouldn't trade it for the world. "Why don't you all go do that," she said to Jake, who had cast her a questioning look. "I have an article I'm working on that I've been pushing off. What better time to do that than when I'm laid up with a gunshot wound in the middle of a hurricane?"

Her comment elicited a laugh, and in truth, it was a bit ridiculous. But also in truth, she did have an article she'd been working on and she might as well make good use of the time.

"Very practical, Doc," Dominic said. "I think you have a keeper, McMullen," he added, rising from his seat.

Nia let out a dramatic huff and rolled her eyes. "Of *course* he has a keeper, Dom. Good lord, I hope you're more insightful than that when you work."

Dominic gave a dramatic gasp and clasped his chest. "You wound me, Doc."

"She's right," Alexis said, pulling away from Isiah. "I really hope that lame observation isn't an example of what we can expect from you over the next few days, Agent Burel."

"My six-year-old godson is more observant," Beni chimed in. Charlotte cleared her throat. "For the record, my three-year-old nephew told me Nia was a keeper when he was here in May. I think it had something to do with the tour of the lab she gave him, but still...."

Isiah, Damian, and Jake stayed silent, but all were not so subtly trying to hide their laughter.

Dominic glared at all of them. "So that's how it's going to be?" he said more than asked.

Jake took pity on the man, and, walking over, he looped an arm around his friend's shoulder. "I know you're a good agent, buddy," he said.

"Damn straight," Dominic muttered.

"You kind of suck at the relationship dynamic thing and you did kind of put your foot in it, but you're a good agent."

"Fuck off, McMullen. You're the king of putting your foot in it," Dominic said, but he didn't shrug off Jake's arm.

"He does have you there, McMullen," Nia said, flashing Jake a grin. "I mean there's always—"

"Do *not* mention that night at Lola's, again," he said, glaring at her.

She pursed her lips and tried really hard not to smile. But in the end, she couldn't help herself. "That night did take the cake," she said, raising her glass in a mock salute.

She saw the amusement in Jake's eyes even as he tried to glare at her. "I think we have some things to do, Burel," he said, leading Dominic away. "Rodriguez, you going to join us?"

Damian flashed a grin at Charlotte, who smiled back at him. "Be right there," he called, then, after grabbing a banana from the counter, he joined his teammates in the living room.

"You all don't need to join them?" Nia asked Beni and Alexis.

Both women shook their heads. "We were working on a few other things," Beni said. "They've got it handled."

Alexis and Beni joined her at the table, and Charlotte spun on her stool to face them.

"So now we wait," Nia said, glancing at the metal shutters covering the windows. She liked how protected they made her feel, tucking the house up all nice and cozy, but she did give a fleeting thought to what they'd find when they were rolled back up.

"No, we don't just wait," Isiah said. "Now we make pancakes and eggs. By the time we're done eating, we'll know exactly how much damage Penelope has done."

That plan sounded better than hers, but when she offered to help, Isiah waved her back down into her seat. Deciding to take his advice, Nia remained at the table and sipped her coffee as Isiah and Alexis leisurely started making breakfast for eight people. The generators were up and running, so electricity wasn't an issue, though the persistent darkness and roar of the wind was enough to put anyone on edge.

"Nia?" Beni asked from her spot across the table.

Nia switched her gaze from where she been half-watching Isiah whisk eggs to Beni. "Yeah?"

"I know we covered some of it yesterday, but is there anything else you can tell me about your cousin? Once we can, we'll see if we can get CCTV footage from places around The Rye and see if we can find Westoff and who he might be spending time with. But I'm interested in Troy. What other kinds of places does he frequent?"

Nia shook her head, "I don't really know. We haven't spent much time together since we were kids. I do know that before the first time he was arrested, he was at that club, you know the one in town that only lasted four months?"

"Ah, yes, I remember that place," Beni said. "It had a high sleaze factor, even for a club."

"I only went once. I have a high tolerance for the ridiculous and even *I* felt like I was an extra on the set of a second rate version of Miami Vice," Nia said.

"Do you know why it shut down?" Charlotte asked.

Beni shook her head. "Seemed to be doing well with the tourist crowd, at least the night I was there."

"Hm," Charlotte said.

"What was that 'hm' for?" Beni said.

Charlotte lifted a shoulder. "I worked with a finance minister once whose son was a bit profligate. He, the son, not the father, got into business with some shady folks and they started doing these pop-up clubs. Nothing as grand as what you seem to be talking about, but the clubs would pop-up in random places for a few weeks then shut down. It was billed as a way to keep the hype, but what it ended up being was a way for dealers to distribute drugs and stay on the move."

Nia looked to Beni, who was tapping her finger on the table. "It would take a lot to do that in Havensted, but it's an interesting idea. I'm going to go get my files for the cases we think might be tied to the drugs and see if any others occurred while that club was in operation."

After Beni disappeared upstairs to the room she'd stayed in, Isiah joined them at the table and set a plate of pancakes down. "Ready for breakfast?"

"We also have bacon and eggs," Alexis said, setting a second platter down. "Now that you've finished your juice, do you want some coffee, Nia?"

Nia nodded but rose from her seat. "I can get it, it's good for me to move a little bit."

Both Alexis and Isiah eyed her but didn't say anything, and Nia had the errant thought that someday, those two would make good parents.

When she sat back down, Charlotte, Alexis, and Isiah were already starting to eat and so she forked a few pancakes onto her plate along with three strips of bacon. "Should we call the others?" Nia asked.

Isiah shook his head. "Those three," he said, pointing to the living room. "Are like locusts with bottomless pits for stomachs."

"It's true," Charlotte said. "I seriously have no idea where Damian puts it."

They had a point, Nia had eaten with Jake and Dominic enough to agree.

"We'll finish ours and then I'll make another batch for them," Isiah said.

That sounded like a good plan and the table fell into silence as they ate—well, as silent as it got when a hurricane was passing through. The eye had passed over them while Isiah and Alexis had been cooking, leaving a few moments of eerie quiet before the near explosive impact of the inside wall of the hurricane had hit the house. But now that Penelope had moved on a bit, the soundtrack to their morning was back to a dull roar.

"We got it!" Jake said, all but jumping into the room and startling the four of them at the table. "You started breakfast?" he said, frowning. Dominic and Damian came up behind him, and Nia couldn't help but laugh at the lost puppy dog expressions on their faces, thinking they'd missed breakfast.

"There's more," Nia said, rising. Isiah, who still had some eggs on his plate, started to rise as well, but Nia waved him down. "I'll cook, you finish eating. You've done all the hard stuff, I think I can make a few pancakes and fry up some scrambled eggs and bacon."

"You're the best," Jake said, snagging her as she walked by for a quick kiss.

"Isiah and Alexis did all the real work," she said, continuing on to the kitchen area.

"I do know how to pick 'em, don't I," he said with a wink at

Isiah, reminding everyone of the mission where Jake and Isiah had played a couple. Isiah rolled his eyes but huffed out a laugh.

"How much longer before we can head out, do you think?" Damian asked, taking a seat beside Charlotte.

"It will still be stormy, but probably an hour or so," Nia said from where she stood behind the counter, pouring batter onto a griddle.

"And what did you find?" Alexis asked Damian, Jake, and Dominic.

"You found something?" Beni said, rejoining them with two files in her hand.

"I'm 98% sure I found the island where the drugs are being manufactured," Jake said, setting a piece of paper on the table. From where Nia stood, it looked like a map. "Once the internet is back up and running, we should look at some better satellite imagery, but I'm pretty sure this is it." As he spoke, he pointed to something on the paper, and both Alexis and Beni leaned forward.

"Why that one?" Alexis asked.

"We started with the area Brian and Lucy gave us to search. There are six islands within the coordinates, but only four have any development on them. From there, we looked at the images and dug into the history of each. There's an abandoned armory on the south side of the island, which is what first caught our attention, but that wasn't what clinched it for us," Jake said.

Beni let out a long sigh. "So dramatic, McMullen. Can you just give us the details? Succinctly, please?"

"You'll never guess who owns the island," he said, ignoring Beni.

"Duncan Calloway?" Alexis asked, hopefully.

Jake grinned. "In a way, but it gets even better."

"For the love of all that is holy, McMullen. Get to the point," Beni groaned.

Damian chuckled and stepped in. "The island has one resort

on it. One of those all-inclusive, exclusive, adult-only places. Both the island and resort are owned by a company registered in Delaware. One of the majority shareholders *is* Calloway. But guess who another is?"

"Seriously? You, too?" Beni said, shooting him a disgusted look.

"Ronald Lawlor," Damian announced.

That name obviously meant something to the team, but Nia hadn't a clue what. Although the sounds of cutlery landing on plates and muttered curses filling the air gave her a pretty good idea of the weight of the information Damian had just shared.

"You're kidding?" Alexis asked.

"'Fraid, not," Dominic said.

"How did you find that without an internet connection?" Beni asked.

Damian shrugged. "When Brian and Lucy gave me their preliminary findings, I downloaded all the intel on the area that I could get my hands on before we lost connection. We just culled through it this morning."

"Who's Ronald Lawlor?" Nia asked as she set a plate of pancakes on the table.

"He's another FBI agent," Alexis said.

"What?" Nia asked, surprised.

"He works in the DC office, and while we don't have any cause to think he's done something wrong, there's something kind of off about him," Jake said, speaking to her as he patted the empty seat beside him. "We think he sent one of his agents down here over the summer to check on us, and Shah said he was all but foaming at the mouth to get one of his pet agents on the task force. He could just be trying to consolidate some power, but he's definitely someone who raises the hairs on our necks."

Nia considered Jake's words as she sipped her coffee. The task force was an elite team. If someone was intent on gaining power, trying to infiltrate the unit seemed a plausible course of action.

"So tell me about this island?" Alexis asked Damian.

Alexis's question interrupted Nia's musings, and she leaned over to get a closer look at the map. No one knew these islands better than she, and she wanted to know which one they'd identified.

"Like I said, the south side has an old armory that could hold a lab. There are tourists on the island, but the resort is on the northeast corner and the only transport allowed is by golf cart. There aren't any paths that stray more than a half a mile from the main grounds, so it's unlikely anyone would wander anywhere close to the old buildings," Damian said.

"There's also a really treacherous reef along here," Nia said, reaching across the table and pointing to the mouth of the bay where the armory sat. "If you know your way in, it's not hard to navigate, but if you don't, that reef will stop you fast. It's one of the reasons the armory was built there. A land attack wasn't likely given the size of the island, and if someone was going to come in by boat, the reef acted as an additional safeguard."

Everyone stared at the printed satellite images for a while, then Beni spoke. "Do we know if there is electricity going to the armory?"

Damian shook his head. "We don't know. There is electricity on the island, of course, but I didn't go so far as to look at the consumption rates or the grid. That will have to wait until we're back online."

"Have you ever been there, Nia?" Charlotte asked.

Nia's gaze lingered on the map, then she nodded. "A couple of times. Once when I was home from college and a couple of my college friends were visiting. We took a boat out and decided to explore the island. The resort wasn't there at the time either. The armory buildings are pretty locked up, but we did manage to crawl through a few doors and windows and explore the compound. The second time was a few years ago when we wanted to check the reef for damage after Irma and Maria."

"Could someone set up a lab there?" Jake asked.

Nia frowned and dropped her gaze back down to the map. "There are a lot of large, empty rooms where they stored torpedoes and missiles and other weapons. I suppose one of those could be made into a lab. I don't really know what goes into making a lab that manufactures drugs, but there's certainly enough space."

"I think it might be time for a little cruise, ladies and gentlemen," Jake said with a grin.

Everyone stared back at him, and Nia started counting in her head. Huh, three seconds before someone called him on his crazy.

"We are literally in the middle of a hurricane, McMullen. I know you're crazy, but are you seriously suicidal?" Beni asked.

Jake turned his head to the closed shutters and frowned. "I guess I kind of forgot, seeing as how we're locked up in here, we haven't lost power, and we have no idea what's going outside."

"You forgot," Dominic said. "You forgot a hurricane?"

Nia patted Jake's chest. "Now, I know you're all thinking I'm jumping to his defense because we're sleeping together, but I'd like to remind you all that Jake has attention span issues and you all know that about him."

"It's true, I do," Jake confirmed, taking her hand.

"I hate to agree, but that's a fair statement," Damian said. After a beat, there were a few reluctant nods of agreement.

"So seeing as how we're mostly in agreement that we won't be jumping in a boat," Damian continued. "I think we hunker down here until the worst of the storm passes, and then we evaluate. If the roads are passable, and if we can get the boat out of dry-dock, and if the seas aren't too rough, then we might be able to make it out there later today."

"May I make a suggestion?" Nia asked.

"Of course, Doc," Dominic said.

"Why don't you try a flyover this afternoon? A plane or a helicopter will be able to get out to the area much better than a boat. Also, if anyone is paying attention, a flyover can be passed off as looking for hurricane damage. On a day like today, if someone sees a boat out, they're either going to think the boat is stranded or that the captain is crazy. Either way, it will raise questions."

The agents considered her comments, then Dominic nodded. "It's a good plan. If we can get close enough, we might be able to gather enough intel to help us formulate a battle plan if we decide we need to raid."

When everyone agreed with Dominic's assessment, Nia let a small sigh of relief. Navigating a boat into the bay where the armory was wasn't child's play, and trying to do it during the tail end of a hurricane bordered on insanity.

"In the meantime," Alexis said, sliding the map over in front of Nia. "Can you tell us anything about the island?"

For the next fifteen minutes, Nia walked the team through what she knew of the small, privately held island. It wasn't a lot, but it was more than they could see on the map. For example, the map didn't show the small harbor on the southwest side of the island. It had been used to bring supplies into the armory rather than risking the reef in the armory bay. There was a small, crumbling concrete dock there that might make for a good spot for them to land—should they need to—so long as they didn't need to tie up a boat.

She also pointed out the good snorkeling and diving spots. Not that she thought they were going to head out on a joy ride, but the fact that those spots were all close to the resort meant that those who stayed there had little need to venture too far... to, say, the south side of the island.

When she'd exhausted her knowledge, they all retired to

their rooms to prepare for the coming day. Twenty minutes later, everyone met in the lower foyer. Despite the heat they all knew they'd step out into, everyone was dressed in jeans and work boots.

"Ready?" Isiah asked. Everyone nodded, and, slowly, he unlocked the massive front door and let it swing open. Alexis's house had a portico, so when they stepped outside, they were protected from the heavy drizzle that was still falling. A gust of wind blew some of the drops their direction and they all turned their backs to protect their faces.

When the wind died down again, they ventured farther out. Debris littered the driveway, lining it with a carpet of palm tree fronds and leaves, but none of the trees themselves looked to have fallen.

"Alexis!" Everyone turned at the voice to see Mac, one of the security guards that lived onsite at the gatehouse to Alexis's home. He was striding toward them from the side of the house, obviously having already taken a look around.

"Mac," Alexis said, stepping out from under the portico. "How's everything looking? You and Teddy okay?"

Mac nodded. "We're good. Not too much damage, and what there is looks mostly superficial. I didn't see anything structural. One of the big potted trees broke loose from its tether and slammed into the back shutter, so we'll want to get that checked out, but other than the mess, it's looking pretty good. You hear from Yael and Eric yet? How's Rachel?"

Rachel was Eric's mom and Alexis's house manager. The three of them lived in the luxury apartment complex up the road.

Alexis nodded. "Yael radioed me fifteen minutes ago. They're all good."

"Good," Mac said, rubbing his hands together. "We'll get started cleaning up here. We'll get the driveway clear first, so if you need to get out, you can. But once that's done, if you hear of anything more urgent than what we've got on our hands here, you know Teddy and I are happy to help any way we can."

"Thanks, Mac. We'll take a look around then help clean up," Alexis said.

"After we scope it out, why don't you and Isiah head on down to check on Rachel and the others and then to The Shack," Damian said to Alexis. "We've got this here," he added, gesturing to the driveway and yard.

Dominic stepped out from under the portico and turned in a circle, surveying the property. "Once we've got this cleared, we can try to make our way down to the office to see if we can touch base with Shah, and then we can try and convince Shorty to take us up," he said, referring to the helicopter pilot the team used. Nia hadn't ever met the woman, but she'd been in the room, listening to the radio, when the helicopter—piloted by Shorty and carrying Damian and Dominic—had nearly blown up some months ago.

Without another word, the group began to circle the house. It was exactly as Mac had reported. Lots of debris littered the yard and the pool looked a mess, but other than the huge pot that had broken free and slammed against the house, shattering it into several pieces—which was what must have woken her and Jake up—the damage didn't look bad.

Once Isiah and Alexis left to check on the others, the rest of them joined Teddy and Mac in starting the clean-up. A little over an hour later, Alexis returned and joined the efforts, then shortly after, Isiah came walking back through the main gates.

"Cell service is back," Isiah said, holding up his phone. "And the reason I know that is because your dad has texted me five times asking what to get you for your birthday, Lex." He stopped in front of his significant other, and the two shared a smile. "He also said you should carry your damn phone after a hurricane so that he can check in with you directly rather than having to go through Yael," Isiah added.

Alexis laughed. "I left it in the house. I'll call them in a bit."

"When's your birthday, Alexis?" Nia asked, stopping her sweeping of the portico.

Alexis made a face. "December."

"And he's texting you *now*? It's only October," Nia said.

Alexis shrugged. "That's my dad. He's been bugging me about it since he was down for a visit in August."

"That's sweet," Nia said.

"It's a little ridiculous, but after thirty-four years, I'm used to it," Alexis answered with a shrug.

Nia glanced over to see Jake watching her. She didn't need to be psychic to know what he was thinking. It didn't help that she didn't even try to hide it from him. His family was as fucked up as hers, and with him, she didn't need to hide her struggles. Because she *was* wondering what it would be like to have a dad, or any parent, that cared enough about her birthday to be planning months in advance. To the best of her memory, and as pathetic as it made her feel, she was pretty sure that once she'd gone to college, her family hadn't remembered her birthday even once.

CHAPTER SEVENTEEN

"HEY, GUYS," Dominic called everyone to attention, pulling Nia from her maudlin thoughts. "Anika said the roads are looking good if we want to try and head into the office." As he spoke, he held up his phone. Apparently, Dominic and Detective Anika Anderson were now on a texting basis.

"Anyone talk to Shah?" Alexis asked.

"On it," Damian said, pulling out his phone. The rest of them continued to clean up while he texted and ten minutes later, he slid his phone back into his pocket. "She can be at the office in an hour and a half," he said.

"The roads may be in good shape, but they're going to be covered with debris. We should think about heading over in forty minutes or so," Beni said.

"I need to check on my boat and get Nia home," Jake said, surprising her with his sudden announcement. Not that she thought she'd be going to the FBI office with him, but there was an urgency in his voice that had her cocking her head at him in question.

"If we head out now and I drop you at home, will you be okay on your own for a little bit?" he asked.

She studied his eyes, then nodded.

"Good, do you mind if we head out?" he asked no one and everyone. There were murmurs of assent and Damian joined in, saying he wanted to get Charlotte home as well. A short while later, Jake pulled his jeep out of Alexis's driveway with Damian and Charlotte in their own car behind them.

Nia said nothing as Jake navigated the roads west toward his boat. After a quick stop at the marina, he assured her that his boat was still watertight—and more importantly, still in its berth—and they headed toward her home on the other side of Havensted.

The roads were as Anika had reported, and while lights were still out and tree branches and bushes were everywhere, nothing had washed out. Still, she kept quiet as Jake navigated the obstacles. But when they got to Havensted and Jake turned north—away from her house—and started driving toward the hill side of town, she asked, "Where are we going?"

He glanced over, his expression not quite grim, but definitely pensive. "You'll see."

She started to ask, but he reached over and squeezed her hand. "Just trust me. It's one more stop and then I'll take you home."

The seriousness of his voice gave her pause, and so she did what he asked and remained silent until they stopped at what looked like a large, cement warehouse. A metal roll-up door faced the hillside, away from the views of the town, and along the tops of the walls were several long windows, though those were shuttered now.

"Where are we?" she asked.

"You'll see," he said, getting out of the car and coming around to her side. Jake was acting so un-Jake-like, that she didn't even tease him about opening her door and helping her out.

With her hand firmly tucked into his, they approached the

main door. Dropping her hand, Jake pulled out a key and dropped to his haunches. He unlocked the padlock, then stood, bringing the door with him. Nia watched as the metal door rolled all the way up, then finally, she dropped her gaze to the interior.

The cavernous room was dark, and Jake stepped inside and hit a switch. Light flooded the space, and Nia sucked in a startled breath.

"Jake?" she asked, stepping into the room. There were several easels holding paintings covered in drop clothes, but on the far wall, six paintings hung at various heights. They ranged in size from no more than sixteen inches by twenty inches to one that had to be at least eight by ten feet.

"Are you a Broussard collector?" she asked, having instantly recognized the style. She might only own one of Marie Broussard's paintings, but she was a big fan.

Jake cleared his throat, but when he didn't answer, she swung back to look at him.

"Jake?"

He crossed his arms and finally met her gaze. "I'm not a collector. I am J. Marie Broussard. My mother's name was Marie, and her mother's maiden name was Broussard."

Nia stared at him—gawked at him, really. Before today, she hadn't thought that gawking was really a thing, but as it turned out it was. She half expected him to suddenly break into a grin and say "gotcha!" but he didn't.

She studied his posture—his folded arms, his closed-off expression, his shallow breathing—and the more she saw, the more she accepted that this was no joke. Not only was it not a joke, but he was showing her something deeply, deeply personal.

And how she reacted in this moment mattered.

"Talk to me," she said quietly as she walked toward the far end of the room.

He didn't answer right away, but after a moment, he spoke. "My mom used to paint all the time. When she died, I refused to let my dad throw her things away. I didn't know what I'd do with them, but I didn't want them tossed away, and so I took them and hid them somewhere safe." He paused, and she heard him take a few steps toward her, but she kept her eyes on the paintings before her.

"I'd painted with her often as a kid. It was just something we did together. I wasn't nearly as good as she was and I didn't really take to it like I think she hoped I would. At least not until after my injury."

She turned away from the massive painting she'd been looking at and looked over her shoulder at the man she'd thought she'd known. Some of his defensive posture was gone, and after a beat, he walked toward her.

"After my injury, I didn't know what to do with myself. I couldn't surf anymore, I couldn't even teach it, and I sure as hell wasn't going to go into the family business. Out of frustration one day, I picked up one of my mom's brushes and started painting."

Nia turned her attention back to the paintings on the wall. He made it sound so easy, and maybe it was for him—at least the painting part. "Did it make you feel closer to her?"

He came to stand beside her.

"Not at first. At first, I was just angry. Angry that she'd died, angry at losing my career, angry at my family for being who they were. But slowly—and I don't even know how it happened —it became more. It did become a way to be close to her, but it also became a way to let how I felt about my dad and brothers and my surfing career fade away. Because once I started painting, nothing else mattered."

She could well imagine that. Jake's paintings were landscapes, but not just simple landscapes. No, in every nook and cranny, in every tree or hill, there were hints of what one might imagine if they were standing looking at the bucolic scene. They were stunningly beautiful from a technical standpoint, but what she loved most was how they evoked a sense of yearning, a sense of adventure, and a sense of wonder.

"And how did you become J. Marie Broussard?"

She heard a small laugh at that. "Other than you and me, there are only two people who know that this is me," he said, waving to the paintings. "My old surf coach and his wife. My coach came to check on me one day and found me painting. I'd never intended to do anything with them, I just used them and the process to bring me some peace. But his wife is an art dealer and he convinced me to let her see them. She did and, as cliché as it seems, the rest is history."

At his words, it truly struck her how poignant this moment was as he shared this part of his life with her. But as humbled as she was by his trust, she had to wonder...

"Why show me?" she asked. "And why now?"

He sighed and stepped closer to her, his shoulder brushing hers. "I come here when I want to, but I almost always come here when my family gets to be too much. Unlike you, I can't step away from my father and brothers. It was the deal I made with the FBI when I joined. So, when my head starts spinning with everything they've done and everything they are capable of, I come here and just, well, let it out."

He paused, and she sifted through his words until she realized what he was saying to her. "But I have a choice, don't I?" she said more than asked.

He nodded. "You do. I'm not even going to pretend to give you any advice on whether or not your family is worth your time—you've been successfully navigating that question for many, many years before we met."

He paused, and they both stared at the paintings before he spoke again. "I know what you told your mom when she came to the hospital, but I saw your face when Alexis was talking about her dad. That's what dads *should* be like, isn't it? They should remember birthdays, and check-in after hurricanes, and generally *care*. But ours don't. I'd ditch my family in a heartbeat if I hadn't made that deal with the FBI or if I didn't think they were the ticket to finding out what really happened to my mother. But I can't. You can, though." He paused then spoke again. "Again, I'm not going to stand here and tell you how to deal with your family, but I guess...I guess I want you to know that whatever you decide—or don't decide—to do, that I understand. You aren't alone and regardless of how your family makes you feel, you are *enough*."

The words were simple, really. Just three little ones—you are enough. But Nia hadn't realized how desperately she'd needed to hear them. And coming from Jake, someone who not only knew her situation but *felt* it too, was enough to bring tears to her eyes.

She sniffled, trying to hide them, but Jake wouldn't let her. Pulling her into his arms, he held her tight, resting his cheek on her head as she burrowed against him and let her tears flow freely. She wasn't crying for any reason in particular, but rather for all the times her parents had let her down, for all the times they'd made her feel different and not good enough, for all the times they simply hadn't cared.

She didn't know how long they stood there, but Jake never wavered. Finally, the tears dried up and in their place, a warm kernel of strength started to take root in her. She'd already cut her mom off the other day at the hospital, but standing here in this warehouse, with Jake at her side, the decision started to truly feel like the right one, and not one she'd made in the heat of the moment. She didn't fool herself into thinking that all her issues with her family were suddenly solved—Jake's paintings were good, but not *that* good—but for the first time ever, she believed that she might be able to deal with those issues in a way that didn't further damage her.

"Thank you," she mumbled.

"You're welcome," Jake said, pulling back enough to look at her. "You okay?"

She gave him a watery smile. "I will be."

"Good. I knew you would be, but what *I* know isn't what's important."

"So, what now?"

He glanced around the space and let out a long breath. "I'll need to clean up in here at some point, but it looks to have weathered the storm pretty well. So what now? Now I drop you off at home and head into the office for a few hours. After that, take-out at your place?"

She didn't fight the smile that tugged at the corners of her mouth. Jake didn't dwell on much of anything, and though in some cases, it might drive her batty, in this, it was exactly what she needed. "How about that Cajun place over at the docks?"

He grinned down at her. "One of my favorites. Do I need to get two orders of hush puppies, or are you going to pretend you don't want any and then eat all of mine like you always do?"

CHAPTER EIGHTEEN

JAKE DROVE NIA HOME, then made sure her generator worked and the outside of the house was in decent shape while she checked the interior. He took a few extra minutes to pull the shutters off her front windows so that she'd have some daylight, though he left them on in her bedroom windows, figuring the darkness might help her sleep.

After helping her get tucked up all cozy in her bed, he left to join his colleagues at the FBI offices. He hadn't been exaggerating when he'd told her she was only the fourth person to know his alter ego, and his nerves were raw and twitchy from showing Nia his studio. He didn't regret it—not for a second—but the newness of sharing what he had shared was an uncomfortable feeling. Like wearing a shirt with too much starch.

But he'd seen Nia's face when Alexis had talked about her dad—yearning, confusion, and anger had flashed in her eyes. He was intimately acquainted with all those feeling and he'd felt her pain as if it had been his own. In that moment, any desire he had to keep his own secrets was outweighed by his need for Nia to know that she wasn't alone in her struggle to sort through the scars left by her family.

What a pair they were.

Jake paused, his hand on the door to the FBI office, with that thought vibrating in his mind. They *were* a pair, he realized. Yes, they were dating and they were a "pair" in that sense, but they were more than that. He was in that mythical unicorn state of relationships that he'd never thought he'd find himself in—Nia was his friend and his lover, just as he was to her. Despite the ugliness they'd both grown up with, they each had careers they loved, friends they enjoyed, and, of course, they'd found each other.

Because of course they had all those things. He and Nia were pretty badass if he did think so himself.

"Agent McMullen?" Steven, their receptionist, opened the door, a quizzical look on his face. "Is everything all right?"

Jake grinned at the man who was holding the door open for him. "Everything is fabulous. I mean, except of course for the hurricane and the mystery drug and Nia getting shot. But other than that, everything is great. And you? How are you? And the hospital? How'd it fare?" Jake walked into the lobby as he spoke.

Steven blinked, then answered. "We're doing fine," he said, referring to himself and Sarah, his doctor-wife. "The hospital had some damage to the top floor, but they anticipated that and had moved all the beds and equipment for safekeeping."

"And is Sarah working this morning?" Jake asked as Steven retook his place behind the desk.

"She is. It's all hands on deck, though from her last text, there haven't been any serious injuries. Just a lot of bumps and cuts and those sorts of things. Everyone is waiting for you. Agent Rodriguez arrived less than five minutes ago, so you're not too late."

Jake thanked Steven then waited to be buzzed through the first door before using his code on the second.

"Agent McMullen," Shah said, walking out of her office. "Glad to see you managed through the night."

"Alexis was a great host. And you?"

"No complaints. We're getting set up in the conference room."

He followed her in and took a seat beside Alexis. Damian was at the front of the room with an enlarged satellite image of the private island they now believed was the location where the drugs were being manufactured.

As soon as the door closed, Damian proceeded to update Shah on everything they'd found the night before, and that morning, along with their idea of conducting a flyover recon mission. When he was done delivering the report with his usual military precision, all eyes went to Shah.

She stared at the image for a long moment, then finally shifted her attention to Damian. "Have you talked to Shorty?"

Damian shook his head. "We wanted to update you first."

She nodded. "And if we get the intel we need, what's the situation with the boat? We'll need a boat for any kind of raid. At least one."

The resort had a small helipad, but aside from not being big enough to land a helicopter that could carry a tactical team, landing at the resort, which was owned by the same group who owned the armory, wasn't a solid option.

"Our boat is dry-docked and it will be a couple of days before we can get it down. It weathered the storm fine, but the winch we need to get her back in the water was damaged. There were also a number of boats that didn't get dry-docked and were tossed around the marina—it's a mess," Damian answered.

"Nia—I mean the Marine Center—has a boat," Jake said. Shah turned to him. "She mentioned it this morning. I didn't ask if we could use it, but she implied it might be an option. Bertha Kitt is in The Center's private marina and she was dry-docked in one of their private buildings. She's big enough to deal with the tail end of Penelope, but small and agile enough for what we'd need her for."

Shah seemed to consider this, then nodded. "Can you ask her?"

Jake nodded and pulled out his phone. He sent a quick text to let Nia know he'd be calling and when she sent a thumbs up, he dialed her number and put her on speakerphone.

"How are you, Dr. Lewis?" Shah asked.

"Doing well. Better than I thought I'd be a couple of days after being shot and then living through another hurricane."

That comment brought a ghost of a smile to Shah's lips. "I understand you have a boat that you might be willing to loan us if the need arises in the next few days?"

Jake could hear Nia setting something down, maybe a coffee cup. "I do. Bertha is a solid boat, nimble but not easily pushed around. Kind of like her name implies."

"And if we needed to borrow her, what would be the process?" Shah asked.

"A requisition form would be the first thing we'd need. The Coast Guard has used her a few times and so we have those available. I can send one to Jake for your review. The harder part is that someone from The Center will need to go with her. I'd argue that it should be me."

Shah flicked him a glance, and he shook his head. He and Nia had spoken about Bertha, but she hadn't mentioned this caveat.

"I'm sure you appreciate that we'd be borrowing her for an official government operation. Since you no doubt know this, but still suggested that you or one of your cohorts accompany her, can you explain why?"

Nia took a deep breath and let it out. "First, we don't let our boats out without one of us on them, ever. Not even when the Coast Guard uses them. Second, and more practical, is that you are going to need someone to pilot her and it makes sense to have someone *extra*, someone who isn't involved in the raid, to do that, so you're not losing resources."

"We could dock her or anchor her," Shah countered.

"You could, but where?" Nia countered. "I can promise you, there is no one on this island except for maybe me and ten other fishermen who can get you into the armory bay. And I'm probably the only one who can do it in Bertha."

Shah cocked an eyebrow at Jake, and he didn't bother to hide his smile at Nia's confidence.

"We could use the supply bay. The one with the old dock," Shah said.

"The dock isn't stable," Nia answered. "It's a crumbling mess. It's still there, but not anything you could tie a boat like Bertha up to. As for anchoring her, you could do that too, but in this weather? Penelope might have moved on, but the tail end of the storm is going to be with us for a few days. I wouldn't trust an anchor to hold Bertha, not in a sandy bay."

Shah turned her attention to Jake and held his gaze as she asked, "So you're proposing you pilot Bertha for us?"

He didn't like the idea of Nia anywhere near a raid—if that's the route they ended up taking—but he was also smart enough not to cut off his nose to spite his face. Nia probably *was* the best person to pilot the boat and there was no one he'd trust more.

"I am," Nia said. "It might be tricky getting into the armory bay, but I can get you there. Or, we could use the supply bay as a drop spot. I could take her back out to sea once everyone's on land, then come back in for pick-up."

"And are you physically able, Dr. Lewis? As you pointed out, you were recently shot," Shah asked. Her tone was dry, but Jake could tell from the glint in her eye that she was on board.

"I'll be piloting a boat, not running a marathon," Nia shot back. This time Shah did smile.

"Send over the requisition form, and we'll get it filled out. We won't know if we'll need Bertha until later today or tomorrow, but can we count on you to be available tomorrow if we move forward?"

"The Center is closed for the week to allow staff time to clean up, so yes, I can be available."

Shah murmured a "thank you," and Jake ended the call. Everyone stayed silent as Shah rolled a pen between her fingers and studied the image still projected on the wall. Finally, she set the pen down.

"Alexis, Damian, and Dominic, I want you three up in the helicopter. Beni and Jake, you stay here and keep digging. I want everything we can find on Carl Westoff, the comings and goings-on at that armory, and anything tied to that club you mentioned, that one that was only open for a few months."

"What about Calloway?" Beni asked.

A dark look flashed in Shah's eyes. "Leave Calloway for now. But only for now. You can be assured we'll get to him."

Jake glanced around. He understood the practicality of Shah's approach. The drugs were the most pressing issue, and they needed to deal with shutting that operation down. But by the way everyone was avoiding each other's gaze, he knew that leaving Calloway out of their investigation, even if just for now, didn't sit well with anyone. Even so, everyone obeyed the order, and thirty minutes later, he and Beni were at their desks while Alexis, Damian, and Dominic were on their way to the airfield.

"You want to take Westoff and the club, and I'll take 'everything armory for $600'?" Jake asked once Shah was back in her office.

Beni nodded. "I'll go back and look at crimes committed during the time the club was open. We already have the files on the cases I pulled the other day, but all of those took place *at* the club where the perpetrator was partying. I didn't look at crimes that might have happened around the area."

Jake nodded, but he was already pulling up records on the armory and the development of the resort. He also wanted to check the reef maps to see exactly what Nia had been referring to when she'd said the approach by boat was tricky.

At some point, Beni stepped out, but he didn't ask where she was going, figuring that if she found anything, she'd tell them when they reconvened later that evening.

He was finishing up his last analysis when Beni returned, followed by Damian, Dominic, and Alexis. Shah walked out of her office, and without a word, all six of them made their way back into the conference room.

"Okay, Damian, tell us what you found," Shah said.

"It was a little touch and go as to whether we were going to be able to get anything with the wind still being what it is, but Shorty came through, and this is what we got." As he spoke, he typed something into a laptop and an image projected onto the large screen hanging on the wall. The image wasn't the sharpest, but it was sharp enough to make out each of the four buildings that made up the compound, along with details such as windows, exhaust vents, and, on one of the buildings, hanging planters.

"It's hard to get a heat signature in the tropics and through a concrete bunker, but this is what we were able to capture," Damian continued, bringing up another image. In this one, there was a dull glow coming from several windows in two of the buildings as well as around what looked like a ventilation pipe. The other two buildings were dark.

"How far underground do they go?" Beni asked.

"Two floors down, two floors up," Jake said, spreading out the printed blueprints that the Navy Archives had emailed him. Everyone stood and leaned over. "I have these electronically as well and can send them out, but I thought it might help to have them printed. The two buildings with the heat signatures are this one and that one," he said, pointing to two buildings that roughly formed a discon-nected "L."

"The signatures on this building are coming from the ground floor windows," Alexis said, pointing to one.

"Here," Jake said, pulling out a few sheets from underneath the one they were all studying. "I have the blueprints for each level of each building. Let's set these two aside for now." He pulled out the sets that covered the two buildings that appeared to have no heat signatures. "Here's the first floor plan for that building." He slid a sheet over to Alexis, and she and Dominic immediately started poring over it.

"But in that second building, the signatures are clearly coming from the second floor. What do those plans look like, Jake?" Shah asked.

Jake rifled through his stack of prints and pulled the correct one out. "It looks like that area was originally designed for offices," he said, shifting the paper for others to see.

Alexis straightened and studied the images. "I think it's safe to say that whoever is staffing the facility is probably staying on the island and in the facilities themselves. The funders wouldn't want to raise any suspicions by having people come and go, and it also prevents anyone from talking. If we go with that assumption, I'm thinking these are the living quarters," she said, pointing to the sheet in front of her. "And those offices have been turned into labs," she said, pointing the other paper.

Beni leaned over to get a closer look. "I think I agree. Look at the ventilation system here." She pointed to the marked spaces on the second-floor plans. "It would have been important when those were offices occupied by people, but it's even better when you need to vent out toxic fumes."

"So we've established the armory is being used by someone, though we don't know who or how many. We also think they are using it to manufacture drugs, but we don't have any confirmation of that," Damian said, then he looked up at Jake and Beni. "If we're going to get a warrant, we need more evidence. Please tell us you got something."

Jake looked at Beni, but she gestured for him to go first. He tossed a couple of files on the tables. "I didn't find a whole lot. The company that owns the island and resort isn't public, but it is a group holding. In addition to Calloway and Lawlor there are twenty-two other shareholders. I have all their names, and I recognize a few, but some of the shareholders are other companies and I haven't had the time to dig into them."

Shah's eyes narrowed at the mention of Ronald Lawlor, but she didn't pursue that trail of thought. "Who are some of the others?" she asked. "The ones you recognized."

Jake rattled off four names. One was a senator, one was a real estate mogul, and the other two were hoteliers he knew of through his father's business.

"Any chance any of them are into the drug market?" Damian said.

"There is a pharma CEO on the list and I was just looking into her when you guys came in. Anyone else recognize any names?" Each of the agents, and Shah, were scanning the files he'd handed them. Jake kept his attention on Shah as she was the one most likely to recognize names, at least the individual names. He wasn't sure she'd recognize the shareholders that were companies.

A few times her eyes paused before continuing down the list, but when Damian spoke, Jake turned his attention to his teammate.

"Fourth one down. Thomas Edwards. He's a weapons manufacturer. When I was in the army, he toured the base once."

"And Clyde Waterson is a Wall Street banker," Alexis added.

Jake glanced at Shah, who had set her file down and was looking at the group. "Everyone, give Jake any details you have on any of these people, or companies, but for now, fill us in on the resort itself," Shah said.

"The island was originally owned by just Clyde Waterson," Jake began. "A few years ago, the company was formed, and the shareholders were brought in. The resort went up pretty quickly after that, and the main lodging area was complete and taking guests within six months."

Dominic let out a low whistle. "I guess when you have money to burn," he said with a shrug, though Jake could see his friend's mind turning—most likely mirroring Jake's own thoughts. In a region where it sometimes took six months to get a refrigerator fixed, building a fully functioning luxury resort in the same time frame was definitely something he was going to look into.

"All this is interesting, and we should dig into it, but there's nothing to help us get a warrant in the next day or so, is there?" Alexis asked.

Jake shook his head. "Like I said, I have lots of interesting leads, but nothing will help us get a warrant by tomorrow. But maybe Beni does?"

Beni made a face. "Unfortunately, I'm in the same boat as Jake. I have a lot of leads, but nothing concrete."

"Walk us through them," Shah said.

"The club that was up and running for four months was owned by DJ Kitt. He's a sort of washed-up DJ from the early 2000s. He was really popular in Europe for six or seven years, then drugs got the better of him and he pretty much lost everything."

"Then how'd he get the money to buy the club?" Dominic asked.

"He didn't, and that's one of the leads we need to follow up. He was approached by a man who said he wanted to license DJ Kitt's name for the club since retro music was back in style. Kitt agreed and signed paperwork that gave him a shit ton of money in exchange for the rights to use his name. Only he didn't look at the paperwork very closely, and it also enabled the man to set up accounts in Kitt's name and make it appear that Kitt was the owner."

"How does someone miss something like that?" Alexis asked.

Beni lifted a shoulder. "When your brain is fried, you've lost all your money, but still have a huge ego, I think things like the details of a business deal might not be something you think about too much."

"Any lead on the guy who brokered the deal?" Jake asked.

"That's the best lead," Beni answered. "He couldn't remember the name of the man and believe it or not, the copy of the contract Kitt has isn't countersigned, but I showed him a picture of our favorite blonde and sure enough, he identified Carl Westoff."

Jake sat back and let out a frustrated breath. "Why has this guy never shown up on our radar before and now suddenly, he's everywhere?"

"Because we don't know what we're looking for until we find it, and then when we do, we see it—or in this case, him—everywhere," Damian answered.

"Again, a good lead, but it's not going to get us a warrant," Dominic said.

There was a knock at the door and everyone turned to see Steven pop his head in. The receptionist's gaze scanned the room then landed on Shah. "That matter you had me look into? Here's what I found." As he spoke, he walked into the room and handed Shah a file.

Jake's curiosity went off the charts as Shah read it and a little smile appeared on her lips. Steven wasn't just a receptionist—he was also retired MI6. Or perhaps not totally retired.

"Thank you, Steven," Shah said. "Any problems?"

Steven shook his head. "No, always happy to help," he said with a cheeky grin.

"And you have. Please thank whomever for this," Shah said, gesturing to the file.

Steven nodded, then turned and left the room. As soon as the door closed behind him, Damian spoke. "Please tell me that whatever it was Steven was looking into for you will help us get that warrant."

Shah smiled and handed Damian the folder. "Ladies and gentlemen, I don't think getting a warrant will pose an issue at all."

CHAPTER NINETEEN

"GREGOR LEV?" Damian asked. "Never heard of him." As he spoke, his eyes went back to the documents, and Jake watched about ten different expressions cross Damian's face before he closed the folder and handed it to Alexis.

"Lev," Alexis said. "That's 'lion' in Russian, isn't it?"

Shah nodded and sat back in her chair. "As you'll see in the file, Lev is both a medical doctor and a chemist. His grandfather was a protégé of Mengele, and Lev has taken up the reins. He fled from Russia when they discovered that not only was he testing out new chemicals to be used in war, but that he was testing them on Russian soldiers, one of whom happened to be the son of a prominent minister. Oh, and they also didn't like that he'd taken funding from a few groups in the Middle East."

"It seems like they might not have wanted him to get away. You know, keep your friends close and your enemies closer, and all that," Jake said.

Shah quirked a brow at him. "Oh, the Russians are still looking for him and he's wanted by Interpol, but he was in the wind."

"Until now," Alexis said, sliding the folder over to Jake.

Shah nodded. "Until now."

Jake opened the file and scanned the contents. "He flew from Argentina to Venezuela then to Tildas Island nine months ago?" He didn't bother to hide the disbelief in his voice. Who would have thought that an insane angel of death that was wanted by the Russians would have popped up in their investigation?

"And look who picked him up from the airport," Alexis said.

Jake rifled through the papers until he came across a photo taken from the airport CCTV. "Carl Westoff," he said, holding up the image. He studied it, then handed it over to Beni.

"While it seems like the drug we're dealing with would be right up his alley, unless we can tie his arrival on the island with the armory, we still might not have enough to get a warrant," Dominic said, taking the picture Beni handed over.

Jake picked up what looked like a bill of lading form and skimmed the list. Then he smiled and held the paper up. "I'm thinking that the fact that Lev's favorite vodka and caviar, along with the chemicals needed to make our drug, is delivered to the island every second week, might be just what we need."

The information turned out to be more than sufficient to get a warrant, and at seven the next morning, Jake and his colleagues, eight members of the Tildas Island SWAT team, and Nia, as their captain, were loading Bertha up.

In addition to the weapons they'd each be carrying—well, everyone but Nia—they had two inflatable Zodiac boats that would ferry the group from Bertha to the shore of the bay used to drop supplies. From there, the thirteen-member squad would walk the mile to the armory, conduct the raid, and, with a little luck, shut the place down. It would be an added bonus if they could find someone involved who would be willing to rat out the operation, but Jake wasn't counting on it.

"Fuel will be topped off in five minutes," Nia called out. She got a chorus of acknowledgments, and a couple of the SWAT team members double-checked the ropes anchoring the inflatables to Bertha's deck while the rest of them checked their gear.

"Everyone ready?" Shah called from where she stood on the dock.

After each of the agents responded in the affirmative, she called out again. "Dr. Lewis?"

Nia glanced over from where she stood, watching the fuel gauge. "All set, Director Shah."

Shah nodded. "We'll stay in touch via the radio in case plans change."

Nia nodded then turned her attention back to the fuel line as she deftly removed it. The plan was that she'd get her passengers as far into the bay as she could and once they were onshore, she'd motor out far enough to keep Bertha safe from the lingering waves and swells, but close enough to move in once the raid was over. Earlier, she'd given Shah the coordinates of where she'd wait, and though it was between the supply bay and the armory bay, given the way the island curved, she'd always be out of sight of the armory in case anyone was on lookout.

Jake still wasn't crazy about her being involved, but at least she wasn't being foolhardy; and, in truth, there was no one he trusted more with a boat, especially on the churning seas they'd be traversing, than Nia.

Twenty minutes later, they were motoring out of The Center's marina and heading into the open waters of the Caribbean Sea. The island they were headed to was located fifteen miles northwest between Tildas and St. Thomas, but because the armory was on the south side of the island—the side they'd be approaching from if they took a direct route— they'd agreed to swing wide, then come back toward the island from the north. From there, they'd skirt around the eastern end and into the supply bay that lay to the east of the armory.

"We clear?" a familiar, but new, voice said from below deck.

"Clear," Alexis called back, and Jake turned to see Isiah jogging up the steps to the deck.

"Uh," Jake said, staring at the man.

Isiah grinned. "Nia called me while you all were getting kitted up. She wanted a co-pilot and figured it would be easier to just ask me directly than to try to get it cleared through Shah first."

Jake's gaze went to the pilothouse where he could see the top of Nia's head as she navigated them around the final channel buoy. He hadn't had a chance to talk to her since they'd left her house that morning, but still, it would have been nice if she'd told him.

"She's right," Jake said. "Though I think Shah would have agreed."

Isiah inclined his head in agreement. Shah had brought the former SEAL in on one other op and had tremendous respect for him, but time had not been on their side that morning.

"I'll walk you up there," Jake said. He didn't wait as Isiah give Alexis a kiss, and instead, he made his way to Nia.

"Your backup has made an appearance," he said, walking through the door. She looked at him over her shoulder and smiled.

"Sorry I didn't mention it to you earlier. It just occurred to me that while I can manage Bertha, if you all need any help with anything, or if something happens to me, then it would be good to have a co-pilot, and I figured Roger wasn't a good option," she said, referring to her second-in-command at The Center and the man who would, under normal circumstances, be the one working beside her.

"You feeling okay?" he asked. It was not lost on him that she was still only a few days away from having been shot. His pride wished she'd told him about asking Isiah, but if she felt concerned, then he was glad she'd taken matters into her own hands.

She lifted a shoulder as she returned her attention to the water and started picking up speed. "I'm okay. I didn't ask him because I think something will happen or because I feel any worse, but I've never recovered from a gunshot wound before, so I figured better safe than sorry."

"And you're right," Isiah said, stepping into the pilothouse. "I'm planning on doing nothing more than take you in a few rounds of poker while we wait, but it never hurts to be overly cautious on an op."

Jake glanced at Nia, but she was focused on watching the water. The swells were peaking at about twelve feet. It was going to be a bumpy ride.

"For the record, if you're playing poker, I'm placing money on Nia taking you in a sweep," Jake said with a grin.

"Aw, thanks, babe," Nia said, her gaze still fixed in front of her.

"She's a card counter. Dominic and I refuse to play with her anymore," Jake added. Nia gasped in mock outrage making Jake grin and Isiah chuckle.

"You know, if you hadn't spoiled all my fun, you could have made a killing betting on me," she muttered.

"Oh, I'm still betting on you, sugar." He walked over and placed a kiss on her temple, trying not to disturb her concentration, but still needing to touch her. "But I get the sense Isiah can be sneaky as shit, too and I'm looking forward to hearing the stories."

"Don't you have some guns to clean or something? And no," she said, holding up a hand to stop him from speaking, although how she'd known he'd been about to respond, he hadn't a clue since she hadn't taken her eyes off the horizon. "That was not a euphemism. Go make sure everything is in order. I want this raid done as quickly and as efficiently as possible so that we can all go drink ourselves silly tonight at The Shack. Or at least so I can drink myself silly...seriously, this is some stressful shit," she added under her breath as the boat tipped down a swell.

She might be joking with him, but Jake could see the intense concentration on her face. Penelope had moved on, but she'd stalled out thirty miles to the northwest of Tildas and the seas were definitely angry.

He glanced at Isiah, who was now watching the approaching swell. The expression on his face didn't change, but the muscles in his arms tensed as the boat climbed it, and for a moment, only the sky was visible through the window. Then with startling speed, the boat tipped and started back down again.

Yes, he had gear to triple check, but more importantly, he needed to let Nia do her job without any distractions from him.

Placing another kiss on her shoulder, he gave her arm a gentle squeeze. "I probably won't see you before we leave the boat. Take care and be safe." As he said these last words, he met Isiah's gaze, and an unspoken agreement was formed between them. Nia didn't need a babysitter, but she did need someone to watch her back, and he was trusting Isiah to be the one to do it.

"You, too," she said, turning her head for a quick kiss. "Stay safe and you might even get lucky tonight," she added.

He dropped his head as Isiah laughed at Nia's comment. He thought by now he was used to her lack of filter, but apparently adding the physical aspect to their relationship just opened up a whole new door of opportunities for her.

But if he couldn't beat her at her own game, then he'd join her. "Counting on it, sugar," he said. Then without another word, he left Nia and Isiah, and maybe even a piece of his heart, in the pilothouse and rejoined his team.

From where he stood beside Nia, Isiah pointed out the window. "We've got a shoal coming up on the starboard side, but then we should be clear to the bay," he said. Despite the rocky ride so far, he was looking as comfortable as a cat on a cushion in the sun as he kept vigil at her side. It wasn't the first time she'd been on a boat in the aftermath—or even during—a hurricane, but it was the first time she was solely responsible for everyone on board. She was good, she was damn good at piloting a boat, but that didn't mean she hadn't had a few heart-stopping moments along the way.

As they skirted around the eastern edge of the island, she kept Bertha as close to the shore as was safe. When the mouth of the supply bay finally came into view, she let out a long breath. They weren't done yet. In fact, everything was just beginning for everyone else, but at least she'd done her part to get them there.

Fifteen minutes later, she was holding Bertha steady as first one, then the second zodiac boat hit the water. The thirteen members of the team—five agents along with eight Tildas SWAT members—climbed in. Another few minutes passed, then they were ashore, tying the inflatables up to the crumbling cement pier. The old dock wouldn't have held Bertha, but there was more than enough left of the structure to hold the zodiacs even with the wave action that the bay was experiencing.

Both Alexis and Jake fell into the rear of the line of agents making their way west toward the armory, and before disappearing into the dense foliage, they both turned and raised a hand. Isiah and Nia mirrored the movement though Nia wasn't sure if the two agents could see them. Still, it did give her a small sense of comfort.

"So, what now?" Nia asked, hoping Isiah, who'd been with Alexis a few months longer than she'd been with Jake, might have some insight.

"Now, we wait."

"I suck at waiting. Just so you know."

Isiah chuckled. "You're dating Jake, I kind of figured you'd have to be at least a little bit antsy in order to deal with his antsy."

"Yeah, we're a good antsy pair," she said on a sigh, though why she was suddenly feeling so melancholy, she didn't know.

"You are, and they'll be fine. Hopefully. In the meantime, why don't we pull out of the bay and find somewhere a little bit calmer to wait it out? I'll even play poker with you."

She looked at Isiah then grinned. "I do count cards," she said.

He smiled back. "So do I."

CHAPTER TWENTY

JAKE SANK onto his heels beside Alexis as they waited for Damian and Dominic to return from their recon pass of the two buildings that they believed housed the lab as well as the people working in it. Beni had taken a few of the SWAT members to confirm that the other two buildings were empty, and the irony that Jake, the antsiest of them all was left behind to wait, was not lost on him.

"You doing okay?" Alexis asked.

He tossed her a grin. "Despite surfing all those years and all that time that I spent floating and waiting for the perfect wave, sitting still isn't my strong point."

Alexis smiled. "We know, but despite that, you do it better than anyone on the team. Well, except for maybe Damian."

He wasn't so sure, but it was true that if he could get past the initial urge for action, his body kind of went into a meditative state. "Do you think Damian's people will come through?" he asked. The couple Damian had sent the tracker to—Brian and Lucy—had confirmed the night before that the signal was being transmitted to this island. At Shah's request, the couple did a little more digging—

apparently, they were super-hackers or something—and had found plans to the armory's security system. With the warrant issued, Shah had asked if they could interfere with that system while the raid was taking place so as to ensure a truly stealthy entrance.

"Damian said they're the best. Dominic's met them, too. I don't think Shah would have asked if she wasn't confident they'd come through."

Just then, their earpieces crackled to life. "All clear in buildings three and four. We're making our way back to base," Beni said. They didn't have a "base" per se, but the spot where he and Alexis, and the rest of the SWAT team, where waiting was the designated holding area where they'd plan the final details of the raid once the recon was complete.

"We're on our way back, too," Dominic said.

Less than ten minutes later, the five agents gathered in a circle with the two SWAT team leads.

"Lucy and Brian will put the security cameras on feedback loops in five minutes," Damian said with a glance at his watch. "From what we could see, and visibility was limited given that there are floors below ground, there appears to be two people in the lab and three in the living quarters. A window was open at the latter, and we heard them mention Lev's name. It's always good to have confirmation that our prime suspect is present and accounted for."

"What about the other security features?" Beni asked. In addition to the security cameras, Lucy and Brian had provided intel on the locking mechanisms on four doors as well as the internal security alarms.

"Once Lucy and Brian see that we're safely inside the perimeter fence, they'll disable everything," Damian answered. "They have eyes on us, so feel free to flash them a grin," Damian added with a smile as he pointed up to the sky.

Jake didn't know who these people were who could access a

satellite to keep an eye on the operation, but he was glad they were on Damian's side.

"So once we're through the fence, Jake, Beni, and I, along with half of the SWAT team, will take the lab," Damian continued, eliciting nods from those in that group. "Dominic and Alexis, you take the second SWAT crew and lead the charge on the residential building. You'll have one more person to contain, but, presumably, a lot fewer dangerous chemicals to contend with, so hopefully, the allocation works."

Alexis, Dominic, and the leader of that SWAT group nodded.

"I know I don't need to say this, but standard procedures regarding the use of force are in play, but the goal is to capture not eliminate, if possible," Damian added.

After having lost Rosen—their only prior lead tied to one of Calloway's schemes—no one wanted to lose Lev, the second.

"All right, everyone," Dominic said, turning to encompass the entire combined interagency-group. "We ready to roll?"

At Dominic's words, adrenaline flooded Jake's bloodstream and his body came alive. It was a feeling he welcomed, having mastered how best to use it years ago while surfing...there was nothing quite like facing, then riding a twenty-foot wave, but working with his team came in a close second.

"Let's do this," he said, and moments later, they were headed into the lair of the lion.

Jake and Beni cut through the hurricane fencing and peeled it back. Once all thirteen were through, they split into the two groups, and he, Damian, and Beni led their SWAT support through the foliage toward the building that housed the lab. There were two functional doors to the building, one at the end of the long, rectangular structure and the other on the side that faced buildings three and four. Not wanting to spend time in the open, the group had decided to use the door at the end of the building—it was closer to the residential building, and if someone happened to be walking from one place to the other at the time, they'd be seen, but the element of surprise would still be on their side.

Pausing at the edge of the foliage fifteen feet from the entrance, Jake glanced at Damian. "We're clear," Damian said quietly, knowing everyone would hear in their earpieces.

Rather than bursting into the building, which was a tactic that sometimes worked when agents wanted to leverage surprise and chaos, they quietly slipped through the now unlocked doors. Based on the heat signatures, the labs were located on the second floor between the staircase at the end of the hall where they entered, and the staircase in the middle of the building.

Damian signaled for Jake to lead two SWAT members to the next set of stairs. When he and his group started up the staircase in the middle of the building, Damian, Beni, and the other two SWAT members started up the other set. By coming at the lab from both ends, they hoped to cut off any potential escape routes of those inside.

As Jake reached the top of the stairs, he hugged the wall and peered around the corner down the hall. He could see three doors open, but only two rooms had lights. Beyond that, he saw Damian also peek around the corner. With the two SWAT members behind him, Jake paused and focused his attention on Damian.

Damian raised his hand, then slowly, rhythmically, lowered his fingers one at a time. On "zero," both he and Damian led their teams down the hallway toward the open doors. As planned, Beni and one of the SWAT members took the first room, Damian and the other SWAT member took the second, and Jake and his band of merry men took the third and closest to them.

He heard Beni call out and identify themselves as FBI, but Jake's focus was on the room he was responsible for clearing. Having slipped across the opening, he once again hugged the wall with his two backups on the other side. He waited a heartbeat, expecting to hear something from inside the room once Beni had announced their presence, but nothing emerged—no sound, no person.

Glancing over his shoulder, he saw Damian and his partner enter the room beside his and he heard scuffling from the office Beni was securing. Jake turned his attention back to his task and nodded to his partners.

The SWAT lead stepped into the large space, moving diagonally until his back was against the other side of the same wall as Jake's. Jake made a similar move, but in the opposite direction and the third member of his group, ducked in to stand beside his teammate.

But there was no one else in the room.

Just then, Beni's voice echoed through the corridor, followed by a shot. Jake signaled his partners to search the room while he bolted down the hall to check on his teammate. As he passed the middle room, he heard Damian reciting the Miranda warning as he cuffed a man lying on the floor. Jake caught his colleague's eye as he passed, and even in the nanosecond of connection, he saw the concern in Damian's expression.

Jake continued on to the first room but paused at the door. "Ricci," he called, hoping to hear her voice.

Relief washed over him like a bucket of cool water when she called back, "We're clear. I had to disable someone, but we're clear."

Jake stepped into the room, his weapon still drawn, but it only took him a second to take in the scene and once he did, he lowered it. Beni and her partner had a man and a woman handcuffed and lying on the floor. The woman had blood seeping through the white fabric of her lab coat, but it looked to be little more than a graze. Okay, maybe a little more than a graze, but nothing life-threatening.

"She tried to throw that at Savoy," she said, gesturing to a beaker that sat on a long lab table. "We didn't want to take any chances."

"Thanks for that," Peter Savoy, from the SWAT team, said with a grin. "I'm getting married next weekend, I'd like to be sure I'm in attendance."

"Congrats," Jake mumbled, looking at the man on the floor. It wasn't Lev. "Alexis?" he asked, knowing she could hear him.

"We're clear. We have three in custody," she replied.

"Lev?" he asked.

"No, two men and a woman, but neither of the men is Lev," she answered.

Jake glanced at Beni. Their count had been off. They'd estimated only two in the lab, but they had three in custody.

"Kellington and Parker?" Jake said, calling the two men who cleared the room with him. "Report in."

"There's no one else here, sir," Parker answered.

"Get down to room one and help with the suspects. Agent Ricci and I have a few things to check on," he said.

"Go," Beni said, gesturing with her head toward the room where Damian was. He needed to confirm that the man Damian had down was Lev because if he wasn't, then that chemical mastermind was in the wind again, and that wasn't a good thing for anybody.

He nodded and exited the room, passing Kellington and Parker before entering the second room.

"Rodriguez?" Jake called, before entering.

"We're clear, come on in," Damian answered.

Jake's attention immediately fell to the man on the floor. The man who wasn't Lev.

"Fuck," Jake said.

"We don't have him, do we?" Damian said, understanding the reason for Jake's dismay.

Jake shook his head, then turned as Beni walked in. She, too, looked down, before raising her gaze—her pissed gaze.

"You got this?" she asked Damian. He nodded. "Good. McMullen, let's go find that asshole. He has to be here somewhere."

"I'll have Alexis start a search of her building, too," Damian said as they left the room.

"You studied the blueprints the most, where could he have gone?" Beni asked even as they started down the hall and systematically started clearing the remaining rooms on the floor.

"The labs are up here, if he's not here and not in the residential building, then maybe he set up an office on another floor?"

The question went unanswered as they cleared the last two rooms—none of which looked to have seen any use in the past several years.

They paused at the top of the stairwell at the far end of the building, and Jake took a moment to wrack his brain. The first floor didn't make any sense—why would Lev set up an office on the floor below where the main labs were when there were several empty rooms in the same hall?

There were two floors below ground, and while an office in that space didn't make sense, would Lev have set up an entirely separate lab? He was about to pose that question to Beni when the light angled through the window at the end of corridor, and an impression near the door caught his attention.

Dropping to his haunches, he examined the area.

"What do you see?" Beni asked, squatting beside him.

"Does that look like a shoe impression? Or part of one anyway?" he said, gesturing to a few lines of drying mud on the floor not much more than a half-centimeter high—as if it had been tracked in.

"And there's another one," Beni said, pulling out her flashlight and using it to light the dim stairwell.

"Rodriguez," Jake said, standing and following Beni down to where she'd stopped on the landing between the floors. "Beni and I are headed down to the lower levels. We'll keep you updated in case we need backup."

"Roger that. Stay safe."

Jake took his own flashlight out and together, he and Beni followed the fainter and fainter footprints down to the first level below ground. They paused at the juncture, silently debating whether to continue down to look for more tread or walk through the metal swinging doors and into the cavernous area that once held all sorts of missiles used by the US Navy.

"There," Beni said, the beam of her light landing on a smudge in the dust on the door—as if someone had placed their fingers there to open it, then let them slide off as the door closed.

"Fun, let's walk through a metal door that has no window and into a room we know nothing about," he muttered. His statement wasn't entirely true, he knew what the room looked like on paper, but that didn't mean he knew what the room looked like—or contained—now.

"It's all fun and games..." Beni said, as Jake pushed open the door and leaped to the side, once again keeping his back to the wall.

Beni caught the door as it swung back, and in that tiny, infinitesimal second when his attention flickered to Beni, out of the corner of his eye, he caught movement coming from a door to his left. Keeping his body against the wall, he rolled to the side, blocking the door to keep Beni from entering and stepping into danger. Beni's shout permeated the metal slab, but it was drowned out in the searing pain that sliced through his right shoulder at the edge of his Kevlar vest.

Glancing down, the sleeve of his shirt was already turning damp and sticky with blood. The knife that had come at him— the knife that would have hit Beni in the face had she come through the door—was lying on the floor.

"Jake!"

Jake stared at the blade for a split second, then moved to

allow Beni through. Beni stepped in, her weapon drawn, her eyes scanning the now empty room. When she confirmed for herself that it was, in fact, empty, she let her eyes touch on him. She was a medic by training, and he saw her calculate the damage to his shoulder. Her gaze dropped down to the knife and lingered there for a few seconds before meeting his again.

He gave her a lopsided smile.

She stared at him, then shook her head. "Guys, we need backup," she said, speaking to her earpiece.

"I've got the suspects. Lex and Damian will make their way down," Dominic answered. Beni relayed their position, told Dominic to have SWAT keep an eye on the stairwells, then turned back to him.

"I know you're not really good and will probably need at least a few stitches, but are you good?" she asked.

Jake rolled his shoulder to check on his ability to move, then nodded. He wouldn't be playing any baseball games anytime soon, but he'd live.

"I didn't catch a full glimpse, but I saw movement that way." He gestured toward a door in the back left corner of the room.

"Any idea where it leads?"

"Two more rooms just like this. The good news is, he's probably cornered," he answered as they started toward the door.

"Meaning?"

"The next room has no way in or out other than through this room or the room after it. The room on the other side has a stairwell, but if we've got SWAT watching the stairs, then there's nowhere for him to go."

They paused beside the door that joined the room they were in with the next, then swiftly, Beni spun to the other side so that they stood sentinel.

"You think it's Lev?"

Jake shrugged his good shoulder. "Logically, it would make sense. We're 99% sure he's here, and we haven't captured him yet." He paused and darted a look around the corner. What he saw almost made him lose his concentration.

"I was going to say that it's possible that it's not him, but after what I just saw, I think the chances of that are pretty low," he added.

Beni gave him a quizzical look then quickly peeked around the door. Her eyes were bugging out of her head when she returned to her position.

"What the actual fuck?" she muttered. Jake couldn't have said it any better because what lay on the other side of the door was a lab that made the ones upstairs look like a five-year-old's chemistry set.

"The good news is, I think we found Lev," he said with a grin, despite the fact that his right shoulder was starting to go numb. It was a good thing he was left-handed.

"The bad news is he's going to be cornered, and while that bodes well for capture, he doesn't have a lot to lose," Beni said, finishing his grim thought.

CHAPTER TWENTY-ONE

"DOM, make sure SWAT guards the east stairwell. If he makes a run, that's his only way out," Jake said, speaking into his earpiece.

"Roger that," Dominic said, then he started issuing orders as Jake checked in with their cavalry.

"Damian? Lex? Where are you?"

"We just hit the landing on the lower level. Is it clear to enter?" Alexis asked.

"It's clear," Beni said.

The door squeaked behind him as the two agents joined the party, but as they did, Jake caught the scent of smoke and his attention zeroed in on the lab. Nothing appeared to be on fire, but if Lev was taking the time to burn something, Jake was pretty sure they should take the time to stop it.

"I'm going in, cover me," he said. Then, before Beni could say anything, he stepped into the adjoining room. Keeping his back to the wall, he moved around the perimeter. The smell got stronger as he moved through the room, but as he passed lab tables filled with equipment, he saw no smoke and no source of the odor.

The thought fleetingly passed through his mind that there were a lot of chemicals in the area and a fire wasn't the only thing that could kill them—he'd been part of enough failed chemistry experiments in college that he was well aware of what fumes could do. But the scent that he kept catching smelled more like good, old fashioned smoke from paper or wood, rather than something noxious.

Out of the corner of his eye, he saw his colleagues enter the room and fan out. As always, it felt good to have them at his back, but the fact that he hadn't located the source of the smell was starting to feel like an itch he couldn't quite reach.

He caught Beni's eye and gestured with his head toward the last room. Unless Lev had vanished into thin air, the man had to be in there. She nodded as they continued to make their way through the room, doing a much more thorough sweep than he had.

Jake paused at the door, took a deep breath, then quickly darted a look inside. He wasn't sure what he'd expected to see, but what he actually saw chilled him even more than seeing a cornered lion.

Gregor Lev stood in the far corner of a room that was devoid of anything except two desks and one whiteboard. He wore a white lab coat and casually raised his gaze from the flaming paper he held in his hand to Jake.

Jake almost issued an order for the man to drop the paper, but seeing a stack of files on the man's desk, he hesitated. If Lev dropped it, all the papers would catch on fire and they might lose valuable evidence. On the other hand, if the files were as sensitive as whatever Lev was currently burning, wouldn't he have burned them all at once?

Lev's calm demeanor rattled Jake more than he wanted to admit. It was creepy as fuck and definitely not in the norm. Then again, from what Shah had told them about Lev, he was anything but normal.

"Step away from the desk," Jake ordered. Lev hadn't made any threatening moves—yet—so while Jake kept his weapon raised, he held fire.

Lev gave him a ghost of a smile but didn't move. His eyes, however, darted up. Jake tracked the movement, then smiled.

"Drop it," Jake yelled with more force this time as he approached the man one step at a time. His shoulder throbbed, but his left hand was steady as he tracked Lev with his weapon. He had the upper hand now that he realized the reason Lev wasn't burning all the papers at once was because it would set off the fire suppression system. Water would pour from the sprinklers in the ceiling and douse the flames. The only way for Lev to ensure his evidence was destroyed was to do it piece by piece.

"I wouldn't come any closer," the man said, his Russian accent carrying a bit of a British lilt to it. "You see that," he said, gesturing to a beaker of fluid on the desk beside him. "All I need to do is drop this in there and we'll all be gone." As he spoke, he waved a lighter that he held in one hand over the mouth of the container.

It was possible the man was lying, but Jake didn't think so. Which meant that Lev was confident that so long as he succeeded in burning the paper, then, even if he allowed himself to be captured, there wouldn't be enough evidence to tie him to anything. Not in any way that would stand up in court.

Which wasn't something Jake was going to let happen.

"I said, drop it," he ordered, taking another ten steps forward. He had a clear shot, but he hoped his advancement would encourage Lev to instinctively take a step back—and away—from the beaker.

Lev did no such thing. He simply picked up another sheet of paper and let it burn, keeping the flame far enough away from the beaker that it didn't pose an imminent threat.

Jake knew what he had to do. He needed to control the situation by taunting Lev into threatening to blow the room up again. The second Lev made a move in that direction, Jake could take a shot. He had no intention of killing the man—he was their best tie to Calloway and whatever schemes that man was putting in place—but there was a lot of room between letting him get away with his crimes and killing him.

"Rodriguez?" Jake said, knowing his backup was close behind.

"Do it," Damian replied, obviously having come to the same conclusion. "We've got this."

Jake walked forward again, bringing him to within fifteen feet of Lev. The scientist watched him as the paper in his hand slowly burned. "You don't want to do that, agent," Lev said.

Jake inclined his head. "Oh, I think I do, Gregor."

"You want to blow us all to kingdom come? Feel free to come a little closer if you do."

Jake smiled, and Lev paused. "Don't mind if I do," Jake said, then took another three steps. "I suggest you put the lighter and the papers down, Gregor. I have no intention of anyone dying today, but I'm not above a little maiming if needs be."

Lev blinked at Jake, unsure what to make of his change in demeanor. If Lev wanted to play it cool, two could play that game.

Slowly, Lev let the remnants of the burned paper drop, and they floated down to land on his desk. His eyes scanned the room, taking in the four people who now had weapons pointed at him. Jake could see the calculation in the man's eyes, could all but hear his mind churning, weighing the odds and outcomes. Then he reached down, but instead of coming up with another document, Lev pulled out a small, but powerful, gun that had been lying, out of sight, beneath a stack of papers.

Well, that definitely changed the dynamics of the situation.

Jake stilled as he watched Lev. The scientist held the weapon loosely in his hand as his eyes skittered around the room. He wasn't aiming it at anyone yet, but it was clear that he'd chosen suicide by cop rather than blowing the place up. Jake was a little disappointed at the man's lack of creativity—and his choice also made Jake wonder what was really in the beaker—but in this moment, neither of those thoughts carried any importance.

"You got this, McMullen?" Dominic asked.

"Yeah, you?" Jake asked. The thing with suicide by cop was that it was as predictable as it could get, and every half-decent team trained for ways to avoid it. When the time came—when Lev raised the gun and posed a clear and convincing threat—Jake would take the shot. But if Lev got one off first, Damian was his backup.

"I'm clear," Damian said.

"Go ahead, agent," Lev said. "Take the shot, if you please."

Jake was well within his rights to do just that—even without Lev pointing the gun at anyone. But he'd never been very good at following directions, and, more importantly, if there was a chance Jake could talk Lev down without any shots being fired, he was going to do his best to do accomplish that. Both he and Damian were excellent marksmen, but in the heat of the moment, anything could happen and Jake did *not* want to lose this witness.

A bead of sweat trickled down Lev's temple.

Jake smiled and took one more step, zeroing his focus in on Lev's hand that held the gun and looking for any movement to indicate he might be getting ready to raise it and pull the trigger.

"Well, Gregor, are you going to do it? Or are you just going to let me walk up and cuff you? I'm looking forward to reading what's in those papers."

His team remained as silent as statues behind him, but he could practically feel Beni and Alexis rolling their eyes at him.

"Is it porn? I know it is," he taunted. "Maybe Russian porn?

You gotta admit, if you're going to look at porn, Russian porn is probably the best. Does it make you miss the homeland?"

Lev's finger twitched and his arm jerked. The gun came up six inches.

"A pity your own government doesn't want you," Jake said. "I mean, I know some good Russians, but you got to be pretty fucked up to have the Russian government after you in this day and—"

And there it was, the moment they'd been waiting for. Lev raised his hand and brought the gun up. His motions were so quick and so practiced that in that disconcerting split second before disaster hits, that moment when everything slows down, Jake recognized that Lev must have had extensive weapons training. But the thought didn't go further than that and without hesitation, he took the shot just as Lev fired his own weapon.

As if from a distance, he saw Lev go down, clutching his shoulder. Damian moved in to manage Lev, and suddenly Dominic, Alexis, and Beni were in his view.

"We good?" he called, or thought he did, to Damian.

"Clean shot through the shoulder, McMullen. Nice one," Damian said.

"Thanks," he muttered, as Dominic's arm came around him.

"Here, let me help you, buddy," Dominic said, easing Jake down onto the ground. Jake frowned at his friend. Where had Dominic come from? Wasn't he supposed to be upstairs? Not that Jake wasn't glad to see his face.

"Are Nia and I going to have matching scars?" Jake asked as Beni started to rip the top his shirt. A few of the SWAT guys entered the room and one dropped what Jake assumed was a first aid kit by her side.

"I hope you have a better handle of anatomy than that, McMullen," Beni said, trying to smile though her voice was grim. "For Nia's sake, if nothing else."

Jake grinned. If he had to get shot, he kind of liked the idea of having a matching scar, but even through the numbing pain —and his inability to move his fingers—he knew Lev's bullet had hit him in the upper arm, right at the shoulder and not far from where the knife had struck. He was pretty sure he'd survive, but it hurt like hell. And if Beni's muttering was anything to go by, it was messy, too.

"Alexis, call for Nia. We need her to bring the boat into the bay to transport him to the hospital as quickly as possible," Beni said.

"I'm fine," Jake said, his breath feeling hot and heavy.

"You will be," Beni answered.

Dominic appeared in his line of sight again, looking unusually concerned. Very little concerned Dominic, so Jake caught his eye.

"What's up, Dom," Jake managed to say, though it was getting harder and harder to talk.

Dominic frowned at him. Beni cleared her throat, and Dominic glanced at her before returning his attention to Jake. "Aside from you getting shot? Russian porn? Really, dude? That's where you had to go?"

Jake smiled, then his vision blurred and he slipped into a deep sleep.

CHAPTER TWENTY-TWO

NIA LAID DOWN her hand just as the radio in the boat crackled to life. It turned out that two card counters playing poker was as fun as watching paint dry.

"Nia," came Alexis's voice.

Nia didn't miss the little sigh of relief that Isiah let out at hearing Alexis's voice. But Nia had caught the strain in it and with a sense of foreboding, she connected.

"We're here," she replied.

"Can you bring the boat into the bay? We need immediate transport to the hospital."

Nia's stomach pitched and she didn't need Alexis to tell her what she already knew. "Jake?"

Isiah was already starting the engines and the smell of diesel fuel filled the air.

Alexis hesitated. "Yes," she said on a long breath. "He's in and out of consciousness, and we don't want to transport him to the supply bay if you can get to the dock at the armory. He has a minor stab wound and a bullet also grazed his side."

A thousand questions filled her mind about Jake and the state he was in, but to ask them would be to waste time. She looked at the weather readouts then gauged the sea. Getting into the bay wouldn't be a problem. Getting out would be tricky. Tricky, but doable.

"We'll be there in ten," she said. Without a word, she took the helm and opened the throttle as they powered to the bay. On a good day, they would have made it in five minutes, and they did reach the mouth in five minutes, but once there, Nia throttled back and studied the scene.

There were several people standing on the dock with a stretcher at their feet. For a flickering moment, Nia wondered where the stretcher had come from, but that thought wasn't worth her attention and she turned and looked out the window toward the open sea. If they could ride a swell in, it would be much easier than navigating the channel between the reefs. They'd have to navigate the channel on the way out, but first things first.

"We going to ride a swell in?" Isiah said, his voice and presence solid and steady.

She nodded, keeping her gaze fixed on the water. Her stitches pulled and the muscles along her back protested, but she ignored them and held her focus. She needed to time the swells, and to do that, she needed to get a feel for them. The speed was more important than the size, though if she could find one that was both large and fast, that would be their best bet.

"What do you need me to do?" he asked.

"I need you to prepare to help get Jake on board. I want both of you up here with me, once he's onboard."

Isiah made a sound beside her just as she spotted what looked like the start of an ideal swell. "It's not going to be a distraction, Isiah. I mean, it probably will be, but he can't be on deck, so you'll need to either be below or up here. I may need your help, so that means both of you need to be up here. Hold on," she said, gunning the motor and dropping the topic as she prayed they'd catch the right spot and be able to ride the swell over the reef.

Isiah gripped the handle on the console and adjusted his stance as the back of the boat lifted with the water. The water was moving faster than she'd anticipated, and for a moment, she feared they'd get left behind. But she wasn't going to let that happen, and she opened Bertha up to full throttle. Five seconds was all she needed, and she let out a long breath as Bertha positioned herself right in the sweet spot and rode the swell right over the reef and into the bay. Throttling back, Nia let the wave move underneath them as she stabilized Bertha.

"Nice driving," Isiah said with a grin.

She muttered a thanks, then eyed the dock. "There are two stretchers, Isiah." Once again, she wondered where the stretchers had come from, but then assumed they must have been in the facility.

He went still beside her, then flicked the radio on. "Alexis, are there two injured?"

"The primary suspect," Alexis answered. "He took a bullet to the upper torso. We figured since you're picking Jake up, it's easy enough to take Lev as well. Damian and Beni will travel with him to stand guard. If you're okay with it, you can keep an eye on Jake. His bleeding has stopped, but he's in and out of consciousness."

Out of the corner of her eye, she saw Isiah glance at her, and she gave a distracted nod. She didn't really care how many people were on her boat as long as she could get Jake to safety. She trusted Beni's care and Alexis's report, but she wouldn't rest easy until Bertha was back in port and Jake in the hospital.

"We can't tie up at the dock," she said to Isiah. The water was too rough, even in this relatively protected bay.

"We'll bring them in by dingy," Isiah responded. Then, after relaying the plan to Alexis, he left without another word. Despite knowing he'd been a SEAL for over a decade, she didn't like leaving that job to Isiah, but at this point, she didn't have a choice. All she could do was hold the boat steady.

She heard the winch kick into action and she knew Isiah was lowering the small boat that lived on Bertha down to the water. How he planned to both get in it from where he operated the winch on the deck, then disconnect it, she'd leave to him. It was hard enough keeping Bertha steady between the reef and the shore.

What felt like ages later, but was probably only a few minutes, she caught sight of Isiah motoring through the waves to the shore like he'd been born to it. That morning, when she'd asked him to join her, she'd done it on a whim—an educated and experienced whim, but a whim nonetheless. But as she watched him run the boat up the beach and expertly hop out, she was more grateful for following her instincts than she'd ever been before.

Two stretchers were loaded onto the boat, then Damian, Beni, and Isiah jumped back in, and Alexis and Dominic pushed them back into the waters. Getting back onboard Bertha would be a little trickier, but through an open window, she heard Isiah shout that he'd climb the exterior ladder and operate the winch, leaving Damian and Beni to hook up the dingy.

As soon as the dingy landed gently on the deck, Nia started turning Bertha around. She hadn't said anything to Isiah—was pretty sure she hadn't needed to—but the truth was, she wasn't entirely sure how she was going to get them out. She'd figure it out—hopefully—but it was definitely going to call on all her skill and a little bit of luck.

She was hovering on the edge of the reef, navigating the swells, when Damian and Isiah brought Jake into the wheelhouse. It took everything in her not to turn her attention to him. Only knowing that lives potentially depended on her getting them through the reef channel safely, kept her focused.

She did glance over her shoulder when the door closed, only

to find Isiah kneeling beside Jake, who was strapped to a stretcher.

"How's he look?" she asked as she dropped her gaze to the depth gauge.

"He looks better than ever. He might need a new shirt, but other than that, he's still the handsomest man you know."

Nia whipped her head around at Jake's voice. He was grinning, though his eyes looked a little glassy. His right arm was secured against his torso.

"As you can see, I think he'll live," Isiah said as she returned her focus to the bay.

"And Damian?" she asked.

"He and Beni took Lev below deck. They know it's going to be a bumpy ride." Isiah's message was clear—they needed to get out and on their way quickly.

"I need to angle for the channel, but time it with a swell so that I don't get turned around," she said, mostly speaking to herself.

"I'm fine, sugar," Jake said, his words slurring a bit. "Take your time."

The wind looked to be dying down a little bit, but she wasn't feeling good about the tides. She glanced down at the depth gauge again. So long as a swell didn't cause too much of a subduction, she should be able to make it through the first part of the channel, then pull hard to the starboard and power out of the second half.

Assuming they didn't get tossed around too much.

"Fuck," she muttered. Her back throbbed with tension and a bead of sweat dripped down between her breasts.

"You got this, sugar. And like I said, I'm cool. Kind of hurts a little, but Beni gave me something. Not sure what it was. I think I was passed out when she did it, but regardless, all's good. Take your time."

"Jake," she said, not taking her eyes off the entrance to the channel. It wasn't visible above the waterline, but she knew exactly where it was.

"Yeah, sugar."

"You know I love you, but you need to stop talking to me. Especially if all you're going to do is tell me how fine you are when I know you've been both stabbed and shot," she said. No sooner had she finished speaking than she saw her opening. "Hold on, Isiah."

"You got it," he said. She didn't know how he planned to keep both himself and Jake steady, but she appreciated his confident, and succinct, response.

Plowing straight through a swell, she entered the channel, having spotted a second swell not far behind.

"You love me?" Jake asked, his voice sounding distant in the roar of Bertha's engines.

Nia couldn't answer. She was too focused on judging the next swell. She'd need to time her turn to the starboard just right in order to not get tossed around.

"I think you do," Jake continued. "And I'm glad. Because I love you, too," he added, his words still not entirely clear, but clear enough.

"Did you hear me, Doc?" he asked. "I said, I love you."

She glanced over her shoulder to see Isiah staring at her. His arched eyebrow brought a smile to her face and his calm demeanor gave her the small boost in confidence she needed to make that last push.

"Great, glad to hear that, Jake. I love you, too. Now stop talking to me," she said, once again, as she opened the throttle to full force and pulled hard to the starboard side.

"Ah, the romance," Isiah said.

"Shut up, Isiah," both she and Jake said at the same time.

And then Nia laughed. She laughed partly because of the ridiculous conversation, but mostly because she'd actually gotten them through the channel. She'd done it. They'd made it.

Now all that stood between her and Tildas Island was fifteen miles of the angry Caribbean Sea.

Nia had grit, she knew this. You didn't grow up with the family she had, in the circumstances she had, then make of her life what she had, without it. But that didn't mean that when she finally pulled into The Center's marina that she wasn't sick with relief. It wasn't over yet—they still had to get Jake to the hospital. But as soon as she tied Bertha up, everything she'd been responsible for that day would be completed. Successfully. The rest was out of her hands. And at the moment, she couldn't wait to have everything in someone else's control, at least long enough for her to catch her breath.

"You doing okay?" Isiah asked quietly as he stood at her side, once again, his solid presence lending her strength.

She nodded. "Not gonna lie, this has not been a day I'd like to repeat." She looked over her shoulder and down at Jake. At some point on the journey home, he'd fallen asleep. Or maybe succumbed to whatever painkiller Beni had given him.

He chuckled. "You done good, and he'll be fine."

"I know," she said on a long breath as she motored slowly toward Bertha's home. "I know it's his job, but that doesn't mean I have to like it, does it?"

"No," Isiah said. "But we do have to respect it, and I know that's not a problem between you two."

He was right. On both counts—she did respect Jake's work, and she'd figure out how to manage her anxiety. "Well, I'm just looking forward to some nice quiet time in the hospital after this," she said, throwing Isiah a cheeky grin. He smiled back and shook his head.

"Shah said two ambulances would be waiting for us. Will you

251

go with Jake?" she asked. "I need to get Bertha bedded down for the night, and then I'll join you."

"I will, but I think he'd prefer to have you."

"No offense, I know he would. But I can't leave you to take care of Bertha. She's The Center's responsibility. Which means she's my responsibility."

"Not arguing that, but I think you have help." As he spoke, he pointed to the berth inside the massive concrete structure where Bertha lived. Standing on the dock were not just EMTs, but also three of her staff and Roger.

"How...?"

"I suspect Shah," Isiah said.

She did, too. Especially when she saw the woman standing behind the gathered crowd.

"She's a good egg, isn't she?"

"She most definitely is that," Isiah answered.

"I didn't even think to ask about the rest of the team. How will they get back?"

Isiah smiled. "Alexis texted that Shah arranged for a couple of helicopters to pick them up."

"Like I said, a good egg," Nia said as she switched the engine into neutral and glided into the bay. "Go throw them the lines?"

"Aye aye, Captain," he said, then slipped out the door and jogged down to the deck.

Once her team had Bertha secured, the first EMTs boarded the boat and disappeared below deck. A few moments later, they emerged, carrying a stretcher, flanked by Damian and Beni. From where Nia watched in the pilothouse, she saw them step onto the dock and immediately, four more policemen—well, and one woman—surrounded the gurney on which they'd placed the stretcher. Beni and Damian stopped to say a quick word to Shah as they passed, but Nia turned away from the scene when the second set of EMTs entered the pilothouse.

They did a quick check of Jake's vitals and as they did, he opened his eyes briefly. "We back?" he asked.

She nodded, suddenly fighting tears.

"Come with me to the hospital?"

She wanted to reach for his hand, but she'd only be in the way.

"Nowhere else I'd rather be."

Jake chuckled, well, he managed a half-chuckle. "Your imagination is better than that, sugar."

The EMTs glanced up at her. One quirked an eyebrow.

"Get him out of here," she said with a smile.

She followed the EMTs out of the pilothouse and off Bertha. As they strapped him onto a gurney and checked a few more vitals, her team rushed up to greet her.

"Oh my god, are you okay?" asked Tom, one of her Ph.D. students.

"You're a hero," Yvonne, one of the resident researchers, said.

"Is it true you got Bertha in and out of the armory bay? In a hurricane?" Joseph, a local college kid who worked for The Center while doing his undergrad degree in Marine Biology, asked.

Nia hugged each of them, then grinned. "Yes, I am okay. No, I'm not a hero. And as to the armory bay, yes, I did. But that's only ever to be whispered about in back rooms of dingy bars after a long night of drinking. I don't want anyone to get any ideas."

They all laughed as Roger stepped forward and wrapped her in a big, but gentle, bear hug. "Glad you're okay, kid. But you know you didn't have to do that alone?"

She glanced at Shah, who stood twenty feet away watching the EMTs work on Jake. "I appreciate the sentiment, Roger. I really do. And while normally, that would be true, this really was something I had to do on my own. Or well, not on my own because I was never alone, but I couldn't have called you." As she spoke, she realized that while in this case, she *couldn't* have called Roger or anyone else from The Center to help, had it been any other situation, she not only could have asked, but she would have. And she knew beyond any doubt that each of them would have stepped up to help without hesitation. Like family.

Just then, the EMTs unlocked the wheels of the gurney, and she turned to see them beginning to wheel Jake away.

"Go," Roger said. "We got Bertha."

She glanced at the boat, then at her staff. Her friends. "Thank you," she said, giving each another quick hug before stepping around the follow the EMTs.

"You'll let us know?" Roger asked.

She looked over her shoulder at him as she walked away. Then she smiled and nodded. "I'll call you as soon as I have any news."

CHAPTER TWENTY-THREE

JAKE TRIED to open his eyes, but his lids were so heavy that he gave up with the strain. Then a cool hand touched his and fingers curled under his palm. He'd know that hand, that skin, those fingers anywhere.

"Nia?" His voice came out a croak.

"I'm here," she answered. A hand came up to brush his brow.

"How come my arm doesn't hurt, but my eyelids feel like someone stitched them shut?"

Little puffs of air hit the bare skin of his neck as she let out a soft laugh. "The drugs they gave you accomplished both of those."

"I'm fine, you know," he said.

She must have risen from her seat because the bed depressed at his side and heat from her body seeped through the thin blanket.

"You're not, but you will be. No permanent damage to your shoulder, but it will take a few weeks to recover."

He was silent for a moment, just enjoying the heat of her body next to his. "Isn't there something you want to tell me?"

Again she laughed. Then she lifted his hand to her lips and brushed a kiss across his fingers. "Open your eyes."

He groaned. "It's hard," he whined.

"Opening your eyes is nowhere near as difficult as I will make your life if you don't, so pick your poison."

"You're cruel."

She laughed again. "Sometimes, but you love me anyway."

He opened his eyes to see hers staring back at him. He smiled. "I do."

The light that came into her eyes filled him, flooding into all the cracked and damaged places. "I know," she said. "I love you, too. Now was that so hard?"

"I'll show you something hard—"

She slapped a hand over his mouth, but she was still grinning at him. "Stop," she said. "It's going to be a while before we can do that, so I suggest we don't talk about it. At least not in public."

"We're not in public. We're in a private hospital room," he said. Though it was somewhat garbled because he was still speaking against her palm.

She arched an eyebrow at him and, as if on cue, the door opened and a nurse walked in followed by his entire team, along with Charlotte and Isiah.

"I couldn't keep them out," the nurse said, waving at the group as he started to check the fluids in the IV bag.

"I don't mind," Jake said. And he didn't. Everyone in that room—except the nurse, of course—was his family, which was a weird, but welcome thought. In the scheme of things, they'd only been together a short time—less than a year—but he was closer with them than anyone else in his life. Except for Nia, of course.

They made small talk while the nurse finished his rounds, but when the door closed behind him, Jake fixed his gaze on Damian.

"Did we get Lev?"

Damian nodded. "He only needed to be stitched up. He's already been transported to an undisclosed location for questioning."

"We have an undisclosed location? Why didn't anyone ever tell me we have an undisclosed location?" Jake asked.

Beni rolled her eyes at him. "Alexis and Shah are going to question him…" she turned to Alexis.

"I agreed to meet Shah there in two hours," Alexis answered.

"And the papers?" Jake asked.

"You done good, Jakey," Dominic said. "Those papers were the only tie between Lev and the actual formula for the drug. If he'd been able to destroy them, we still would have captured him, but all we would have had were a bunch of chemicals that, on their own, were controlled substances but otherwise completely legal. Would have been a hard case to make."

"Anything on Calloway?" Jake asked.

"Not yet," Alexis answered. "But we haven't had a chance to go through everything with a fine-tooth comb."

"And Carl Westoff?" Nia asked.

Alexis shook her head. "Nothing yet. But we still have a lot to unravel."

Everyone turned with a surprised jerk when the door opened again. Shah paused in the opening, then smiled.

"I see you're all here. Good," she said. Damian and Beni moved to the side as Shah walked to the end of the bed. "How are you feeling, Jake?"

He tried to shrug with his good shoulder, but it was hard in his supine position. "Fine. But I'm drugged up, so…"

"And you, Nia?"

"Much better now, Director Shah," she said. He rolled his head and looked at her. She hadn't been hurt during the trip, but the day they'd had couldn't have been good for her own recovery.

"Are you sure you shouldn't be at home resting?" Jake asked her, squeezing her hand.

"I'm fine. Though I suspect I'll crash hard tonight. Adrenaline will do that to a girl," she answered with a smile.

Shah's gaze swept the room. "You all did well today, but unfortunately, it's not quite over. All the suspects except for Lev are being held in county jail. Damian, Beni, Dominic, I'll need you three to head over and begin questioning them." The three agents nodded, and Jake felt a pang of regret at not being able to join them. Then again, doing anything more than squeezing Nia's hand felt nearly impossible, so maybe he should suck it up and let it go. There would be other suspects and other interrogations. Besides, that meant he got to hang out with Nia, which was definitely one of his favorite things to do.

"Jake, you're on 'rest and recovery leave' for at least three weeks. After that, the doctor will evaluate you, and we'll go from there."

He wasn't thrilled with that proclamation—taking a little time off to heal was a far cry from three weeks of forced non-work. Maybe he could sneak some desk work in.

"Three weeks," Shah repeated, giving him a hard look.

He narrowed his eyes. "Are you reading my mind? Because if you are, I'd suggest you stop unless you want to be truly shocked."

Shah let out a surprised laugh. "Contrary to what you might think, I have very little interest in what goes on in your mind 90% of the time, though I doubt it would shock me. But I do know that a lack of stimulation and Jake McMullen does not make for a good mix. However, we're also inching closer to The Summit next May and I need all of you in top form. Not that you haven't been," she hastened to add, "But we don't want to risk it. So I'd rather you take the time you need for a full recovery now than spend the next several months partially recovering."

Jake's gaze held Shah's. Her reasoning was sound and though her delivery was light, the look in her eye told him everything he needed to know.

He sighed in acceptance. "I wouldn't dream of countermanding your order, Director Shah." Sometimes retreat was the better part of valor.

How she managed to roll just one eye as she shook her head was a trick Jake thought he might want to learn. Good thing he had three weeks to practice.

"All right, everyone. Once again, good work today. Hopefully, we'll know more tonight about the extent of the network and production, but I think we can all feel good about closing the lab down. There might be others, but this one was clearly a major source of the product, and if nothing else, it will slow production down considerably." She paused as if considering what to say next, then she shook her head. "Let's get moving so you all can celebrate tonight."

There were murmurs of agreement, and, after wishing him well, his friends followed Shah out the door. The door clicked shut behind them, leaving him and Nia in silence.

He turned his head to look at her, the sub-par hospital pillow crinkling under him. "So, I guess it's just you and me?"

She smiled, then reached down for something. When she straightened, she held up a distinctive rectangular black box. "You, me, and this, McMullen," she said, wagging the box of Cards Against Humanity. "And you're going down this time."

He laughed, then winced, though he kept laughing.

Lord, he loved this woman.

EPILOGUE

SHAH SAT BACK in her chair, her legs crossed, her fingers resting on a file. Gregor Lev, his arm in a sling, sat across from her. After two hours of questioning, Lev had said nothing. Alexis had left five minutes ago, leaving the two of them alone. Exactly the way Shah wanted it.

It wasn't that she didn't trust Alexis, or any of the agents she'd handpicked for the task force, but Shah had years of experience on each of them and the situation they were finding themselves in was a sensitive one. A situation that had the potential to rock the foundations of American democracy—depending on who was on which side.

And that was at the crux of her issue. Shah saw the chess game unfolding before her—she'd even caught glimpses of it before she'd accepted the role as the head of the task force. In fact it was *why* she'd accepted the role in the first place. But despite the fact that she could see the game, she couldn't see who was moving the pieces.

"I want to know who funded you," she said. She had too many years under her belt to *hope* for anything, but it was possible Lev might know something.

The doctor just looked at her.

"Did they pay you, or were you going to split the proceeds? Was there a buyer already?"

Again, Lev looked at her.

She stared back. His eyes were dark and empty, and though his expression was carefully blank, it wasn't hard to see the contempt and arrogance under the surface. As a follower of Mengele, Lev had barely been able to handle being questioned by two women, not to mention two women of color. It had been rather fun to watch him cope with being in such close proximity to her and Alexis while still trying to stay calm and nonresponsive.

But for Shah, this game had run its course.

She made a show of looking at her watch. "Your transport to Russia will be here in fifteen hours. You'll remain here until then." She uncrossed her legs and started to rise, all the while noticing the little things that gave Lev away.

His eyes flashed with surprise, then fear. His body went still as it absorbed the statement. Then he adjusted his feet under his seat.

"They'll kill me," he said. His first words since she'd stepped into the room.

"Most likely," she concurred as she rose from her seat.

"I don't know who was behind it," he said.

She turned, studied him, then retook her seat. "How did you get involved?"

Lev shook his head, not in refusal, but in defeat. "A man. He came to me while I was in Argentina."

"His name?"

Lev gave a tiny shrug. "I don't know. He had blond hair and a little, what do you say…stub of a nose?"

Shah removed a picture of Carl Westoff from her file and slid it across the table. Lev's gaze darted down, then he nodded.

"Yes, that's him."

"And what was the deal?"

"I make a drug that could control people, and they'd fund it."

"Who was 'they'?"

A sad laugh escaped Lev. "You think they told me?"

No, she didn't think that, but it had been worth a try.

"So that was the full deal? You make it and they fund it?" Lev may be interested in science, but he was also interested in money. Having the opportunity to develop a new drug would have some appeal, but he'd want more.

Lev's gaze jerked down again to the picture. "They just wanted the formula. Once it was complete, we'd both have it."

That sounded more like Lev. "You planned to sell it to the highest bidder, didn't you? It's not hard to imagine what a regime or terrorist organization would pay for such a drug."

"Or your own government," he shot back.

Now they were getting somewhere.

"What makes you say that?" she asked. Shah had no illusions that the entire project was funded by an American and she had a pretty good idea who—the whole team did. But was Calloway the master or just another pawn?

Lev studied her for a long moment, then finally, he spoke. "There was a man who came to the compound one day."

"When?"

Lev shrugged. "Maybe three weeks ago?"

"And?"

"I didn't see him, not his face. But he was tall. Wore a light-colored suit, maybe off white or light brown? He had blond hair, cut short, and I remember his neck was sunburned. It stood out against the color of his hair."

"And what makes you think he was an American?"

"I heard him talking on his phone. His accent."

"Come now, Lev, don't make me keep asking," she prodded.

His gaze wandered to the corner of the room as he recalled

the conversation. "He was telling someone that progress was being made and that the fraternity would be pleased."

"He used that word?" she asked. "Fraternity?"

Lev nodded. "He said everything would be in order to restore power."

Shah gave him a hard look. She was getting awfully tired of pulling information from him.

Lev shook his head. "That's all I heard. He walked away, and I heard no more."

"What about Robin Spencer, the young man you left at the bottom of the sea?"

A sneer formed on Lev's lips. "Some spoiled kid the American brought with him. He was supposed to help in the lab, but instead he started sampling."

"And you couldn't have that, could you?"

"He wasn't trustworthy," was all Lev said, making Shah almost, but not quite, smile.

"What about the drop points and trials being run on innocent people?"

Lev shook his head. "As I said, I don't know any more. The man with the tiny nose managed all that."

Shah studied Lev, and, unfortunately, she believed him. He looked to be pondering the words he'd overheard more than thinking about what he might tell her next, which he'd be doing if he had more to tell.

It wasn't much, but it was more than they had before. If what Lev had said was true—and she believed it was—then Calloway might be a major player but he wasn't the one pulling the strings; he reported to someone else, or perhaps, a group of someones.

The pieces of the puzzle were starting to fall into place, and it was creating a picture she didn't like. But when had she ever really liked the things she'd seen or heard in her job? The day she did was probably the day she'd need to quit.

"Thank you," she said, reaching for the picture of Westoff as she rose.

"What now?" Lev asked.

She slid the picture into the folder and signaled for the guard. "Your transport to Russia will be here in just under fifteen hours."

Lev's eyes looked about to bug out his head. "But you said... you implied that if I answered your questions..."

Shah smiled. It wasn't a nice smile. "I said nothing of the sort. I simply told you what was going to happen. That you inferred otherwise is hardly my fault."

Lev lunged at her but came up short. The chains they'd used to secure him held.

"You stupid bitch," he sputtered. "You will regret this."

She smiled as the guard opened the door. "There are a great many things in my life that I do regret, but I can assure you, this won't be one of them. Now have a nice trip home, Dr. Lev."

THE END

Thank you for reading A TOUCH OF LIGHT AND DARK! I hope you enjoyed Nia & Jake's story.

In the (next to last) installment THIS SIDE OF MIDNIGHT, the team continues its preparations for the big summit on Tildas Island, but they have more adventures in store for them. Especially Dominic and Anika! Read on for a sneak-peek!

EXTRACT OF
THIS SIDE OF MIDNIGHT

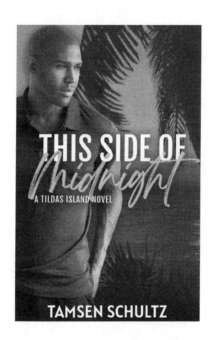

PROLOGUE

DECEMBER

Dominic leaned against the wall and tried to strike a pose that conveyed both confidence and calm. The hospital had done its best to disguise the odor of antiseptic and anxiety, but that particular scent had worked its way into his nostrils, and now he was pretty sure that every time he smelled it from this day on, it would bring him back to this moment.

He glanced over at his family. His mom and dad sat side-by-side, gripping each other's hands, his mom's head resting lightly on his father's shoulder. His two sisters and their husbands sat in remarkably similar tableaus. He was the only one standing. The only one alone.

The clock on the wall clicked over a minute and Jeremiah, his oldest sister's husband, leaned down and spoke quietly to Pamela, his wife. With her head resting against his shoulder, Pamela nodded, then sniffled. Jeremiah pulled a tissue out and handed it to her.

Dominic's gaze traveled to where his other sister sat, her hands intertwined with her husband's. Pamela was older than he was by five years, but he and Katherine were only eighteen months apart. They'd been close as kids, but when he'd left home to join the Air Force and she'd gone on to law school, they'd let the distance—and their respective jobs—be an excuse to drift apart.

He stifled a sigh and glanced at the clock. He'd come home to Louisiana for what was supposed to have been a couple of weeks of R&R from his job as part of a special FBI task force stationed on Tildas Island in the Caribbean. What he'd walked into was a nightmare—a possible cancer diagnosis for his mother, the matriarch, and center of their family.

His eyes traveled to his mama. He hadn't lived in Louisiana for more than a decade, and it was true that he and Katherine had drifted, but his family was tight. They always had been and always would be. That love, that loyalty, and that bond had come from his parents, and in particular, his mom.

She'd been a stay-at-home parent for most of his early years, while their father, a professor, had taught at the nearby university. Even managing three kids and supporting her husband's career, she'd had dreams of her own, though. Dreams she'd made come true when Dominic had been ten and she'd opened her first restaurant.

Dominic still remembered his mother's smile the day she opened the door to her home-style breakfast cafe and the way his father had teared up at her achievement, so moved to see the woman he loved so happy. Now, twenty-five years later, Korryn Burel was one of the most celebrated chefs in the state. It was well deserved, and no one—and he meant *no one*—could cook like his mama. But to him, she'd always be the one who prodded him to do—to be—better, the one who'd bandaged his scrapes while dispensing life lessons, the one who held the family together with her love and light and drive to make the world a better place every day.

And now they were waiting to see if she'd die.

Dominic blinked and looked away. When would the damn doctor arrive?

"Dominic, baby, why don't you sit down?" his mother asked.

He met her gaze, and in her dark eyes he saw the mother he'd always known. She was the one who might be getting the cancer diagnosis, and yet here she was taking care of him.

"She's right, son," his dad said. "Why don't you have a seat?" As George Burel spoke, he patted the empty chair to his right.

Dominic switched his attention to his dad. Other than Dominic's bright green eyes that he inherited from his mother, he was the spitting image of his father—tall with a lean build, smooth, dark skin, and a killer grin. While Dominic deployed his smile to influence and encourage witnesses and suspects alike, the elder Burel had used his to sway and inspire students. After almost forty years of teaching, he'd mostly retired from his professorship of Literature at the university, but that hadn't slowed Papa Burel down. He still played tennis three times a week, helped out at the restaurant when asked, and his world still revolved around his family. He'd aged, though. In fact, the amount that his father's black hair had turned grey since Dominic's last visit had been Dominic's first hint that all was not well.

Dominic shook his head. He didn't want to sit. He wanted to stay standing, he wanted to stay alone on his side of the room. Perhaps it was childish, perhaps he was being weak, but if the doctor gave them the news none of them wanted, his mom would have his dad, Pamela would have Jeremiah, and Katherine would have her husband, Michael. He needed the steady wall at his back to offer cold comfort because he had no one to lean on and he wasn't about to burden his family with his grief when they'd all be struggling with their own.

The shuffling of feet in the hallway and the garbled words of a quiet conversation happening on the other side of the closed door drew everyone's attention, and the question of whether he'd sit or not became moot. His sisters straightened in their chairs and in almost identical moves, Jeremiah and Michael wrapped an arm around their respective wives. His dad leaned over and kissed his mom's head. It was a sweet gesture, but Dominic saw the man's eyes close for a moment and in that moment, Dominic's heart broke. His father was being faced with the reality that the love of his life might be taken from him.

The door swung silently open and the doctor entered. Dominic's family all leaned forward a touch, as if bracing themselves for an assault. He pressed his back to the wall, hoping it would hold him up if his world collapsed around him.

The doctor was young, close to his own age, and she wore a gentle smile.

"Mrs. Burel, thank you for coming in today, and I'm glad your family is with you," she said.

Dominic hated that she'd led with that ambiguous statement. What did that mean?

"Dr. Joachim," his mom said, her voice wavering.

Dr. Joachim's eyes quickly took in the room, then landed back on his mother. "It's good news, Mrs. Burel. The tumor is benign. Once we remove it, you should have no further symptoms and, after a short recovery, you should be able to resume your normal life."

A beat passed, a flickering moment in time when everyone in his family held their breaths as they absorbed the words. Then everything erupted. His sisters curled into their husbands and tears and words of relief flowed. His parents simply held each other though Dominic knew they'd be praying, giving thanks, in their silence.

As for him, the wall he'd hoped would hold him failed, and he sank to the floor. Acknowledging how close a call they'd just had, a string of four-letter words flowed through his head, releasing some of the pressure of the past few days. Knowing that his mother wouldn't appreciate him letting off steam in that way, though, he kept his special embodiment of relief to himself. But he didn't stop himself from crying. He couldn't remember the last time actual tears had fallen from his eyes— maybe when he'd been ten and dislocated his shoulder? There was no shame in them now, though. Fuck no. His mama was going to be okay.

Then just as quickly as the tears of joy started, laughter followed. First his mama, then his dad, then soon, his sisters and their husbands had joined in. Dominic smiled, too, as he looked up and watched his family. Watched them hug their partners, then hug each other, then come together in a group hug.

The room filled with love. His sisters held on to their husbands and his parents stayed wrapped in each other's arms. Gratitude and grace coursed through his body. But from where he sat, alone on the floor, he wondered if maybe, just maybe, something was missing from his life.

Made in the USA
Columbia, SC
18 April 2023

15443373R00169